THE SECRET

ARRANGED BOOK TWO

STELLA GRAY

ALSO BY STELLA GRAY

~

Arranged Series

The Deal

The Secret

The Choice

Convenience Series

The Sham

The Contract

The Ruin

Charade Series

The Lie

The Act

The Truth

ABOUT THIS BOOK

On the day I was married, I promised to love, honor, and obey my husband Stefan.

Little did I know how literally I would mean obeying.

Stefan tells me what to do, and I do it. There are questions asked, but I always submit in the end.

It would hurt less if I hadn't started falling for him.

It was supposed to be pretend. But the secrets we now share are too real, and they're crumbling every piece of who I thought I was.

If only Stefan was the man I thought he was.

If only I weren't so powerless.

But there's one thing I have that he wants.

My body.

And I'll do anything it takes to right the wrongs I've discovered.

PROLOGUE

STEFAN

I awoke in the middle of the night to the sound of Anja's heavy breathing, the now-familiar distressed moans escaping from her lips. Another nightmare.

"Anja," I whispered, reaching for her shoulder. I tucked her lithe, naked body into mine, curling around her protectively from behind.

She gasped for air and turned to face me in the bed. I could see her fearful expression in the glow of the streetlight coming from outside, her eyelids fluttering rapidly as she glanced around my room and struggled to get her bearings.

"Shh. It's me," I said.

Her hands reached up to frame the strong lines of my jaw. "Stefan." Her exotic Romanian accent never failed to send a shock of lust through me, even at times like this.

"You're safe," I soothed her, kissing each palm. "You're with me. I won't let anyone hurt you."

"I know," she said, but I could still feel her heart pounding as her chest pressed against mine.

I had no idea what the nightmares were about; Anja

refused to give me any details. She said there were certain things about her history that I was better off not knowing. I respected this need for privacy, but I also fucking hated it. Whoever had hurt her, I'd give anything to hunt them down. To make sure nobody else ever touched my girl again.

But now she was climbing on top of me, her lips hungrily seeking mine. That long black hair falling like a sheet of silk against my chest, my fingers instinctively reaching for the soft curves of her breasts. We'd fucked for hours earlier, before falling exhausted into bed, but our bodies were like magnets and I was hard and ready for another round as she straddled me.

"You sure you want to go again?" I teased, nudging my cock against her. "Pretty sure if I make you scream as loud as you did earlier, you're not gonna have a voice tomorrow."

"Who needs one?" She leaned back, spreading her thighs, and looked down at me with a smirk. "I don't have the kind of job where it pays to have a voice."

Despite her smile, the words had an edge that sent a chill through me. I pulled her mouth down onto mine, wishing my lips could make her pain go away. As we kissed I rolled us over, pinning her to the bed. She reached for my cock.

"Wait. We need to talk first," I said. My adrenaline was pumping at the thought of telling her my plan, but it was now or never.

She pouted. "Talk is boring."

I laughed. "I hope what I have to say won't bore you."

I'd met Anja Borjan in the fall, at a fashion show in Paris where the models had been painted in gold leaf. Even still, Anja had glowed like no one else on that runway. Her eyes, the bluish-green color of an ocean during a storm, had locked onto mine as she'd pouted her sultry way down the catwalk. I knew in that moment: I had to have her. I soon found out she was one of the up-and-coming new talents recruited by my father for his agency, KZ Modeling, and had quickly become a favorite among his clients. All of his clients.

But as the son of KZM's owner, I was used to getting what I wanted.

Within a week she had been in my bed, and in the months since, she'd barely gone more than a few nights at a time without returning—even if she sometimes texted me after 2 am so I could sneak down to the lobby of our luxury apartment building and let her in. And to my surprise, I'd become addicted to her. I hadn't grown tired of Anja as I had with other women.

And I didn't think I ever would. Something about her anchored me, made me see a future where we were happy together. It didn't matter that I was seventeen and she was in her twenties, or that her career was on fire and mine hadn't even begun yet, or that she was so much more worldly than I was (despite my money and my travels and my experiences with women). We just...fit.

My mother had died when I was six, and my father was a lifelong workaholic. Anja had immediately nodded with understanding when I told her how I'd had to grow up fast. My younger siblings and I had been brought up by a series of nannies but they'd always seemed to take little interest in me, probably because I was such a strong-willed, independent child. In many ways, I'd raised myself.

I'd been sleeping with the models from KZM since I was thirteen. As far as I was concerned, it was the best way to gain maturity and life experience, to learn about pleasure and beauty. The talent my father employed were experts in both, and I made it a point to seek out their expertise. Espe-

cially in the bedroom. Anyone who didn't return my interest, though few and far between, was politely passed over in
favor of someone who was more attracted to what I had to
offer. With my father so focused on running the business,
there was no one around to dissuade my particular form of
sexual education. It had always been fun. And easy.

But everything had changed with Anja. I'd found
myself opening up to her. I trusted her.

What we had going on, though—it wasn't enough for
me anymore. The sneaking around, the incognito coffee
dates on the other side of town, these little sexual interludes
in between the various jobs she was sent on. I wanted more
of her. I wanted *all* of her.

I was in love and I was going to marry her.

I'd even picked out a ring and everything. Right now it
was burning a hole in my bedside table—it was set with a
huge, heart-shaped diamond that would sparkle on her
finger. I was ready to make her mine, to take our relationship out of the shadows and into the light. I wanted to stop
hiding and make things official. She loved me too. I was
certain.

She'd said the words, yes, but it was more than that. I
could tell how she felt by the way she looked at me, the way
she melted into my arms, the way she kissed me...the way
she relaxed at the sound of my voice whenever she woke
from her nightmares. She wanted this, too. Something
permanent. Something safe. Something...real.

I cleared my throat, checked my nerves, and looked
down into those stormy eyes.

"I'll be graduating from high school soon," I began, my
tone serious.

Anja's hand froze mid-grope. "I know this..."

I nodded, unable to read her neutral expression. "So.

So I've been thinking that...that the timing is right, now, for us to start thinking about the future. What's ahead of us—"

"You are saying you are ready to move on from this?" She was frowning now.

I couldn't help myself; I laughed. "No! God, no. Anja, I —I love you." I stroked her cheek, tucked a strand of hair behind her ear.

"And I love you," she said. She wrapped her legs around me and propped herself up on her elbows to drop kisses down my throat, along my collarbone, moving toward my chest. My cock jumped against her thigh eagerly, but I gently pushed her away. I needed to focus.

"*Anja*," I said.

She looked up at me, her angelic face wearing a frown of confusion.

"You don't want to—?" she gestured to my cock.

I did. I really did, but I took her hand in mine instead.

"I love you," I said again, slowly, "and I want to marry you."

Her eyes widened in shock. We'd spoken about it before, in passing—I had made my intentions clear—but for some reason this was still a surprise to her.

"But—what is wrong with what we have?" she asked. "Are you not happy?"

"I am happy," I said. "What we have is amazing. But...I want more. Don't you?"

"Stefan." She laughed softly. "You can't be serious."

I looked into her eyes. "I am. I want to be with you. I want to marry you."

She gently pushed me aside and wriggled out from beneath me. Before I fully realized what was happening, she was getting out of bed, pulling on her clothes.

I leapt to my feet, stopping her with a hand on her shoulder. She stilled but didn't turn toward me. "I can't."

"Why not?" I asked. "I can take care of you. You wouldn't even have to keep modeling if you didn't want to, or you could stay focused on your career as long as you want. Either way, we'd get on a good path—together. Build a life of our own."

Anja finally looked back at me. "You are a wonderful boy. But you know we cannot."

That word, "boy," stung. But I wasn't going to take no for an answer. "This can work. My trust fund has enough money to live off of for years, and once I have my MBA I can provide for us even better. If you don't want to come with me to U Penn, maybe we can—"

"Your father would never allow me to stop working for him," she cut me off.

I was confused. "You don't have to stop. You can keep modeling."

Her shoulders slumped under my touch. "I am not referring to the modeling," she said.

Of course.

I knew that my father employed his models for more than just print work and runway shows, that some of the clients who came to him expected the women to work in the bedroom as well. I'd always known this. As someone who was naturally curious and expected to take over KZM when I was older, I'd made it my business from a young age to learn everything about how the agency operated. And I did. I knew where to recruit models, how to woo them, what their contracts looked like, how to entice new clients into the fold and keep the established ones. I had no illusions; I knew exactly how our company was run. Including all the things my father kept out of the press. The sex work was just another part of the business. A part that we never discussed, that was kept secret from most of the world, but a part of KZ Modeling nonetheless.

I never judged the models that supplemented their income this way. After all, I had been the grateful recipient of many of the tricks and treats they had doled out while earning additional money. They could live their lives as they saw fit.

And even though I knew it wasn't entirely legal, I didn't judge that either. Everyone was making more money, everyone was having a good time, everyone was gaining something. As far as I was concerned, it was a win-win situation. My father made more profits and connections this way, and the models earned more to send home to their families, as most of them were supporting their relatives overseas.

But if Anja and I got married, she wouldn't need to make that extra income. She would be part of the Zoric family, and all the wealth and perks that that included.

"You don't need to keep doing that kind of work once we're married," I told her. "I meant what I said. I'll take care of both of us. Of your family, too."

She pulled away and resumed dressing, zipping her jeans and reaching for her T-shirt.

"That's not how it works," she said, her voice quiet.

I didn't understand her stubbornness, but I wasn't going to let Anja's hesitation stand in the way of our happiness. It was a problem I could fix. She just didn't realize it.

"Don't you love me?" I asked.

"Just because I love you, it doesn't mean we can be together. Not like you're asking. Even though it sounds like a fairytale." Her voice caught in her throat, and I could see her eyes glistening with unshed tears.

I felt triumphant. She *did* want to be with me. "If you love me, then trust that I will find a way to make this work," I said. "Can you do that? Can you just...trust me?"

Finally, her eyes locked on mine. I saw the glimmer of hope there, and felt a surge of emotion go through me, my chest swelling.

"I trust you," she said. "But...I need some time. Okay?"

I swept her into my arms and kissed her, holding her tightly. I never wanted to let her go.

And if I had my way, I wouldn't have to.

When she left a few hours later, she had agreed to think about my proposal, just as I had promised to fix whatever problems she was afraid of encountering. I was on top of the world. My whole life was ahead of me, my future bright, and now I'd have Anja at my side.

I still felt that way when I got a text from her a few days later saying we needed to talk. I was certain she was ready to officially say yes, so I rushed over after school, making a stop at home first to grab the engagement ring I was eager to slide onto her finger.

But when I arrived at the apartment KZ Modeling had set her up in, I found it empty. Completely stripped bare. Besides the sparse modern furniture that had been there when she moved in, I found none of her books, no clothes, not even a toothbrush. Even the many vases of fresh flowers that I had delivered to her place each week—which she never threw away—were gone. It was as if she'd never been there at all. None of the other models who lived in the building or on her floor could tell me anything. None of them knew where she had gone.

I texted her and called her, but there was no response.

Unsure of what to do, my adrenaline pumping hard, I

got in a cab to go see the one man who had the power to fix anything—and everything. My father.

When I arrived at his office in the KZM building, it was almost as if he'd been waiting for me.

"Anja Borjan is missing," I said, not caring that I was out of breath. "And everything of hers is gone from her apartment. Something's not right. I talked to a few of the other girls, but nobody knows where she went."

"Yes, I know," my father said disinterestedly.

He had never been a warm man. Never been especially kind or fatherly, but the coldness in his voice at that moment stopped me in my tracks.

"Wait—you knew about this? So where is she?"

He glanced down at the paperwork on his desk, barely paying any attention to me.

"She's been deported."

It felt like the ground had dropped out from under me. I sank down in a chair, my knees failing me.

"How? Why? We need to get her back," I told him.

My father shook his head. "She was here illegally. There's nothing we can do."

"But I'm in love with her," I said, the words coming out of me in a rush. It wasn't how I had envisioned telling my father about our relationship, but there wasn't time for that now. "I'm in love with her and I'm going to marry her, so her immigration status won't be a problem. She'll be a full citizen."

My father looked up at me, his gaze hard as diamonds. "You think I didn't know about your little tryst?" he asked. "You think I haven't known about every single one of my models you've fucked around with?"

I flinched at his words. "This is different," I said. "*Anja* is different. I need you to get her back."

He smiled, and I finally felt myself relax. It was going to be okay.

And then he spoke.

"Why would I get her back?" he asked. "I'm the one who had her deported."

"*What?*" I said, my chest caving in. "Why?"

"Because no son of mine is marrying a whore."

The room seemed to spin as despair turned into fury. I wanted to reach across the desk and grab my father by the lapels of his Armani suit, punch the smug look off his face.

"You hypocrite," I choked out. "Treating your employees like they're worthless trash, after all they do for you. For our business. You were an immigrant too, Dad. How could you do this?"

He shrugged, cutting the end off a fresh cigar. "It's just business. Don't be naïve, Stefan."

I shook my head in disgust, disbelieving. "This is how you do business, how you treat our models? Like they're inferior beings? I can't believe any of them chose to work for you."

My father laughed. But when he looked at me, there was no humor in his eyes.

"What makes you think they had a choice?"

It was a punch to the gut. I felt numb in my chair as I watched him light his cigar and take a few languid puffs.

All this time, I had assumed that the women were sleeping with clients of their own free will. That they saw it as an opportunity to help themselves and their families. I never in a million years imagined that they had been coerced into sex work. Never would have imagined that *my father* had coerced them into it.

I had been a fool. An ignorant, childish fool.

Why hadn't Anja told me? Why hadn't she confided in me, as I'd confided in her?

Fury filled me. Not at her, but at my father. The monster in front of me, smoking his cigar and casually flipping through a series of photographs from a recent high fashion shoot.

Fuck him. I was going to find Anja. I would bring her back. I would make things right.

Almost as if he could read my mind, my father set down a photo, the smile slipping.

"Don't even think of going after her," he said. "You had your fun. It's time to grow up."

I didn't say anything, just returned his gaze, my jaw tightening in order to keep myself from saying things I couldn't take back. Because as much as I hated my father in that moment, I was aware that I was still a minor. Still just seventeen and completely dependent on him and his money. Money I would need access to if I was ever going to get Anja back.

"If you want any part of this business, boy, you need to get in line with what's best for the family. Or I'll make sure you never get a cent of KZM's profits. Is that clear?"

I was trapped. Like a caged animal. I only shrugged, not wanting to assent.

He went on, "You want to be a partner? Take charge someday, when I retire?"

I did, but it killed me to admit it. "Yes," I finally ground out.

"Then you'll do exactly as I say." He came around the desk, leaning against it so he could look down at me as he smoked. "Zorics always look out for each other. You understand?"

All I could do was nod. One tight, short nod.

"Good. I'll hear no more of this," he said.

With a wave of his hand, he dismissed me.

I trudged out of his office defeated and at a loss. And furious.

My father had won this battle, but what he didn't realize was that the war had just begun. From now on, I would play smart and I would play quietly. Because I had to get Anja back. I had to fix what my father had broken. No matter what. The stakes were too high, the victory too important. There was no other option.

I was going to destroy him.

TORI

CHAPTER 1

earing my eyes away from Stefan's cold glare, my hand scrabbled for the door knob behind me. I burned with rage at the sight of my husband standing there beside my father, both of them completely impassive despite my horror over the explosive, dark secret behind KZ Modeling's business—a secret I'd just revealed that I had figured out on my own.

"Tori," my father began.

"Just—don't." I shook my head, fury making my voice tremble. It was almost like I was watching the scene from outside my body. My logical mind had retreated, gone somewhere else. I had never felt more betrayed in my life.

My gaze shifted between my father and Stefan, the reality of the situation still sinking in. How could they have known about this, been a *part* of this? And god, all those women. Scores of women. Degraded and discarded by powerful, careless men who used them for their own gain.

I was disgusted with the men standing before me, but I was also disgusted with myself. For trusting them. For trusting Stefan. For falling in love with him. I felt sick.

"You're not my father anymore," I choked out.

My father shook his head at me gently, his expression disapproving. As if I was merely a child throwing a temper tantrum, instead of a grown woman whose father had married her off to a family that used its employees as sexual playthings to be bought and sold.

"I'm going to the authorities," I said, finally regaining some control, my voice like ice.

They exchanged a glance.

"I'm afraid that won't go well for you," my father said. "And you have zero evidence."

That stopped me cold. He was right. It would be my word against his, against Stefan's, against the entire Zoric empire. I knew what I had seen with my own eyes, what I had heard from Konstantin's mouth, but would any of the models agree to back up my story and tell the truth? Would they testify if there could be retribution, if they could lose their jobs or be harmed for talking? Could they find strength in their own numbers?

"I have witnesses," I bluffed. "They'll stand with me."

"It won't *work*, Tori," my father said, his voice like steel.

"You're not outside the law," I spat. I glared at my husband. "And neither are you, or your father, or the whole fucking KZM agency. I'm going to burn all of you to the ground."

I took out my phone, my hands still shaking, but neither of them looked concerned.

"I could call 9-1-1 right now," I said. "Tell them everything."

"You're welcome to try," my husband taunted me. "See how far that gets you."

"It would be best to avoid any embarrassing scenes," my father tsked. "I'd hate to see this on the news later...Senator

Lindsey's daughter making a frantic emergency phone call, raving about delusional scandals and international crime rings. Her mental health called into question."

He was disgusting. They all were. I lifted my phone, but I couldn't get my fingers to move. What if he was right? What would I say? What would the authorities do? Anything at all?

"Keep her in her place," he told Stefan, a warning note in his voice.

My "place"? It was the last straw.

I turned around, flung the door open, and slammed the door behind me before storming toward the bank of elevators.

I wasn't sure if I could stand to see either one of them ever again.

But when it came to my husband, I didn't have a choice —because before the elevator could close, Stefan thrust his hand between the doors and stepped inside with me.

I didn't want to look at him, let alone be in a confined space with him. And still, I hated the way my pulse leapt when he looked at me. The way my body responded as he moved closer.

"Don't touch me," I warned as his hand came up to reach for me.

Thankfully he listened, his hand hovering between us for a moment before he let it fall at his side. "I can't let you leave here alone," he said. "I won't let you process this by yourself."

I scoffed. "Really? Pretty sure I just heard *Senator Lindsey* tell you to keep me in my place. So if that's what you're here to do, forget about it. I'm calling the cops. If I were you—"

He grabbed my shoulders and slammed me back against

the wall, not hard enough to hurt but hard enough to shock me into shutting my mouth. I couldn't read the expression on his face as I looked up at him, but what else was new? He was just as inscrutable as ever. But at least he wasn't wearing the same smug look my father had been.

"The thing is..." he said, his body pressing against mine, "my father and your father both have friends on the force. *High up* in the force. You understand? Calling the police won't work."

"I'll go to the FBI, then," I shot back. "You won't get away with this."

He sighed. "Tori, listen. KZM is operating under the knowledge—and protection—of people in the highest levels of law enforcement in the country." He paused a moment, letting his meaning sink in. "No matter where you turn, you won't find a sympathetic ear. And you won't be helping any of those girls, either. If anything, they'll be endangered. I can guarantee you that my father wouldn't bat an eye at making them disappear. And I'm worried about you, too."

"Is that a threat?" I asked. I tried to sound tough, even though I was scared.

"It's a promise—and a warning," he said. "You know how my father is. You've seen it with your own eyes. You'll do more harm than good trying to blow a whistle. So don't try to play the vigilante, please. You won't be safe. I swear to god, I'm telling you the truth."

And god damn it, but he was. I could tell that much.

The elevator dinged and Stefan stepped back.

"I want to be alone," I said, walking past him and out into the lobby.

I needed a chance to process this information, to figure out what my next move was. I wasn't going to just let this stand, but I had to come up with a plan. Flying off the handle in a hot rage like this wouldn't help anyone. Not those women and definitely not me. My own father was against me, and Stefan was right about Konstantin as well—he was a dangerous man.

I felt helpless and hopeless. I was just one person up against a huge and evil corporation that had a powerful politician—and the law—in its corner. What could I do? Who could I trust?

Back on the street outside, I tried to hail a cab, but Stefan grabbed my hand.

"We're going back to the apartment," he told me, punching a text into his phone.

I glared at him. "I'm not going anywhere with you."

"You need to grow up," he snapped. "Did you listen to anything I just said? These women's *lives* are at stake. And if you threaten KZM's livelihood, you threaten theirs too. So you'll keep your mouth shut and accept the reality of the situation." He looked around and then lowered his voice. "Because if you don't, we're all *fucked*. Their careers, the families they care for, our income and apartment, my job, your education, your father's Senate seat—"

"I can't believe you're on their side," I said, fighting back tears. "How could you?"

"You have to understand, Tori—everything is on the line. For all of us."

Stefan's private car pulled up to the curb, and the driver got out and held the door open for us. With a scowl, I slid into the backseat. Stefan climbed in beside me.

As we pulled into traffic, he leaned close, his voice hot in my ear.

"This is how it has to be," he told me. "You've known from the beginning what your life would be, what this agreement would be—so stay in your box. Your role is to go to college, play nice at social events, and at the end of the day you come home and suck my dick every night. You can't dwell on the men's business. This is the only way you'll be safe. Understand?"

I stared at him, unable to speak. How could this man be two completely conflicting people at the same time? Kind and caring one moment and cruel beyond belief the next?

"Just keep your head down and be the obedient wife you were raised to be," he went on. "You know your place."

I didn't say anything, just stared down at his hand wrapped tightly around my arm.

"Tell me you understand, and that you're not still thinking about endangering yourself or anyone else," he demanded, his green eyes blazing.

I managed a nod, even though my heart was breaking into a million pieces. Finally Stefan released me. I turned away to stare out the window at the Chicago streets flashing past us. I could feel my pulse finally start to relax, and I took a deep breath, exhaling slowly.

As much as I loathed to admit it, he was right. His life, my life, and the livelihoods of these women depended on KZ Modeling and its success. So until I came up with a brilliant plan that would keep us all safe and see justice served without interference, I would have to bite my tongue and play the part they all wanted me to play. I'd be the obedient wife Stefan wanted.

The thought of doing so nearly killed me, but I knew that I had no other choice—not yet, anyway. Not with Konstantin keeping an eye on me, not with the law in his pocket, not with my own father willing to stop at nothing to keep me silent.

But I wouldn't stay silent forever.

TORI

CHAPTER 2

People love saying that the secret to lasting relationships is compromise. But what the hell did they really know about it? By keeping KZ Modeling's secret, I'd be compromising more than just my wants or needs; this was about human rights, moral standards, basic decency.

As we sat in traffic just a few blocks away from our condo—*Stefan's condo*, I corrected myself—I thought hard about the word *compromise*. It had originated in the early fifteenth century, and its Latin roots could be traced back to the combination of the words *promittere*, "to promise," and *com*, meaning "together." My relationship with Stefan, in this respect, had always been a compromise—since the very first time we'd met, at my eighteenth birthday party—a promise we'd made together.

I hadn't gone into my marriage impetuously, despite the fact that we'd gotten engaged within minutes of being formally introduced. We'd talked it over first, weighed the implications of the union that our fathers were trying to force us into. Stefan swore that if we got married, we'd make our own lives and our own choices, independent of our controlling fathers' wishes. We'd forge our own paths. We'd live for *ourselves*. We'd both get what we wanted. But now here we were, completely at the mercy of the decisions and actions—or inactions—of our fathers. And Stefan had known all along. From day one, my husband had lied to me. Played me.

Not only that, but now that I knew he'd purposely omitted the truth about the back-room dealings that his family's agency engaged in, it had completely shattered my trust in him.

I wasn't going to let this stand.

As we stepped into the foyer of the condo, I cleared my throat and leaned against the doorway, blocking Stefan's route into the living room.

"I've made some decisions," I told him.

He nodded, his mouth set in a firm line. "Let's hear them, then."

"There are things I can't control or change about my situation, and I recognize that," I began. "We're married, at least for the next few years, as we discussed, and I'm dependent on you financially, in many ways. My tuition at UChicago, this condo, transportation, Gretna—"

My reference to our personal chef got a smile out of him, and I was glad. Let him think he was winning. Let him think I liked having my meals prepared for me more than I liked protecting women from human trafficking. Let him believe I was just a spoiled, selfish princess with no cares beyond my own comfort and well-being.

"—but while it's one thing to accept my role, you can't force me to embrace it," I finished.

Stefan's expression reverted to its scowl. "I don't expect you to. Just play the part."

"Oh, I fully intend to," I said, my voice low and as cold as I could make it. With that, I twisted off the huge diamond ring on my finger, and the pavé gold band that matched, and placed them both on the entryway table. "When I leave this house, I'll put them on," I said, gesturing to my wedding rings. "But when I'm here, at home, I'm not your slave."

"Is that what you think?" he growled, reaching to pull my body hard against him.

Our eyes locked, and I desperately fought against the desire spiking through my veins.

"It is," I said, twisting out of his grasp and storming down the hallway.

Just because we were married, and would remain so, it didn't mean I had to sleep in the same room as a monster. And I sure as hell wouldn't be sharing a bed with him.

"What are you doing?" he asked.

I didn't answer as I marched into the master bedroom. Stefan's bedroom. Because from now on it would be his, and his alone.

He stood silently in the doorway, watching me as I started angrily pulling clothes out of the closet and piling them in my arms. When I turned toward him, he didn't move.

"Why don't you put those down," he said, his voice deceptively reasonable.

"No," I said, shocked to hear the word fly out of my mouth so fast. I was defying him.

"No?" he repeated, and all the gentleness was gone.

I clutched the clothes I was holding more tightly, not sure what he would do. Would he pull the pile out of my hands, force me to hang everything back up? Would he tell me I had to stay in his room, continue sleeping beside him?

Even though I felt a tremor of fear, I held my ground. I

wasn't going to back down. After everything that had happened, I needed a victory—I needed to feel like I had some control, no matter how small.

I braced myself for him to start yelling, or for him to grab my arm and try to force me and my clothes back into the master closet. But instead of just standing there waiting, I set my jaw, lifted my chin, and walked past him into the hallway.

He said nothing, following me as I went down the hall and deposited the clothes in the guest room. It was half the size of the master, with a tiny closet, but I didn't care. I was going to have my own space, whether he liked it or not.

Back in the master bedroom, I gathered more of my things. Toiletries, underwear, my comfy T-shirts and leggings that I liked to wear to school so I could fit in with all the other co-eds. That load, too, got deposited on the bed in the guest room, along with my laptop.

"Stop," he finally said, blocking me in the hallway.

I looked up, almost daring him to touch me, directing all my fury toward him with my gaze. "Don't treat me like I'm a prisoner here," I said, even though it felt dangerous.

I was surprised when he backed down, stepping aside to let me pass.

"Fine," he said from behind me. "You obviously need some time to come to terms with our arrangement. I understand that."

Ignoring him, I walked back into the master to fill my arms with the rest of my nice clothes: the designer jeans, the flashy dresses I'd bought in Vienna during our honeymoon, the blue party dress I'd worn the first night we'd met. But even though my things were moving, I knew that the memories attached to them weren't going anywhere. As if they were woven into the fabric of every single dress I'd worn in his presence.

Turning toward the doorway, I caught him watching me, and for a split second I could've sworn I saw something in his face—regret. But it was gone so fast I doubted it had been real.

"Just do yourself a favor, Tori, and realize that I'm allowing you to do this as a kindness." He strode over to me and placed his hands on my shoulders. "And when I require my wife to behave as such, you *will* obey me."

His size overpowered me, reminding me how small I was compared to him.

My pulse kicked, and my cheeks went hot. Part of me wanted nothing more than to leave this nightmare behind, drop everything and get on my hands and knees, let him fuck me right there on the floor. Forget about our fight and the sordid truth behind KZM's business dealings—and my father's role in keeping them out of the public eye. But I couldn't forget any of it. If I performed my "wifely duties" going forward, they'd be exactly that—duties.

"Tell me you'll obey," Stefan repeated.

There was no room to argue. I nodded my consent.

After I dropped the rest of my things onto the guest room bed, I shut the door behind me. Then I set about hanging everything up in the empty closet and formally claiming the space as my own. But every item I picked up reminded me vividly and irrevocably of Stefan.

The simple black sheath dress I'd changed into after our wedding. All I could think about was how nervous I'd been unzipping it in the bathroom before changing into the white lace wedding night lingerie he'd done his best to resist. The sexy black cocktail dress I'd bought in Vienna, that even the shop girl had called *vavoom*, with all its complicated straps across the back. I'd worn it right out of the store in an effort to make Stefan jealous, to make him notice me. And here was the gorgeous gown I'd worn the night we had gone to the opera, with its daring neckline that plunged almost to my ass in the back. I'd worn it without a bra, to tempt him. The slinky, ice-blue silk gown I'd worn the night he stood me up, when we had fought and he'd finally kissed me the way I'd wanted him to. Hard and rough, his tongue fucking my mouth, my pussy instantly wet for him. It had been hot. So fucking hot.

And then there was the beautiful designer dress with its petal-scattered skirt that I'd worn for my eighteenth birthday party—the first time Stefan and I had met. A night where I had felt like a princess. Where he had called me Cinderella.

Where we'd shared our first kiss.

Blinking back tears, I abandoned the dresses and tried to focus on putting my underwear away in the top drawer of the dresser. It was hard to hold those beautiful, silky, sexy things and not think about how good it had felt when Stefan ripped them off of me.

I'd noticed that there was no lock on the guest room door. Which meant that if he wanted to, he could come into this room, into my bed, and take what he wanted. Take me however he wanted. Whenever he felt like it.

Standing there, a hot ache growing low in my belly, my hands tangled in lacy lingerie, I couldn't help imagining what it would be like; Stefan's intense, authoritative way of handling me playing out in an intensely sexual way. I couldn't deny that it made me hot. I knew it was wrong, knew he was a monster, but I couldn't erase the memories of him dominating my body. Just the way I liked it, the way he'd always been toward me. Controlled, confident, commanding.

But that part of our relationship, that intimacy, that intensity...it was all done and gone. Things were different now. If and when I fucked him, it wouldn't be the same.

I hadn't been trapped before. Back then, I had been a willing partner in a marriage—one of convenience, but one that I thought I understood. Now, I was trapped. Trapped in this life, this marriage, and now in this guest room. At Stefan's mercy and command. Because he was my captor.

And my enemy.

There was nothing I could do to change the situation yet, but it wouldn't always be this way. My husband had been right about one thing: I did need some time to come to terms with our arrangement. He just didn't know that I would be using that time to figure out my next move.

So I would play the good girl, the good wife, and I'd bide my time. Meanwhile, I'd find a way out, gather evidence, come up with a plan to save myself and all the other hurting women involved in this.

I felt powerful to have separated myself from Stefan already, even in this small way. To be drawing battle lines, fighting back, no matter how small the gesture was. It made me feel strong. Like I would survive.

Because this war was far from over.

TORI

CHAPTER 3

My strongest memory of Harper Memorial
Library on the UChicago campus wouldn't be
that first sight of the building's gorgeous,
medieval castle-like exterior with its walls covered in ivy
and two crenelated turrets, like someplace out of Harry
Potter or a King Arthur tale. It wouldn't be the gothic chandeliers overhead, the geometric patterns of the buttressed
ceiling, nor even the tall, narrow windows with their protective grates that filtered the sunlight pouring in.

It would be the instant, all-encompassing peace of the
space.

My first day of linguistics classes had been overwhelming and I'd been full of stress about whether I'd be
able to keep up with the work, and whether I'd be able to
measure up to my professors' expectations (and my own).
But when I walked into that library, the silence wrapped me
up like a soft blanket and all the weight on my shoulders
just floated away.

I could still remember the way my shoes made the
tiniest echo as I tiptoed across the gleaming parquet floors

toward one of the empty study tables. It was a quiet like I had never known.

Finding out the place was open 24 hours a day was a godsend. It quickly became my favorite haunt on campus, and I spent many hours between and after classes doing my homework at the long tables or catching up on my recommended reading on the third floor. You couldn't actually borrow any books there, but it didn't matter to me; I brought plenty of my own.

I sat in my favorite corner spot with my ASL homework spread out before me, practicing the careful signing of the alphabet as I faced a bookshelf. But my hands were clumsy, and my brain felt fuzzy. I'd thought this class would be fun, would help me communicate with the Deaf community if given the chance, but halfway through the semester I could still barely manage my ABCs. No, that wasn't true. I knew basic words, phrases like *thank you, hello, my name is*...but lately everything had just gotten harder. Thanks to my home life with Stefan, I was a distracted mess. I was lucky to have school as a sanctuary, but I needed to get back into my studies.

Someone pulled out the chair across from me and I glanced up with annoyance, knowing there were plenty of other empty seats at this hour. But my classmate Gavin slid into the seat, and I felt a smile immediately pull up the corners of my mouth. He'd been a late enrollment, transferring to our school from a great program at UC Berkeley. I still wasn't sure why he'd left UCB—every time we brought it up, he'd just make a joke about the hippies or the Silicon Valley crowd getting to be too much for him, or how the weather in California was too horribly perfect.

Hello, he signed.

Hello, G, I signed back. This was one way around the library's no-talking policy.

He raised his hands again to say, *How are you?*

I shrugged. It hadn't escaped his notice that I'd been sulking around ever since the huge fight with my dad and Stefan. Despite my mood, though, I'd spent even more time at group study sessions with Gavin and my best girlfriends Lila, Diane, and Audrey. Anything to keep me from having to go back home. Gavin especially had been a balm to my frayed nerves, grabbing coffee with me between classes and talking with me for ages in the commons.

Evening meal now, he told me. It was dinner time.

Glancing at my watch, I realized he was right. It was almost seven, and I hadn't eaten for hours. I nodded and began packing up my things, but as I stood he gently took my arm and signed, *Go with me?* His warm brown eyes were hopeful.

To evening meal? I gestured.

He nodded, flashing that contagious, dimpled grin that my friends couldn't seem to get enough of. I might have been married, but I had to admit it was a nice smile. Boyish. Charming.

With friends? I asked.

Me and you, he answered, pointing first at himself and then at me.

I hesitated. We'd hung out alone at school plenty of times before, but when it came to going somewhere off campus, it had always been a group activity with at least one other friend. Was this like...a date? But no. Gavin knew I was married. Knew we were just friends.

I nodded and flashed him a thumbs-up, using my left hand to make sure he got a good look at my wedding rings. Just in case.

Why should I worry, anyway? It wasn't as if anyone would be waiting up for me at home, besides maybe Gretna...and by now our personal chef was used to packing up our meals when neither Stefan nor I could make it home in time for dinner—which had been frequently as of late, since school had turned into my place of exile.

Plus, Gavin was born and raised in Chicago, so he knew all the best spots to hang out in the city. I was sure I'd be in for a treat.

Wordlessly, I hooked my arm through Gavin's and let him lead me out of the library.

"So where are we going?" I asked as we walked across campus.

"It's a surprise," he said. "You cool taking the L? My car's at home today."

"I suppose I could endure a bit of public transportation," I teased. "But this restaurant better be worth it."

"Don't worry, princess," he said, using the nickname all my friends threw at me whenever I wore designer heels to class or got picked up by a private car. "It will be."

Everything with Gavin felt easy and fun. Why couldn't it be this way with Stefan?

We took the subway downtown, which (despite my joking) really was a novelty for me, since I mostly traveled via Stefan's private car or one of my ride-sharing apps. I hoped Gavin was taking us somewhere exciting and energetic, because my eyelids felt heavy as I stared at the Chicago skyline out the train windows and allowed my thoughts to wander.

Despite the nightmare my life had become, and how difficult it was to fall asleep by myself in the big, lonely guest room, Stefan and I seemed to have reached an uneasy truce. One where we mostly avoided each other. I spent my days in class, studying at Harper, or hanging out with my school friends. Then I'd return to the condo as late as possible each night, knowing he could track me through my cell phone at any time if he wanted to know where I was. Though I doubted my husband cared enough to bother.

I was certain he was cheating. His days seemed to go longer and longer, half the time he didn't even come home at all, and the other half he'd get in after midnight. I told myself I didn't care, that it didn't matter who he was slept with. I didn't want him anyway. Not really.

When he was home, we didn't speak unless it was to say there was fresh coffee, or that Gretna had the day off. We were basically just roommates, and for all Stefan's posturing about how I was still expected to obey him when he "required" me to behave as his wife, he hadn't tried to put a hand on me.

Those first few nights, I'd tossed and turned for hours, waiting for him to slip into bed after midnight the way he had always done. I kept stirring at every small noise, thinking that it might be him, coming to claim my body, pound into me with that punishing cock until I came.

I was ashamed that I had such thoughts. That I got hot and wet thinking about it. That I still wore my same silky, lacy lingerie, just begging to be torn off of me. That part of me was even entertaining the possibility that things could go back to normal—that I could forget the reality of our situation. Of my situation. But old habits die hard.

My life seemed to float by in a haze. It was almost a dance, the two of us orbiting each other in the same space, but on two separate continents emotionally. It stung, even though I knew I should be happy the monster was staying away from me. I was just lonely, that was all.

Sure, I missed kissing him and touching him and

fucking him, letting him fuck me and own me and make my toes curl—but that was because I'd only recently come to realize how good sex could be, and I'd become accustomed to his touch. Plus, I'd never slept with anyone else. Who else would I even fantasize about when I touched myself in the shower? Gavin Chase?

I glanced over at him, feeling myself blush, hoping there was no way he could read my thoughts.

"Next stop's ours," he said, as the train slowed.

I looked up at the name of the station. "Navy Pier Terminal? We're going to Navy Pier?" I thought about the Centennial Wheel there, and my stomach lurched with unbidden memories of the ferris wheel that Stefan had taken me on during our honeymoon in Vienna.

He shot me that winning, dimpled grin as we walked through the terminal. "I know, I know—it's got a bad rap. The number one tourist attraction in Chicago, yada yada. But trust me, it's changed over the past few years. And there's a restaurant in the botanical gardens with an amazing rooftop bar."

I was skeptical. "A rooftop bar? In this weather?" I gestured at the cloudy sky above us as we stepped out onto the street. "It looks like it might snow."

"It's barely November," he said. "We'll be fine."

I was shivering, though, so he wrapped a friendly arm around my shoulder, pulling me close. I let myself lean into his warmth, but kept my arms crossed over my chest as we walked toward the lights of the pier.

"You don't need to worry about the weather, honestly. It's an enclosed rooftop—all glass. You'll love it," Gavin promised. "It's got incredible views of the skyline and you can see all the city lights reflected in the water. Plus, if you really do hate it, we'll leave. Cool?"

It was a novelty. Someone asking me where *I* wanted to go.

"Cool," I said, returning his smile. It was hard not to. "But if I hate it, not only are we going somewhere else, but you're buying me the pinkest, frilliest cocktail they have."

"No can do," he said. "You're underage."

"Who told you that?" I asked, indignant.

"Lila may have spilled about the "strip club incident" earlier this semester," he admitted, smiling. "I heard your husband showed up all mad and dragged you home before you saw even a single oiled-up six pack or bow tie."

I felt my face go hot. "I can't believe they told you that!"

He laughed. "College hijinks. We all get into 'em. No judgement here."

"Then you'll have to get yourself a drink so we can share it," I suggested, elbowing him in the side. "You can make it a double. Double pink frill."

He shook his head. "Sorry, princess. I'm happy to buy you a Shirley Temple, though."

"Who do you think you are, my father?" I teased. The second I thought about my dad, though, my good mood dissipated. I took a deep breath and tried to banish my frown.

Gavin seemed to notice. "What's wrong?" he asked, pulling me to the railing and out of the flow of pedestrian traffic. "Talk to me."

"Nothing," I said, staring off into the choppy water.

"You got all quiet and pensive," he pointed out. "I know your tells. It's not nothing."

I took a breath. Gavin could read me so well. It was one of the things I really liked about him. He was always so attentive to the people around him.

"I guess it's not," I admitted. "I...had an argument

with my dad a few weeks back. Over something he did. Or didn't do, but should have. We still haven't fixed things between us, and I don't feel good about it. It's been on my mind." I shrugged. There was more to it, of course, but I didn't want to bring Stefan into it. Didn't want to give Gavin any indication that my marriage was in trouble.

He was quiet as we stared out at the waters of Lake Michigan together, his arm still warm around my shoulders, the icy air drying my tears before they could fall.

"That's one of the things about growing up," Gavin finally said. "You start to realize that your parents are people, too. They're not perfect. Just people. Even senators like your dad. They have flaws, they make mistakes..."

"This was a pretty big mistake," I said. "I don't know if I can forgive it."

He nodded. "Give it some time, then. No rush. Your heart will know what's right."

I couldn't help smiling. I had no idea if things between me and my father would ever be okay again, but what Gavin had said was exactly what I needed to hear. "Thanks, Gav."

"Any time."

The rooftop bar and restaurant at the Crystal Gardens was beautiful, and it took my breath away. Panes of glass arched overhead, fountains and twinkling lights and palm trees abounded, and even the flagstones under our feet all made it obvious we were in a huge tropical greenhouse.

"This place is gorgeous," I said, my voice hushed in awe.

"I thought you'd appreciate it," Gavin said.

We chatted about our classes at school until our food arrived, a delicious spread of shrimp and linguini and a steak cooked so perfectly it practically melted in my mouth.

"This is way too fancy," I said in between bites. "I shouldn't have let you order."

"It's the least I can do after you tutored me back up to a B+ in Latin," he said. "Those conjugations kill me every time."

"You never seem to struggle during our sessions," I pointed out.

"That's because I have such a good teacher," he said, reaching across the table to take my hand. Our eyes locked. "Do you have any idea how amazing you are?"

I felt my pulse quicken and I pulled my hand away. "Gavin, I—I really, really like you. But...as a friend. This isn't a date."

I couldn't help wondering, though, what it would be like to date Gavin. He didn't just call me princess—he treated me like one. And almost anyone would treat me better than Stefan had been lately. Gavin was also handsome, there was no denying it. He didn't have the same confidence and polish that Stefan carried himself with, the same animal magnetism that made my knees go weak, but who did? Stefan was a breed in and of himself—I knew I would just be disappointed if I tried to compare any other man to him.

But Gavin had other things going for him. For one, he didn't seem like the kind of guy who broke the law. He certainly wasn't involved in running a trafficking ring, but I doubted he had ever even jaywalked. He had that all-American, squeaky clean persona going for him. The kind of guy who wore faded, well-fitting jeans and a T-shirt. He was casual. Laid-back. Simple. Easy.

Exactly what I needed right now.

Yet all I could think about was my traitorous, cold, but incredibly sexy husband.

"Of course it's not a date," Gavin said, laughing it off

casually. "We're just two friends out for a celebratory meal. I didn't mean anything by it." But his gaze slid away from mine.

"And anyway, I'm not amazing. I'm just awesome at Latin because I spent four years studying it obsessively in high school," I said, trying to deflect the tension between us. "Total nerd status."

"You're not a nerd," he said. "You're brilliant."

I blushed all the way to my toes.

"And besides, look how far it's gotten you," he went on. "*Labor omnia vincit.*"

"'Hard work conquers all'," I translated with a sigh. "All except my mental health. This semester is actually making me crazy. I can't believe midterms are already coming up."

"Then maybe the more relevant phrase is, '*panem et circenses*'?" he said, raising a brow.

"'Bread and circuses'?" I asked, mopping up a bit of melted butter with the last scrap of French bread.

"They're said to be the basic requirements for human happiness," he said. "You know. Food and entertainment."

"Well, we've got half of that covered," I said, gesturing at the now-empty plates.

He grinned. "Then let me take you to the other half."

The other half turned out to be the Funhouse Maze, full of twists and turns and glowing fluorescent lights, room after room of glow-in-the-dark landscapes, tunnels, mirrors, and galaxies splashed across the floors. There was also a game where you chased colored lights for points. I didn't even realize I'd been clinging to Gavin's arm the whole time until we were finally out of the place and back on the pier. I was completely out of breath, and couldn't stop laughing despite how brisk the air had gotten, how bracing the wind was.

"That was so fun!" It had been so nice to get outside my own head for a while.

Gavin grinned, and gently let my arm go. "My mom used to take me and my brother Frank here when we were little. We used to race to see who could get out of the maze first."

"Well thanks for showing me," I said.

We had a quiet moment, just smiling at each other contentedly. It was so relaxed between us, so warm. So different from what I had been experiencing with Stefan these past few months. Here was someone who was kind to me, who asked for my opinion, who listened to me. Who seemed to genuinely like me.

I broke our gaze and realized a single snowflake had dropped onto my coat. And then another. And then two more. "It's snowing," I said. "I told you! First snow of the season."

We looked up at the sky and watched a million little flurries come down, catching the light from the pier attractions as they floated toward us like feathers. I closed my eyes and tilted my head back, letting the soft flakes tickle my face. When I laughed, I realized Gavin's lips were almost brushing mine, the heat of his mouth so close I could feel it.

I imagined myself tilting closer, closing the gap between our lips and finding out what kissing Gavin felt like, seeing if I could lose myself in it—but suddenly all I could see was intense green eyes, dark hair, that chiseled jawline. Stefan.

I pulled away abruptly.

"I can't," I said.

"I'm sorry, Tori. God, I'm an idiot. You just looked so..." Gavin shook his head, running a hand through his hair, and I could tell he really hadn't meant to lose control. "No excuses. That was strike two. I better put you in a cab."

We walked down the pier wordlessly, until we finally reached the street where the taxis were queuing up.

"Listen," I said, as my cab pulled forward. "I had a great time. Let's just forget about the...what happened. Water under the bridge."

He nodded. "Still friends?"

"Of course." I smiled and ducked into the back of the car. "Maybe we can do this again sometime. Invite the others, too."

"Yup. See you in class."

I gave a final wave and rolled the window up, burrowing into the warmth of my coat in the backseat.

As we pulled away from the curb, I turned to watch him. He stood there, hand still raised in goodbye as tiny snowflakes drifted onto his shoulders. I couldn't believe what a complete idiot I was being. Here was a kind, handsome, smart, and equally studious man who liked me, word-nerdiness and all. Why couldn't I like him back? Why couldn't I kiss him? Why couldn't I go out with him and have fun without guilt?

But try as I might to get lost in my not-date with Gavin, I still hadn't been able to erase Stefan from my thoughts. All night I'd been thinking about his kiss. His cock. I told myself that it was normal to feel like this, to have confusing, conflicting emotions, to desire him physically and emotionally even when I knew who he really was. What he was capable of.

But I still hated myself for it.

It wasn't fair. I never would have followed through with my marriage to Stefan if I had known what it really meant. But they had all kept the truth from me—my father, Konstantin Zoric, Stefan himself—all of them had obscured the reality of what I was agreeing to.

My brain knew this.

My heart on the other hand...

My heart seemed to be having a much harder time letting go of the fantasy I had imagined on the night of my eighteenth birthday. The night where I had been dressed like a princess and promised a fairy tale wedding. A romantic future. A marriage of possibilities. I had considered myself and Stefan a team, working together to break free from our fathers' machinations for our respective futures. I had never imagined that Stefan was part of those machinations. That he was just as much the enemy as my father was.

A tear slipped down my cheek and I quickly swiped it away. I was tired of crying over Stefan, but I couldn't help myself. A part of me was still grieving for the fantasy that had died. The fantasy I had built out of a look from a handsome man across a ballroom. The fantasy I had built from a kiss. From a promise.

It had all been nothing but a lie.

My mind knew it. My mind knew exactly what had happened, what was still happening—and exactly how fucked up the whole situation was.

I just needed to convince my heart of the same.

TORI

CHAPTER 4

Though it was a cold, overcast November day in Chicago, as far as I was concerned, the sun was shining, the birds were singing, and everything was on the upside.

I'd been stressing for weeks about a big project for my Linguistic Landscapes class, a group assignment worth 30% of our grade. Luckily I'd been partnered with Gavin and Diane, my good friend and hippie classmate from Vermont, both of whom took the class as seriously as I did. And today, the results were finally in. Our geo-tagged map of Chicago and the accompanying research paper on the usage and display of language at specific spots in the city had earned us all a big fat A. Praise Jesus.

We'd worked our tails off, taken field trips all over town to snap photos of signs, subway maps, informational displays, and place markers, and the paper we'd all taken turns writing examined the way language was used to communicate with the public via these signs. With midterm exams looming ever closer, it was a huge relief to know I had this class practically in the bag. Professor Angstrom, for all her enthusiastic and brilliant lecturing, was not known to grade gently.

"We kicked its ass!" I yelled. With a whoop of triumph, I spun away from the grade sheet posted on the bulletin board outside our lecture hall. It took all of my self-control not to rip the paper off the board and kiss it—or run back inside the classroom to kiss our professor—but instead I threw my arms around Diane and Gavin, pulling them in for a group hug.

"Angstrom gave us an A!" I crowed. "You guys really came through for me. I owe you."

It felt like a huge victory—despite the fight with my father and the awful situation at home with my monstrous husband and our cold relationship, I'd managed to double down on my studies and lean on my school friends so I could keep up with my program. It was so much easier to focus on schoolwork than it was to think about Stefan and everything going on with KZM.

"Angstrom didn't "give" us anything—we *earned* that A. We make a great team." Diane laughed in her gentle way, readjusting the hemp backpack that I'd knocked off her shoulder. "And you definitely don't owe us anything. We all contributed equally."

"I disagree about the owing," Gavin said warmly, looking straight at me. "I think we've earned ourselves a celebration. You do owe us that."

If he was holding a grudge for the almost-kiss that I'd rejected on our not-date at Navy Pier, he kept it well hidden. If anything, he'd been treating me with even more kindness lately. When we studied with our group, he was always checking in to make sure I had everything I needed, occasionally asking how things were going with my father or if Stefan's late nights at work had eased up at all (in both cases I had no news to report). I'd never had such an abundance of highlighters, study snacks, or sympathetic ears in my life. Gavin was actually kind of perfect.

Just not perfect for me.

"You're coming out tonight, right?" he asked after we had gotten out of our last class later that evening. "Diane said Audrey is in, too. And Lila's bringing Tucker, so we'll have a little friendly testosterone to balance us out at the bar." He shot me that winning, dimpled grin.

"I don't know," I said, still debating.

I knew it was stupid, but part of me wanted to be at home tonight waiting for Stefan, so I could tell him about my A. I'd mentioned the project in passing, since it had required me to ask for help using the printer in his home office, and I had stressed that it was a huge part of my grade. I couldn't help wanting to brag, hoping he'd maybe say he was proud of me. I still wanted to believe that the man who had attended the program's first semester mixer with me, who'd played the perfect, supportive spouse in front of the dean and my favorite professor and all my classmates, was still in there somewhere. That it hadn't all been an act. That some of it was real.

But I knew I was setting myself up for disappointment.

"Come on," Gavin urged. "You've been hitting the books nonstop lately. Which, don't get me wrong, is awesome. I'm incredibly impressed with you. Totally in awe."

There he went, making me blush again. "Everybody studies," I deflected.

Gavin squeezed my shoulder, sending warmth through me. "Not like you do, Tori. But my point is, you need a break. You've earned it. *Panem et circenses*, remember?"

Bread and circuses—the Latin phrase he'd taught me on

our not-date. And he was right. I needed food and entertainment to be happy, to live a full life. I'd been hibernating for weeks.

"Are you saying there's food involved?" I asked.

"Absolutely there will be food," Gavin said. "I'll pick you up around eight."

"Oh, no," I said. "Thank you. But I can take a car. Really. It'd be better if...well. I prefer to do my own thing."

I didn't want to tell him that I was afraid Stefan might see me leaving with Gavin, might get the wrong impression. Even though making my husband jealous might be a smart move, all things considered, I didn't want to add to our marital struggles right now.

"Is this just your way of bailing out?" Gavin teased. "I can tell you're still waffling."

I thought about it for a moment, weighing my options. I could go home, eat alone and hide in my room until Stefan came home, ultimately tossing and turning until I fell asleep alone...or I could go out and have fun, celebrate my academic victories with a group of friends who genuinely liked spending time with me, including one very handsome man who would probably kiss me the second I gave him the go ahead. Not that I would.

But I could. If I wanted to.

"I need to go home and shower and change," I told Gavin. "But I'll be there. Text me the address where you guys are gonna be and I'll meet up with you."

"Promise?" he asked.

I grinned. "Promise. I can't wait."

I was still smiling when I got home, but that smile dropped when I got to my room and found a complete outfit laid out on my bed.

And not just an everyday outfit or something that had

been pulled from my closet. No, everything on my bed was brand new, obviously expensive, and very, very classy.

I saw an elegant Chanel evening bag, black with a gold clasp, and a matching pair of heels beside it. There were several velvet jewelry boxes, containing a diamond cuff bracelet that almost looked like a piece of lace with all its intricate filigree work, two more delicate gold bangles to match, and an opera-length pearl necklace. And then there was the dress.

There was no denying it was absolutely gorgeous.

It was a black Gucci gown, perfect for the late fall season with its bracelet-length, longer sleeves and floor-length hem. The fabric was sleek, with a hint of sheen, the waistline ruched and the back open. Besides the daring back and a subtle, thigh-high slit up the skirt—that could expose either none or most of my left leg, depending on how I was standing—the dress was fairly modest. That perfect combination of sexy and respectable. I couldn't help touching the fabric gently, not sure why this outfit was on my bed.

Then I heard footsteps behind me.

Stefan hadn't just come home before to set all this out for me—he was still here.

I whirled to face him.

Annoyingly, and unsurprisingly, my heart started pounding at the sight of him. He was dressed in one of my favorite suits of his, a black Armani with a satin collar that fit him impeccably. His dark hair was combed, but a stray lock had already fallen over his forehead, giving him a devil-may-care appearance that made my pulse leap and my core go hot and liquid.

I told myself that it wasn't my fault for reacting this way. He was an attractive man. My body, therefore, was attracted to him. That didn't mean anything had changed between us.

"You're home," he said, his tone expressionless.

His cool tone and minimal words were typical at this point, but his deep voice still made goosebumps rise on my skin. It was impossible to forget all the things he had ever said to me in that voice—all the flirting, the teasing, the sexy words he'd groaned into my ear when he fucked me. The intense sexual commands he had enjoyed issuing. Commands I had enjoyed following.

Before we'd stopped touching each other. Before I'd learned the truth about him.

"What's this for?" I asked, gesturing toward the bed.

"That's what you'll be wearing tonight," he said. "We're leaving in less than an hour. You'll need to wear your hair up, and minimal makeup. No lipstick."

I blinked at him.

"Wherever you seem to think we're going, I can't," I said flatly. "I have plans."

He narrowed his eyes. "You do have plans. With me. We're going to a fundraiser."

"What? I never agreed to this," I sputtered.

"Don't act like a child," he said. "This event has been on your calendar for months."

"What is this fundraiser even for?" I asked. Maybe I could go with Stefan to make a brief appearance and then just sneak out early to meet my friends, as I'd intended.

"It's a very important, highly publicized event that raises money to fight human trafficking all over the world. KZM is a huge supporter."

My mouth dropped open. "Is this your idea of a joke?" If so, it was a sick one.

The look on his face told me he was dead serious. "All our executives attend every year."

"Well then you can attend yourself," I told him, folding my arms. "I'm not going."

He didn't even blink. "It's not up for discussion. You will get dressed, fix your hair and makeup, and be ready to walk out the door in—" he checked his watch, "—forty minutes."

"*Seriously?*" I felt hysterical, caught between a sob and a laugh. "You think I'd actually attend a fundraiser for *sex trafficking* with someone who runs an illegal prostitution ring?"

Saying the words out loud to Stefan felt good, defiant and strong—but that lasted all of two seconds before he advanced on me, his green eyes cold and intimidating. I shrank back.

"You will do as I say. You will wear exactly what I tell you to wear, and attend any and all events that I schedule for you," he commanded. "My father is watching us, so put on a good performance tonight and pretend you're on the right team. You have no other choice."

Even though I could feel my knees shaking, I forced myself to meet his gaze. I knew he'd already won. I hated it, but there wasn't anything I could do about it. And when it came to what Konstantin Zoric was capable of, I knew better than to cross the man. As much as I hated this whole situation, I did believe that Stefan truly was trying to keep me safe—and alive.

I just felt so defeated. It had been hard enough to come to terms with who my husband was when I was dealing with it in private. When I could focus on school and friends and pretend that this all wasn't happening, that I hadn't been betrayed by my family. Both of my families. But now I had to go out in public with Stefan. With his family. To a sham of a fundraiser like this. It felt like they were rubbing it in my face, and I couldn't do anything about it.

"Never forget who you are," he warned, standing so close I could feel his body heat.

It was completely different from how I felt when Gavin was next to me. My friend was warm, comforting, but...right now I could feel Stefan's anger, his passion, his intensity. It scared me, but it also turned me on. I wish it were different, or that the men in my life were reversed.

"You are my wife," he reminded me. "You will do your duty. You will fulfill your responsibilities. And you will *obey*. That is the bargain we made."

It was. But it was a bargain I never would have agreed to if I had known the truth.

"Forty minutes. No lipstick."

With that he left the room, slamming the door behind him. I sank down on the bed, my knees no longer able to hold me. Warring emotions flooded through me. Anger, frustration, desire. And desire, both emotional and sexual, that never seemed to stop burning deep inside me.

What would I have done if Stefan had kissed me? Would I have kissed him back?

I didn't know. I didn't know myself around him anymore.

I looked at the dress I was expected to wear, running my hands over the silky fabric. Next to the dress was a bag I hadn't noticed before, from an expensive lingerie shop. He had even chosen what was I supposed to wear underneath the dress. Typical of his controlling nature.

Opening the bag, I found a gorgeous pair of underwear, a web of delicate lace and satin that would be invisible underneath the dress. There was also a backless, adhesive

46

bra with ribbon laces down the middle. It looked like a set of angel's wings. I had never seen anything like it.

I rubbed the fine lace of the panties, the satin like water against my fingertips. Stefan had picked these out specifically for me. I tried in vain to banish my sexy thoughts.

Even though I was furious at my husband, I was smart enough to accept that this was a role I would have to play. I texted Gavin to say I couldn't make it due to a scheduling conflict, promising a raincheck soon, and began getting ready. This was my life right now. I had to play the part until I could figure out an alternative.

The clock was ticking. I undressed, pulling on my robe before quickly doing my hair (in a demure twist, as commanded) and makeup, keeping it as subtle as possible. Then I put on the lingerie. The bra felt like nothing at all, the lace giving my cleavage an unexpected lift, and the panties were just as weightless—and undeniably sexy. I couldn't help wondering if Stefan would be thinking about the lingerie he'd bought me, hugging me under my dress all night.

And I couldn't help wishing that at the end of the evening, he'd be the one taking it off.

TORI

CHAPTER 5

"*Take on meee...*" Luka was singing in a corner, getting increasingly louder even amid the din of the lavish hotel ballroom. *"Take me ooon..."*

This fundraiser was a train wreck. Not necessarily in terms of raising the intended funds, since it seemed to be packed full of wealthy, influential people who were clearly happy to throw money at a problem rather than actually thinking about it. But Stefan's family seemed to be imploding in a very public way—or at least, Luka was.

I had spotted him quickly after we arrived, slouching by the open bar serving wine and a few types of classy but small-sized cocktails. But he must have thrown back a lot of them, because he was clearly drunk. Very, very drunk. And with no sign of Stefan or Konstantin in the immediate area, I knew it was up to me to do damage control.

As I made my way toward the bar, I consciously forced a relaxed smile onto my face. Stefan had not uttered a single word to me before we'd left the condo, barely even glancing my way when I came out of the guest bedroom dressed exactly as he had ordered from hair to heels. It was typical of him lately, but I still felt disappointed—and upset that I'd had to cancel my plans with Gavin and my girl-friends. I hadn't even told Stefan about my A. Not that he'd care.

"Luka," I said, taking his arm and adopting a soothing tone as I interrupted his singing. "Maybe we should go get some air. It's getting a little hot in here, isn't it?"

I glanced around. Nobody seemed to be taking much of an interest in my brother-in-law, but I'd noticed a few people looking his way when he'd started singing and I was hoping to convince him to leave quietly. Maybe the air outside *would* do him some good, sober him up enough to come back to the party and go through the motions along with the rest of the Zorics.

"You wanna drink, Tor?" he asked, flipping open his blazer to reveal the flask bulging from the inside pocket. "I brought my own. Iss' always all bougie wine here, you know?"

I felt my smile grow tighter. "I don't drink, Luka. Not in public, at least. I'm still only eighteen." But oh, how I wished I could. It'd certainly make the night easier.

"Seen you drink at home," he argued. "C'mon, take it. No one's looking." He tried to pass the flask, but I took a step back, worried someone would see and it'd be all over the news. "Zorics know how to keep secrets, didn't you know? We're professionals at hiding things."

Despite Luka's slurring, his words were sharp. It was obvious to me that he was still angry and bitter in the wake of his own recent revelations about KZ Modeling's covert activities. I could hardly blame him. My brother-in-law may have been a little spoiled, a player and a partier, but up until a few weeks ago he'd had no idea that his father was a glori-fied pimp.

If only my husband cared as much. But then, he'd known all along.

"Let's step out for a minute," I suggested again.

"What for? Is my little sis not enjoying the rager? Iss' kinda dull for me, too."

"I think I need a short break, is all," I said, looping my arm through Luka's. "Come on."

But just then a fur-wrapped older woman with huge diamond earrings hobbled over and placed a hand on Luka's shoulder. "You're Luka Zoric," she cooed with a huge smile. "Gosh, don't you look just like your father! And what fabulous contributions he's made this year."

"You have no idea what my father has contributed to human trafficking," Luka said. Then he started giggling. Loudly. "No idea at all!"

The woman looked confused, and taken aback.

I cleared my throat and intervened as best I could. "I'm so sorry, but my brother-in-law here has a touch of the flu tonight. He's not feeling like himself." She immediately murmured her understanding, stepping back. "I'm going to find us a quiet corner now, if you'll excuse us."

But he refused to be herded away, ordering from the bar even as I tugged him toward the exit. I could smell the liquor rolling off him. The last thing he needed was another drink.

"Luka, please," I begged.

His sloppy grin turned into a tense scowl, and I followed his gaze across the room and saw his father, Konstantin, schmoozing up a group of men in suits. All of them were laughing.

"Victoria, we have a number of other guests to speak with," a cold voice commanded from behind us. I whirled to find Stefan standing there, glaring between his brother and me.

"But Luka—" I protested.

"Is an adult who can handle himself," Stefan cut me off, detaching my grip from Luka. "I suggest you get yourself in line, brother," he said quietly, his voice like steel. "You look sloppy."

"You don't like my tie?" Luka slurred, lifting it up for inspection. "It's a Ferragamo."

Stefan grabbed the tie, pulling Luka close. "This is a PR event, not a frat party. Get your act together. And you can start by going to the men's room to freshen up. You're a mess."

I watched them stare each other down, until Luka shook his head and stormed off.

Stefan said nothing more, steering me firmly toward a sophisticated-looking couple who were holding court and surrounded by others of their ilk. Obviously my husband was more concerned with keeping up appearances and impressing people than taking care of his brother.

This wasn't the attention I'd been hoping for. Stefan had ignored me in the car on the way over, hadn't even touched me until we arrived at the fundraiser, which was being held at one of the five-star hotels that the Zoric family was connected to. The moment we pulled up to the curb, where there were a crowd of reporters and photographers, Stefan's entire demeanor had changed. At that moment he'd put a toothpaste ad of a smile on his face and taken my arm.

I'd gritted my teeth and played along, feeling betrayed at the way my pulse still leapt at his touch. The way it was doing again right now.

"Try to look like you're having a good time," Stefan hissed under his breath.

I heard the threat in his words so I whipped out my well-practiced public smile. No doubt there would be pictures of us splashed all over the news tomorrow, the happy, glamorous couple, working the room like pros at this laudable and worthwhile charity event.

Stefan kept a firm grip on my arm as we made our way around the ballroom. But as he chatted up yet another older white businessman and his dolled-up Stepford wife, I felt his body stiffen almost imperceptibly next to mine. I looked up to find his father, Konstantin, stalking over in his signature monochromatic grey. Like a black cloud bearing down on us.

My stomach dropped. Konstantin was the last person I wanted to interact with right now. But I could sense Stefan already turning us toward the man, so I put that fake smile back on my face and waited for my father-in-law to reach us.

"Stefan," he said, nodding his head at his oldest son before giving me a long, lecherous once-over. He didn't even bother to properly greet me before turning his attention back to my husband. "Your brother is passed out drunk in the men's room."

"I sent him in there to sober up," Stefan said. "Clearly he failed to do so."

"No matter. Send him home," Konstantin ordered. Stefan responded with a curt nod.

I felt fury rise inside of me. I'd never thought I'd side with Luka over anything, but his drunken misbehavior seemed like a perfectly appropriate reaction to the hypocrisy that we were all participating in. Who would have guessed that my husband's womanizing, arrogant, inappropriately behaved younger brother would have a stronger grip on morality than Stefan?

Konstantin walked off, probably to hobnob with some more rich people with shady ethics. I turned to Stefan, angry beyond belief. Wasn't he supposed to be the good guy? Wasn't he supposed to protect his brother? Instead, he was just doing whatever his father told him to do.

"Better run off in a hurry now and do what daddy says," I said, smiling all along so that anyone looking at us would think we were having a pleasant conversation. "And while you're at it, don't forget to write a check to support this organization. An organization that would give anything to shut you and your father down. How many zeros will you add to this check to assuage your guilt, by the way? I'm a little fuzzy on the cost of a clean conscience these days."

Stefan leveled an ice-cold look in my direction.

"Don't talk about things you don't understand."

"Trust me, I understand perfectly. I understand that you'll go to work tomorrow, probably starting your day off with a blowjob from one of these poor, exploited women, before sending them off on a "job" to service the next well-paying gentleman. Oh, but how silly of me. You don't have to pay."

"*Stop*," Stefan ordered, his grip tightening until it started to actually hurt.

But I wouldn't stop. "Do the models even know you're all here?" I goaded him. "Hiding behind your filthy donations? Rubbing elbows with Chicago's elite while you eat fucking hors d'oeuvres and pretend to actually give a shit about their welfare?"

"You have no idea what I'm trying to do here," Stefan said, leading me to a corner.

"You're a hypocrite," I hissed. "Do the women working for KZM have any idea that you're spending the money *they* earned on a fundraiser that's ostensibly for *them*? A fundraiser that will never be able to help them because you and your family are fucking liars?"

"Shut. Your. Mouth." His eyes flicked around the room, but I didn't care who saw us.

"Is that what you tell your girls?" I taunted. "Nah, it's the opposite. Open wider, right?"

Stefan swung me around and pressed me hard against the wall so I had nowhere to look but up at him. His eyes burned with fury, his fingers still gripping my bicep hard.

"If you don't shut your mouth, I'll shut it for you." His voice was threatening, but low enough that only I could hear it. "I'll push you down on your knees and force my cock down your throat. You won't be able to say one more word while I'm fucking your mouth—while everyone sees that you're just as much of a whore as the women benefiting from this charity."

His words were coarse. Disgusting. Unbelievably cruel. But somehow, it was hot anyway.

"Don't you have enough women's mouths to enjoy?" I spat back at him, clinging to my rage in self-defense.

He laughed. "Jealous, are we? And here I thought your own mouth was too busy with your little friend's cock for you to even think about mine. What's his name? Gavin, isn't it? You two having a lot of fun these days?"

My pulse pounded in my ears. So he knew about Gavin. Not only that, but he knew and he didn't care. He was making jokes about us.

The truth stung more than I thought it would. Would I ever stop being disappointed by Stefan? By this sham of a marriage we shared?

"For a senator's daughter, you've been shockingly indiscreet," he went on. "In fact—"

"*Tori?*"

I looked up and my lips stretched into a huge, genuine grin as I saw Grace Toussaint, my former SAT study partner and private high school bff, beelining toward us with her signature curls bouncing wildly around her expressive face.

"Look at you two little lovebirds," she squealed, giving Stefan a brief side hug before throwing her arms around me and squeezing. "I thought I'd die of boredom tonight. My parents donated like a million dollars to this charity and then didn't even want to come. So here I am."

"We're so glad you're here," Stefan said. "We haven't seen you since the wedding."

"I know," she sighed. "I've been so busy learning all about my parents' company and taking online courses in business. I'm starting to think I should have taken a gap year in the Mediterranean and partied instead of trying to jump into all this work training stuff. It's not just about purses and belts and leather samples, you know? Running a business is *hard*."

"Very true," Stefan agreed warmly. As if we hadn't just been in a tense, ugly fight.

Grace smiled again, and I gestured at her bag, leaning into the pleasant distraction.

"Is that one of your designs?" It had a vintage vibe, almost like one of those buckled train cases that women used in the 1950s.

"Yes!" she said, glowing with pride. "My parents are letting me develop a line on my own, but it won't be out until next year. This is just a prototype. *Tres chic*, don't you think?"

I nodded. "If this is any indication of what you're capable of, you're going to do great."

"Thank you," Grace said, her cheeks going a little pink.

"I've hardly had time for anything but the whole "handbag empire" thing. When can we get coffee? Just us two."

Stefan was polite enough to drift away and give us some space to chat, but he was still close enough that I couldn't have managed much beyond small talk even if I'd *wanted* to tell Grace how bad things had gotten with my marriage, which I didn't. Soon enough, Stefan pulled me away to mingle more, leaving me and Grace promising each other we'd hang out soon and catch up. But I wasn't sure we really would. The situation was too complicated, too horrible, and too dangerous to share with anyone, even one of my oldest friends. It made me even angrier. Even more determined to find a way out of this mess.

I spent the rest of the evening at the fundraiser biting my tongue and plastering a smile across my face that grew more and more forced the more people we encountered. Especially the women, who were more than happy to drape themselves over Stefan, fawning over him for being such a "strong supporter of this wonderful cause." The whole thing made me sick. Especially the way that Stefan would respond to them.

They got the full extent of his charm. *They* got the smooth, charismatic man who had once convinced me to marry him the first night we met. A man who smiled and doled out compliments like roses. A man who made them laugh and smile and blush.

And all the while his wife stood at his side, a well-mannered, modest statue.

I began counting down the minutes until midnight, when the event was over. As if I was Cinderella, waiting for the ball to end. Ready to leave Prince Charming behind to charm his next princess. Because I knew it wasn't me. I knew Stefan didn't care for me, or anyone else but himself and his family and his company and his money. That was all that mattered to him.

Still, I played my part. I was the sweet, silent arm candy he wanted me to be. I looked good, but there was nothing behind the smile. Nothing of substance to share. It was just like it had been with my father. That was the extent of my worth to men like him and Stefan. All sugar and zero redeeming value. A human prop.

When I made a trip to the ladies' room, I noticed I had a text from Grace.

Everything okay? her text said. *I've been watching you guys and am a lil concerned re: your body language?*

I couldn't help smiling. She was right. And of course she'd noticed things were tense between me and Stefan, she'd just been too polite to say something out loud earlier.

Still, I had to deflect. *Everything's fine*, I tapped out, glad she couldn't see the lie on my face. *Just a lovers' quarrel. No big deal.*

I watched the ellipses flash across my screen before her reply popped up on the screen. *Oookay, but if you ever need to get away for a few days—come stay with me. I mean it.*

You have ice cream? I responded, adding a thinking-face emoji.

YAS! All the ice cream. Grace sent a barrage of dessert emojis and a pair of devil horns to go along with them. *My apartment's huge and there's a jacuzzi tub in the guest bath. You know you deserve some girl time. Or maybe I just miss u? xo*

I miss you too, I typed back. *And I'll reach out if I need to. Thanks. <3*

Gotta go mingle with our fellow philanthropists, Grace replied. *Let's coffee soon.*

I went back out and joined Stefan for one final lap

around the ballroom, making small talk with the various donors he wanted to say goodbye to. I complimented outfits and marveled at the beauty of the hotel hosting us, at the amount of donations that were being racked up. Every mention of the purpose of the fundraiser made me cringe inside, but I kept it together.

Then, in the middle of a conversation with an older couple—some big-name Chicago society types who'd made their fortune in real estate development and had donated a ridiculous amount of money tonight, bragging egregiously and basking in their goodwill—Stefan's phone buzzed. I could feel it in his jacket pocket.

He discreetly slid the phone out just enough to check the screen. Then, without a word, he dropped my hand and walked away.

I stared at his retreating back. Had he really just left me standing here with a couple of strangers?

"Is everything alright?" the older gentleman asked.

"So sorry about that," I said politely, reverting to my years of social training as a senator's daughter. "Stefan was waiting for that call. He's very...committed to his work."

The man nodded generously. His wife gave me the same kind of bland smile I was giving both of them. No doubt she had dealt with the same kind of thing in the past.

There was a brief, awkward silence before I managed to excuse myself and head in the direction that Stefan had exited in. He had left the ballroom and made his way out onto one of the balconies. It was freezing out, and the cold seemed to go right through my thin dress.

Glancing around, I didn't see him at first. The balcony seemed empty, most of the guests too smart to venture outside into the night's frigid temperatures. But then, in a dark corner, I saw Stefan's broad shoulders. I took a step and then froze.

My husband wasn't alone.

He was with a woman, a KZM model by the looks of her, the two of them pressed up against each other. Her eyes were closed, her head resting on his shoulder as he shielded her body from the icy wind. I heard myself gasp as I watched him reach up and wipe her tears with a brush of his thumb. I knew what it was like to be on the receiving end of that kind of care—even though I was well aware by now that it was all part of his act. Still, my stomach turned seeing how gentle he was with her. They weren't kissing, but they were close enough to at any moment.

I turned away before I saw any more, tears prickling my eyes.

My heart had been cracked wide open. I'd known he was probably cheating with one or more of the agency's models, but there was nothing like seeing it with my own eyes to force me to accept the truth.

The part of me that had put on the lingerie he had bought, hoping he'd want to see me in it when we got home, the part of me that had hoped there was still a chance for reconciliation, for a real marriage somewhere beyond the horrible revelations and unforgivable behavior, had officially died.

Stefan was sleeping with other women. He didn't care about me. He didn't love me. He didn't want me.

It was time for me to wake up and let go of the fairytale version of my marriage that I'd been clinging to.

It was time to get over him. Permanently.

TORI

CHAPTER 6

How ironic that I spent so much of my time studying language, drowning myself in words, only to realize that none of those words I was so obsessively diving into could properly describe how I was feeling. None had the power to break the spell I was under.

Words had always been the one thing in my life that never failed me—until now. The hell I was experiencing was beyond language. I was desperate for something I knew I couldn't have. Stuck in a cycle of longing and loathing for the one man I never should have touched.

I wished I could scrub Stefan from my memory completely. Walk away, make a new life. And maybe one day I would.

But for now, there wasn't anything I could do.

After the night of the charity fundraiser, I'd gone home and curled up alone in bed, more furious than ever at my inability to do anything to help the women or find a way out of the mess that my life had turned into. Stefan never came to my bed that night, which was no surprise, but I'd been completely unable to sleep, my mind racing. And then an idea had come to me.

I went to my desk, opened up my laptop, and spent hours staring at the screen glowing in the darkness, researching organizations and charities that worked to fight sex trafficking on a global scale. I found out who they were and what they did, how they served, rescued, and advocated for victims of human trafficking. Operation Underground Railroad, The Emancipation Network, Polaris Project, Stop the Traffik. The price of my silence—my continued role as an accessory to KZM's actions—was going to cost Stefan dearly. It was the least I could do.

With my husband's credit card held tightly in my hand (I was an authorized user), I signed him up for monthly automatic donations to as many legitimate organizations as I could. The fundraiser we'd attended was a slick PR move, I knew that, but the fat donation check that KZ Modeling had written wasn't enough to atone for their sins. Yet no matter how many thousands of dollars I signed Stefan up to donate, it still didn't make me feel better. It wasn't enough. It was just a band-aid. Those women were still trapped. As trapped as I was.

Though I knew I couldn't tell my stepmother the truth about KZ Modeling, I figured it wouldn't hurt to call Michelle and see if she had any advice for dealing with a relationship that was constantly on the rocks. I'd seen first-hand that her marriage to my father hadn't always been rosy, but somehow she'd managed to weather all the storms. Maybe she could help.

"So what do I do?" I asked her, after vaguely outlining the way Stefan and I barely saw each other anymore, how we didn't seem to have anything to say to one another, how I always felt an underlying, unresolved tension between us.

"I'm not expecting things to be perfect, and I know it'll pass...but in the meantime, I just want things to feel...less fraught."

I left out that the reason I knew it'd pass was because I planned to leave him someday.

To my surprise, her advice wasn't just to give him more attention in bed (she had no idea we slept in separate rooms) or to pour on a heavy dose of feminine charm. Instead, she said, "Well, you two have very busy but very different lives, Tori. And that's okay. It's very normal. But sometimes the answer to too much space is to find even *more* space—for yourself."

"Wait, what?" I was shocked. "I don't think I can get much further away as it is." Thoughts of running away to Grace's apartment and staying there for a few weeks flitted through my mind, but I knew it would only be a temporary solution—and might make things even worse.

"I'm not saying you should move out," Michelle clarified. "But maybe a weekend vacay with your friends, or even a long girls' night out, could help you reset. Give him a chance to miss you, wonder about you. Then when you get back home, he'll treat you more respectful-like."

"Does that actually work?" I asked. I couldn't imagine my workaholic father noticing if Michelle disappeared for a few days. Then again, maybe I wouldn't know.

"It works every time!" she said, laughing. "Sometimes men just need a reminder that their wives are real people with wants and needs, too—and that they're lucky to have them."

Maybe Michelle was right. Maybe Stefan would be more respectful and kind if I took some real time away. Not just going to school and studying late, every single day like clockwork, but actually packing a bag and leaving for a little while. Yet when I casually brought up spending a few days at Grace's apartment one morning, he barely acknowledged me.

"Do whatever you want," he said, breezing out the door with his coffee in hand. "I'm gone all weekend anyway."

So much for that.

I went back to throwing myself into my school work, desperate to kill any remaining attachment I felt toward my husband. I studied harder than I ever had in my entire life and watched my grades bounce back to their former glory. But I still wasn't happy. Not at all.

Even though I had seen evidence of Stefan's cheating with my own eyes, I still couldn't shake the memories of all the good times we'd had. And though I hated to admit it, the thought of our marriage truly being over was even more painful than the thought of him running around with other women. But I couldn't just stand by and ignore the fact that he was being unfaithful. Would I ever be able to forgive him, even if he wanted me to? God, what was wrong with me?

I'd been reading the same paragraph over and over again in my Intro to Psycholinguistics text, but I couldn't stop thinking about Stefan, huddled close to that model at the fundraiser.

"You okay?" Gavin's voice startled me out of my moping. We were at the end of one of the long tables in the dining commons, and this late at night the place was practically empty.

"Fine," I lied, avoiding eye contact. I stared up at the UChicago phoenix banners hanging from the ceiling, rubbing my eyes against the deep splashes of maroon and white.

"You seem distracted," he said. "You've been on the same page for the last twenty minutes."

I laughed bitterly. "Okay. Maybe I'm distracted."

Gavin smiled. "Well, I've got some bad news for you. I just found out I'm averaging an A- in Latin now, so I'm gonna have to officially break up with you as my Latin tutor."

It was easy to smile back. "Congratulations. This is the best breakup I've ever had."

"Oh, you're not getting off that easy," he said. "I'd bet anything you'll be asking me for help next semester with Code Making and Cryptanalysis. It just so happens to be my specialty."

"You definitely are cryptic," I teased, though of course nothing could be further from the truth. That was the thing that I loved about Gavin: he was just so direct and straightforward. He didn't play games. You always knew where you stood with him. Nothing at all like my husband.

Gavin dropped his voice a little lower. "In all honesty though, I'm worried about you."

I sighed. No doubt I looked terrible. I'd barely been sleeping. I would look at myself in the mirror some mornings and see someone who was just floating through life. The dark circles under my eyes could no longer hide under makeup, and there was a fatigue to my whole body that had me slumping over my desk in class. I looked—and felt—completely worn out.

"It's just midterms," I bluffed. "Getting through them all will be a big help."

Gavin's frown deepened. "How's Stefan?"

Bingo. He got me every time. "He's great," I said, not bothering to hide my sarcasm.

Gently reaching over and closing my textbook, Gavin

leaned closer. "I know you're a private person, and I respect that, but if you ever wanna talk...I'm all yours. Okay?"

His voice was so sincere that I could feel tears stinging my eyes. All I could do was nod.

"I'm just so..." But I couldn't say it. Couldn't admit how defeated I felt, how awful my husband was treating me, how illegal and morally bankrupt his family's business was. It would snowball way too quickly if I tried to tell Gavin even a partial truth. "So tired," I finished lamely.

Gavin stayed quiet for a minute, hesitating before finally resting a warm, comforting hand on my forearm. It had been so long since someone had touched my like that. Carefully. Respectfully. With kind, selfless intentions. I felt my breath calm, my pulse slow. It was good.

"A bunch of us are going out clubbing tonight," he said. "Come."

This man could not have been more Stefan's opposite, and yet I still didn't want him. I wished I did. I wished my attraction was more than just friendly. That he made my heart pound, my insides feel tight and hot, my life feel complete. It would have made things so much easier.

"I'm not really in the mood," I said apologetically. "I don't want to be a downer."

I also didn't want to do what I had to do with Stefan—pretend that everything was okay. It had also gotten exhausting having to dance around the details of my personal life, my husband, or the most recent popular topic of conversation among my classmates: KZ Modeling. Once the other students had found out that Stefan was the son of Konstantin Zoric and set to take over one of the most famous modeling agencies in the world, I had become a bit of a reluctant celebrity.

It was literally the last thing I wanted. Because now

people wanted to talk about Stefan. They wanted to talk about Konstantin. They wanted to talk about KZM and all the exciting, exotic, expensive adventures a connection like that must afford me.

And I didn't want to talk about it. Not now. Not ever.

"You're not a downer to me," Gavin said. "But I won't push you."

"I appreciate it," I said truthfully.

Even if Gavin was cool, I knew that if I went out with a group, everyone else would get drunk and loquacious and start asking questions. They wouldn't be polite about it, either. They'd dig and dig and I'd have to evade and pretend and smile and act like I loved my life when right now, nothing could be further from the truth. All I could think about were the scores of women I wasn't helping, and how every day I didn't go to the authorities was another day they suffered.

"Tori," Gavin said, seeming to search for his words, "You don't have to pretend for me. If you want to deal with stuff on your own, I get it, but I don't need you to lie. Just be you. It's obvious you're going through a lot right now, and... Like I said, I'm here. Whatever you need."

I nodded. Gavin was so sweet I could barely stand it.

"If you do change your mind, though," he added, "we'd be happy to have you."

He started packing up his bag, and I followed suit. I had just zipped up my backpack when my cell buzzed in my pocket. Pulling it out, I saw I had a text from Stefan.

My traitorous heart gave a little leap in my chest. Apparently, I'd learned no lessons.

Family dinner tonight. Be at the penthouse @7pm. Clothes laid out in your room.

Don't be late.

I clenched my jaw. How *dare* he. How fucking dare he.

I wasn't in the mood to take orders from someone who'd abandoned me for his latest mistress in the middle of an event that I hadn't even wanted to attend. An event he'd dressed me up for just to parade me around like a show pony, all to make himself—and KZM—look good.

He had humiliated me and now he wanted me to come to dinner with his family? To pretend that everything was fine? To eat dinner across the table from his father, one of the most vile human beings I'd ever met?

If I'd dreaded the idea of pretending to be happy for my classmates, I downright refused to do so for my father-in-law. I'd much rather go out drinking and dancing with normal, decent humans than be forced to sit across the table from Konstantin and Stefan, acting like everything was grand.

Stefan could take his text message orders and shove them right up his ass.

He could have dinner alone with his family for all I cared. He could stare at his father's cruel, leering face and think about the life he had chosen.

I was going out.

Smiling up at Gavin, I saw the surprise in his eyes at my complete change in demeanor.

"Actually I'd love to join you guys tonight," I said, barely recognizing the sultry, friendly voice I was speaking in. "But I'll need your help with one tiny little thing first."

"Anything," he said, sounding a little dazzled.

"I need a new fake ID," I told him, holding my breath for a moment. "I know I don't need to drink to have a good time, but with the semester I've been having, it'd sure help."

"I don't know," he said. "I mean, I want to, but—"

"Pretty please," I said, signing the word in ASL for

emphasis. "I'd get one eventually anyway. But if I have one tonight, I could really let loose. And I think I need that."

"Well..."

He was weakening. I could tell. I batted my eyelashes and leaned closer. "Plus, you can babysit me if I get too tipsy. I'll even stop if you tell me I'm cut off. Okay?"

This time he didn't hesitate. In fact, his smile grew. "Okay," he said, making the sign for 'okay' back at me. "Let me just make a few calls."

As he stepped away from the table to do so, I looked down at my phone, frowning at Stefan's text messages. I wasn't going to respond. He could be left to wonder. See how it felt.

Not only that, but I wasn't going to let him ruin this night.

Impulsively, I powered off my phone completely. Feeling the tiniest hint of victory, I slipped my cell back into my pocket. Tonight, for once, I was free.

There was no way Stefan could follow me now.

TORI

CHAPTER 7

Spinning across the dance floor, I reveled in the high energy and party atmosphere of the club. So far, the night had been a crazy whirlwind of drinks and dancing. The loud music and crush of writhing bodies were a thrill, exactly the adrenaline rush I needed to get my mind off of everything that was happening in my life.

Still, despite the fun I was having—shaking my ass alongside Lila and Audrey as the bass thumped deliciously in my ribcage—I couldn't help wondering what Stefan's reaction had been when I hadn't shown up for dinner at seven. When the outfit he'd laid out for me remained there. Unworn. Untouched.

Was he still waiting for me, at home or at his father's penthouse? Was he worried that something might have happened to me? Somehow I doubted it. He was probably just pissed.

I tried to forget about him. To throw myself fully into the music, the sweat and the crush of the club. The pink cocktails Gavin was happy to buy me, how happy my friends were.

A familiar pop song came on, reinvigorating my hip shakes, and I spotted Gavin dancing toward our trio across the packed dance floor. I flashed him a small wave, figuring he was just mingling in the crowd, but he took it as an invitation to beeline past Audrey and start dancing up on me. Laughing, I turned the other way. I hoped he'd take the hint that I wasn't interested in male attention. But his hands were hot against me as they circled my waist from behind, and then I felt his body pressing into me along with the beat. It felt good, but it also felt wrong.

Wriggling away, I tried to keep a few feet of space between us as we danced. Every time he'd move closer, I'd take another step back. I wasn't sure why I still cared about propriety after seeing Stefan practically dry hump that model at the fundraiser, but my wedding vows still meant something to me. When I found myself pushed by the crowd back into Gavin's arms, I finally ducked away to a new spot on the dance floor and dragged Lila with me so I'd have a partner.

Lila loved being the center of attention, and she didn't mind putting on a show. As we danced, she put her back to me and slid down to the floor as if I were her personal stripper pole. Then she danced back up and locked her arms around my neck, snaking her hips suggestively against mine. She flashed me a wink and licked her lips and I couldn't help but giggle.

"You see that hot guy over there?" she shouted. "Three o'clock, black button-down."

I glanced over and saw exactly who she meant. "Yup. He's definitely checking you out."

"Mission accomplished," she said, turning to give him a head nod.

When he started making his way toward us, I gave Lila's shoulder a squeeze. "Go get 'em, tiger," I told her. "I'm going to get another drink!"

Though I tried to avoid our bodies making heavy contact on the floor, it was still fun to flirt with Gavin between songs. When I got to the bar, he had a round of bright blue shots ready and waiting. Diane, who I'd only ever seen dance to Tori Amos, perched on a stool sipping hers.

"It's a shot!" I said. "You're supposed to knock it back all at once!"

She smiled. "I'm taking it easy tonight. Got an early class tomorrow."

I nodded. "Well I'm glad you're here," I told her. "I know it's not your scene."

"Always happy to be with my friends," she said warmly, sliding a shot over to me.

I grabbed it and held it up toward Gavin. "Cheers to friendship," I said.

He grinned and raised his own shot. "Cheers, Tori," he said. We clinked the tiny glasses and down the blue liquid. It tasted like passionfruit.

"What is this stuff?" I asked him.

"It's delicious!" Diane agreed, still drinking hers in baby sips.

"Some kind of fruity French vodka?" Gavin said. "I figured you'd think it was pretty."

"It's very pretty," I said, laughing. Then I downed another.

There was something very sweet and chivalrous about him—the dance floor grinding notwithstanding. He was kind and attentive to me and all my friends, making sure we had a drink in hand and a smile on our lips. And amid our innocent flirting, there were moments where I could forget what my life had become and let myself fall into the fantasy of starting over.

The stool beside me opened up and Gavin dropped into it. Diane drifted off toward Lila.

"You look incredible tonight," he said, his lips hot and close to my ear as he leaned in to be heard over the loud music.

I shook off the goosebumps and looked down at my outfit. "This old thing?" I joked.

It was the same thing I'd been wearing to class, the same thing he'd seen me in all day—a pair of tight but comfy designer jeans and my favorite high-heeled boots. But I'd shed my modest sweater and coat, revealing a black body-suit with a deep neckline that clung to my curves. I'd never really intended to show it off when I'd left the house all bundled up that morning, but it was my only option when I'd gotten here and the heat of the club had hit me. Most of the other girls had gone home and gotten dolled up, with big hair, big heels, and short, flouncy skirts. I knew I still looked a little out of place, but the way Gavin was looking at me— with real appreciation in his eyes—I didn't mind standing out too much.

After weeks of being completely ignored by my husband, having someone look at me like that was a real ego boost. Although I couldn't help noticing that another guy— one of the bouncers, judging by how huge he was, with his shaved head and Popeye muscles—had been checking me out all night as well. But that guy had an almost predatory look to him, as if he was studying me. With Gavin, it was all appreciative smiles and those warm brown eyes.

"You're stunning, no matter what you're wearing," Gavin said. "Especially when you're on the dance floor. It's nice to see you let loose. You deserve to have some fun tonight."

The suggestive tone of his words and the sudden intensity of his gaze implied that he'd be interested in doing any number of other "fun" things with me tonight. But even though his intentions were clear, the whole thing felt very innocent. I allowed myself to imagine for a moment what my life would be like if I'd never met Stefan. If I was meeting Gavin for the first time here, and we were both single.

It was how I imagined my love story would begin. With this kind of innocent but charged chemistry, the kind of chemistry that could maybe build to something more over time. It would be romantic, falling slowly in love like that. With someone gentle, who really understood me.

Twirling my empty shot glass on the bar top, I looked over at him and blurted, "What's your favorite word?"

"Favorite word?" Gavin repeated.

Immediately I felt childish for asking, but then he said, "In which language?"

I grinned. "Latin. Let's see how good my tutoring this semester has really been."

He looked off for a moment, and I wasn't sure he'd have a real answer until he shrugged his shoulders a little and said, "*Cohibeo*. It's the purposeful repression of grief. We don't have a specific word for that in English."

I knew the word. It made me ache. "Why such a sad one?" I asked.

"I guess because...my dad died when I was young," he admitted. "And my mom had a string of bad boyfriends, one after another, the whole time I was growing up. A lot of them were abusive. So I don't know, I guess I feel like my childhood could be defined by the word Cohibeo. I worked hard to put on a brave face. My brother and I both did."

"Oh, Gavin, I had no idea," I murmured, my heart instantly going out to him. "But you *were* brave. It wasn't just a face. And look at you now. You've come so far."

I took his hand for a moment and squeezed. I'd mentioned losing my mother in passing, but he had never told me about his dad. Still trying to act like a tough guy all this time.

"What's your favorite Latin word?" Gavin asked, clearly wanting to change the subject, his hand warm on my lower back as he moved closer.

"I have so many," I said. I picked up the last shot, the one that Lila had never come to the bar to claim. "But I think the one you need to hear right now is *bumastus*."

"What's that?"

I cleared my throat. "It means, "having large grapes." A shame it's gone out of use."

Gavin threw back his head and laughed, and I joined along with him. When we settled down I realized he was looking at me with so much amusement and awe that I blushed.

"What?" I asked, a little self-conscious at his obvious admiration.

"You're just...great," he said, shaking his head. "Not at all what I expected. I've never met anyone like you. It's not just that you're beautiful. You're brilliant and funny and kind, too."

I blushed even harder. No doubt I was red enough that Gavin would be able to tell even in the dark club. Our eyes locked and I could tell he wanted to kiss me right then.

"Latin's the best," I said lamely, trying to break up the moment.

"Yup. Ancient and inaccessible," he joked. "Just how I like my women."

I slapped him playfully on the arm.

"Are you calling me ancient?" I teased.

"Not at all," he said, his eyes sparkling. "You're practically a babe in the woods compared to some of us in the program."

I noticed he hadn't refuted the inaccessible part.

What if things could be different? What would it be like to date someone like Gavin? Someone who genuinely admired me, laughed at my jokes, and liked the same things that I did.

What if he could be my new start? I'd never cheat on Stefan, regardless of his own actions in that regard, but I couldn't help imagining what would happen after my divorce.

I looked up at him again, trying to imagine what sex would be like with someone other than my husband. Would it be as hot and intense and fulfilling as it had been with Stefan?

Almost as if he could read my thoughts, Gavin's gaze sharpened, focusing on me, his stare direct and enticing.

I swallowed.

Is this what I wanted? I didn't know anymore.

Thankfully, Taylor Swift came on and it was the perfect excuse to change the subject.

"I love this song," I shouted to him, the speakers pumping it through the club. I wasn't ready to hit the floor with the amount of alcohol I'd just downed, but I bopped on my stool.

"This is extremely nerdy," he said, passing me one of

the fresh mixed drinks the bartender had just brought us, "but sometimes I like to translate pop songs into other languages."

I grinned. "That *is* extremely nerdy," I told him. "But I like it." I gulped the cold drink.

He leaned closer and began singing along to the song. In Spanish.

"Porque los jugadores van a jugar, jugar, jugar. Y los que odian van a odiar, odiar, odiar."

I laughed. He had a pretty decent voice but it was hard not to giggle at an adult man singing "Shake It Off" in another language.

"Not bad," I told him, waiting for the chorus to come back around before I began singing along with the repeated words I could pick up. He joined in with me until we ran out of words.

"You nailed it!" Gavin exclaimed, sounding delighted. "How many languages do you speak?"

"Fluently?" I said. "Not that many. Latin's not so much a speaking language, though I try, and I'm getting better at ASL. But I don't know much Spanish—I was just following along with you. Definitely interested in learning more in the program, though. How about yourself?"

"Eh," he said, waving a hand. "Only about half a dozen or so."

"Half a dozen?" My mouth dropped open. "Fluently?"

Gavin gave a casual shrug. "I've always liked them. I took Spanish and French in high school and studied Mandarin in my spare time. Turns out I have kind of an ear for languages."

"Apparently." I was deeply impressed. I took a few more gulps of the too-sweet mixed drink and stared off into space, deep in thought.

Maybe if I was honest with Gavin, if I told him everything about my current situation, we could build something out of that. If he knew the truth about my marriage, about the kind of man I was married to and why I'd agreed to the marriage in the first place, maybe he'd be willing to wait for me. Wait until my marriage was officially over. And I was free.

It would only be a few years. Would he think I was worth it?

But god, could I really leave Stefan? I hated that I kept thinking about him. Kept fighting the temptation to turn my phone back on and check if he had called or texted. No doubt he'd have things to say to me when I got back home tonight. But I didn't need to leave any time soon.

Especially since I was having such a good time with Gavin. He leaned even closer to me.

"*Eisai poly omorfi,*" he said.

"You speak Greek, too?" I asked, astonished.

He shook his head. "Only a little," he said. "But I was hoping more to impress you with what I was saying, not how I was saying it. I said, 'You are very beautiful.'"

I flushed. "Ef-kha-reesto," I said, thanking him in Greek. "That's the only Greek word I know."

He moved closer, and suddenly the club felt even more hot and crowded. It wasn't Gavin, though. It wasn't his proximity to me or the chemistry that had been pinging between us all evening. This was something else.

A wave of nausea rolled over me, and I placed a cold hand to the back of my neck. I was pretty sure I was going to be sick. How many shots had I had? And how strong was the fruity drink I'd just downed in the last five minutes?

"I'm feeling a little off all of a sudden," I said apologetically, sliding off the stool. The room tilted on its axis. Whoa. "Kinda dizzy. I'm going to hit the ladies' room. Excuse me."

"Are you okay?" I heard him say behind me, his voice worried and already fading away as I moved through the crowd toward the bathroom.

Faces seemed to swarm around me, unsteady and out of focus in the flashing lights and semi-dark. My stomach roiled, and my mouth was dry. I'd been drunk before, but this wasn't at all like Vienna. I felt almost detached from my body, and I could barely feel my feet on the floor.

In fact, my legs didn't seem to want to work at all. It was like they were encased in concrete. I stumbled, barely staying upright as I moved toward the glowing bathroom sign.

It was when the sign became blurry as well that I realized something was very, very wrong. My hands groped blindly, looking for something, anything to grab onto, but there was nothing but confused faces turning my way and then dancing bodies moving away from me.

My pulse skyrocketed. The edges of the room were going black. I was going to pass out.

I tried to turn back, tried to find Gavin in the crowd, but I couldn't focus on anyone or anything. My head was pounding, my tongue heavy in my mouth. *Everything* felt heavy. My legs couldn't hold me up.

This whole night had been a terrible idea. I never should have come here.

I'd been trying to escape Stefan, to forget him, to force my heart to get over him, but that hadn't worked at all. Instead, as my knees hit the floor, the tiles suddenly hot against my cheek as I slumped over, I saw my husband's face in the crowd. Impossible.

But as I lay there on the floor, the darkness creeping in,

it was his face I saw again, leaning down over me as he reached out a hand.

Even in this state, I couldn't escape him.

His blazing green eyes were the last thing I hallucinated before I completely passed out.

"Do not take your eyes off my wife for one second until I get there," I growled into my phone, after directing my driver to take me straight to the club. "And whatever you do, do *not* let her walk out of there with that piece of shit."

I had to go after her.

And if Tori thought she was going home with Gavin tonight, she had another thing coming.

At first I hadn't cared when she didn't show up at 7 for dinner at the penthouse; despite my father's fury at her absence I'd believed my own excuses for why she'd stood us up.

"She's got midterms coming up," I had said. "All she does is study. It's not the kind of program you can just skate by in, and she cares about her grades. She's learning sign language."

"Sign language? What the hell's she gonna do with this degree anyway?" my father scoffed. "Plenty of cheaper decorations if she wants something pretty to hang on the wall."

"I think it's cool," my sister Emzee had cut in. "And I'm glad she has her own passion. The way she talks about linguistics, it really does sound like it's worth exploring."

I had shot my younger sister a grateful look, knowing she'd intentionally interrupted the argument to try getting us back on track to a peaceful evening.

Sure, I was pissed that my wife had disobeyed a direct order. But I hadn't been lying about her intense study habits, and to be honest I would have gladly skipped out on dinner with my father too, if I'd been able to get away with it.

The meal dragged on, my brother Luka unusually sullen and refusing to contribute much to the conversation. Emzee did her best, regaling us with stories about her most recent trip to Istanbul for a photography assignment, but I was relieved when I finally got a text from Dmitri, the secret bodyguard that I'd hired to follow Tori around. I excused myself to read it.

She's at the 312 Club, his text read. *Popular with college kids. Not dangerous.*

Studying, my ass. She'd have a lot to answer for when she got home tonight.

I had returned to the table and tried to play the role of good son and brother, even though I'd lost my appetite. The wine helped.

But when Dmitri texted me again soon after to say Tori was getting handsy with that Gavin asshole, I couldn't not go after her. Especially when I watched the videos that he sent. The sight of Gavin grinding up on my wife's ass, the way she held his hand at the bar, their easy laughter—all I saw was red. There was no way I was letting her get away with this.

I left dinner early, citing a non-existent business

meeting I had to prepare for the next morning, and whipped out my phone to call Dmitri as soon as I got into my private car. And now I was on my way to confront her.

If anything, I was more pissed about the fact that she'd turned off her phone, intentionally making it impossible for me to track her with the app I'd installed. I didn't like the idea of her being out there in the city on her own, without me able to protect her, but that's exactly why I had contingencies in place. Contingencies like Dmitri.

I leaned back into the plush leather seat of the Town Car and scrolled back through the photos Dmitri had sent. Fucking Gavin. I really didn't like that guy. There was something about him that made me want to punch him in the face. Probably something to do with the fact that he knew Tori was married and underage, yet he kept asking her out to dinner and taking her out to bars and clubs she wasn't even old enough to get into. He had a lot of nerve.

I almost crushed my phone in my hand when I zoomed in on the pictures of them dancing. Sure, she was also surrounded by her female friends, but that didn't stop Gavin from putting his hands all over her. That was *my* wife he was touching. I could kill him.

The Town Car couldn't get me to the club fast enough. Adrenaline surged through me as I fantasized about putting my fist through Gavin's face. But when I got there, I couldn't find him or Tori. They weren't outside, they weren't at the bar, and they weren't on the dance floor.

I scanned the room, looking for Dmitri's shaved head.

At least he wasn't hard to spot—he was over six-foot-four and built like a brick wall. He was standing off to the side, barely blending in to the crowd, his eyes focused on something near the bathroom. My eyes followed his gaze, just as his expression became focused and concerned.

That's when I spotted Tori.

She was weaving through the crowd, but not in her usual, graceful way.

No, she was stumbling and reaching out for stability. Something no one around her would offer. They all ignored her, despite the obvious physical distress she was in.

My blood boiled as I pushed through the crowd, needing to get to her.

Something was obviously wrong. How could no one be helping her?

I watched helplessly as she stumbled, her movements slow and uncoordinated. Was she that drunk? She seemed intoxicated, but I'd seen her drunk before—and it was nothing like this. I couldn't imagine my wife drinking to the point of practically passing out in a crowded club.

It wasn't until I got closer and saw her slumped on the floor that I realized she wasn't drunk at all. She was barely conscious, her eyes glazed over. Totally incapacitated. It was obvious she'd been drugged. Someone must have put something in her drink.

As I pushed my way toward her, my heart pounding, my anxiety spiking, I was beyond livid. I was ready to murder the person who had done this to her.

I scanned the crowd, looking for Gavin. The asshole who had apparently roofied her and abandoned her in the middle of the dance floor. There was no sign of him, so I focused my attention back on Tori, on reaching her before something happened.

"Get the fuck out of my way," I ordered the people around me, all of whom were too busy laughing and grinding on each other to pay attention to the woman slumped on the floor.

When I finally reached her, our eyes locked for a brief

moment before she passed out completely, her head rolling back against the tile.

"Tori," I yelled, my voice getting lost in the heavy bass pounding through the speakers. "Tori!" But she was out cold.

Dropping to my knees, I cradled my wife in my arms, holding her against me. Her breaths were shallow against my neck, and I thanked god I had gotten here in time. I was sick to my stomach. I should never have let Tori out of my sight. It was too dangerous for her to be out without me. Even Dmitri hadn't been able to keep her safe.

This was what my secrets had wrought.

With a growl, I stood up and pushed through the mass of moving bodies, Dmitri at my side as I carried Tori through the crowd. She felt so small and delicate tucked up against me, and despite the emergency I couldn't help but savor it. It had been weeks since I'd touched her.

But those feelings of relief at finding her, and any comfort I felt as I held her, were all washed away when I saw Gavin heading our way. Immediately I passed Tori over to Dmitri, who could handle her with one arm as I pushed my way over to Gavin.

"What the fuck did you do to my wife?" I demanded, grabbing him by his shirt and yanking him toward me.

"Get your hands off me," he shot back, but he couldn't wrest himself out of my grip.

"What did you give her?" I needed answers. I was about five seconds away from beating the shit out of him in front of an entire club full of people.

"I didn't give her a damn thing," Gavin said. "Nothing she didn't want, anyway."

I released him to gesture at Tori's prone body, still draped over Dmitri's arm.

"Does this look like alcohol to you? She was *drugged*. And you're the one who's been feeding her drinks all night. Don't lie to me again, asshole. Is this how you get women in bed?"

Gavin glanced over at Tori, his expression softening. Then he got up in my face, his eyes cold and flat. "Look. I don't know what the fuck is going on here," he said. "But the thing is? I wouldn't have to roofie her to get her in bed with me. Can you say the same?"

My fist came up, but before I could slam it into his smug face, Dmitri blocked me.

"Let's get her out of here, boss," he said, gesturing to Tori, who was pale in his arms. There was a light sheen of sweat across her forehead, and her breathing was still shallow.

I looked back at Gavin, whose face still looked like it deserved a good punch. Or twenty. But I'd deal with him later. Dmitri was right. I had to get my wife home now. Take care of her.

"This isn't over," I told Gavin.

He shook his head and walked away.

I clenched my jaw, wanting more than anything to go after him. To beat him to a bloody pulp. And if it weren't for the fact that Tori needed me, I would have.

Back in the car, I held my wife tightly against my chest. She'd murmured a few nonsense words and I'd managed to get some water into her, so I knew she would be okay. As angry as I was, though, it was myself that I was really furious with. If only I could be honest with her. Keep her protected and safe at all times.

After Anja's disappearance all those years ago, it was impossible for me to feel comfortable with Tori out of my sight. I couldn't let anything happen to her. She didn't belong in my world, even if she deserved all the good things it afforded her. If only there wasn't so much tension between us. If only she could trust me. If only I could trust her. But there was no way I could tell her the truth. It would only put her in more danger.

At least I could hold her in my arms, even if it was only for the moment. It might be the best I could get, considering all the bad blood between us.

I couldn't stop thinking about how I hadn't been able to protect Anja. How she'd been taken from me right when I thought we'd finally found our freedom in each other. I hadn't been able to save her. But I had been a child then, just seventeen, with no resources of my own.

Things were different now, though. I was a powerful man. I had money at my disposal. Money and connections and ways to protect the things I cared about.

I would keep her safe. That's all I needed to focus on. And if I had to hire a million bodyguards or keep her locked up in our condo in order to do it, then that's what I'd do.

She just needed to trust me. Needed to trust that I was doing all of this for her own good.

The truth hit me hard.

I cared about her. A great deal.

The worst thing I could imagine was losing her.

And it scared the shit out of me.

TORI

CHAPTER 9

I woke with a jolt, blinking rapidly at my surroundings. It took a second to realize I was home. In the guest room—my room. The last thing I remembered was feeling sick at the club, the way the floor had rushed up to meet my face, the image of Stefan that had burned itself into my mind as the world went black. But no. It had to have been wishful thinking in my state of panic. There was no way my husband had been there last night. How had I even gotten home?

Gavin. He must have dropped me off. I'd said he could babysit me, and I knew he'd taken the job seriously. He definitely would have gone looking for me after I disappeared on the way to the bathroom. Thank god for him. I'd turned my phone off last night so Stefan wouldn't know where I was, and look what had happened. It was something I now regretted, in light of the awful night I'd had. But hindsight was 20/20 like that.

Why was my mind so obliterated? How many drinks had I had? I couldn't remember. In fact, I couldn't remember much of anything at all. Not clearly, anyway. Just random flashes.

I'd gone out dancing with friends from school, that much was certain. There was dancing, I was pretty sure, and plenty of cocktails and shots, which Gavin had been in charge of.

Gavin.

We'd danced a little. Flirted a lot.

After that, though...

It was all a blur. Except Stefan's face, the one clear thing I'd seen in the crowd before I passed out. I'd definitely fallen, though—I looked down and saw I had bruises on my knees, and when I gingerly rubbed the side of my sore head, I found a knot there from where I must have hit it against the floor. Yet all I could recall about the night's end was the nausea that had swept through me and the hazy image of my husband looming overhead.

Unsteadily, I got to my feet, but sank right back down on the mattress as a massive headache pounded against my skull. My whole body felt weak and shaky. What the hell had happened to me last night? There was nothing but blank space where most of my memories should have been. I had so many questions, and zero answers.

There was a glass of water on the bedside table and I drank it down, gulping greedily, my mouth dry and vaguely sour. My phone was sitting there too, still turned off. I thought about turning it back on, but I really wasn't in the mood to see the angry, disapproving texts Stefan had undoubtedly sent me when he realized I wasn't coming to dinner. We were probably in a huge fight now, and since it was Saturday I wouldn't even be able to hide out at school all day. The last thing I wanted to do right now was face him over the breakfast table, silently seething at me from three feet away.

So I took a long, hot shower. Maybe he'd be out of the house by the time I was done.

When I got out, I felt slightly better. It was almost 10 am, the time I was usually heading out the door to go to yoga. If Stefan was here, he'd be at the kitchen table with his coffee, reading the news on his tablet, but I crossed my fingers and hoped I was home alone. There was no way I'd make it through the day without my coffee.

I picked up my phone, debating whether I was ready to turn it back on.

I couldn't face the embarrassment of texting Gavin to ask what had happened. Had I thrown myself at him in my state of intoxication? And if so, had he reciprocated? What if we'd hooked up on the dance floor, right in front of everyone? What if my friends had seen me cheat on my husband? There was no way I could text them now and ask. Even if it wasn't true, they'd think it was if I claimed to be too hungover to remember what I'd done the night before.

God, this was such a mess.

Yet it seemed unlikely that Gavin and I had gotten physical. Ever since our almost-kiss that night at Navy Pier, I'd made an effort to be extra clear about the boundaries of our relationship. And Gavin was a good guy—a great guy, actually. He wasn't the kind of person who'd take advantage of me in the state I'd been in at the club. I was more sure than ever that he'd been the one to get me home safe last night. I hoped I'd taken my own pants off, though.

What would I say to my girlfriends when I saw them in class on Monday? I was pretty sure Lila had been there—she never missed a night out—but it was humiliating that I remembered absolutely nothing prior to my collapse. I'd have to just pretend it was a great time and hope I hadn't done anything too mortifying or disgraceful.

I could smell bacon all of a sudden, faintly hear the sizzle from the pan. It made my stomach turn. But that must mean Gretna was here, cooking up one of her big Saturday breakfasts. Stefan had probably given her the night off yesterday, what with the Zoric family dinner on the calendar. At least I had one friend to comfort me today. And coffee was a must.

Putting my phone back down, I threw my robe on over my leggings and T-shirt and padded down the hall and into the kitchen.

"Gretna, I didn't know you were here tod—" I stopped dead in my tracks as Stefan turned around, still pushing bacon around in a pan on the stove. "What are you doing?" I asked.

He stared at me, his mouth pressed into a firm line as he gave me a judgmental once-over. "What's it look like?"

My husband never cooked. It wasn't that he didn't know how—the few times he'd actually whipped up a meal, it had been effortless and admittedly delicious—but that he wasn't home often enough to bother, and we both took full advantage of our gourmet personal chef. Something weird was going on.

"You're...making breakfast," I said, still confused. "Why aren't you at work?"

He didn't answer, just handed me a cup of coffee. I sat in a chair at the table and took a deep inhale of the steam, letting it revive me a bit.

"I poached two eggs for you and there's toast," he told me, just in time for me to hear the slices pop up in the toaster. "Do you want it dry or with butter?"

I sipped the coffee, thankful it was piping hot and black,

and tried to get my head to stop spinning. "I'm not hungry," I said truthfully as he set a plate and fork down in front of me.

"You'll eat," he commanded, his voice going from neutral to vicious in a split second.

I pushed the plate away. "I can't eat this."

Stefan stood over me and folded his arms. "Then I'll make you something else. What do you want?"

Why was he acting this way? "I don't want anything," I said.

He was barely able to contain his fury, I could tell by the way the muscles in his jaw were twitching. "I'm not going to let you sit there and starve yourself," he said. "I'm making you a smoothie."

He turned away and went to the counter, slamming cabinet doors and knocking things around in the refrigerator as he searched for protein powder and god knew what else.

Suddenly it hit me. This had to be his way of punishing me for not showing up to dinner last night. Did he seriously think I was on some kind of hunger strike? Rebelling against this marriage by not eating? As if I'd ever do that. He really must think I was a child.

"Look, about dinner last night—"

"Forget it," he said. "It's done."

"I just—" But the roar of the blender cut me off before I could get another word out.

That made me feel even worse. Like I'd fully fucked up, ruined my one chance at getting our relationship back on track. My stomach rolled with nausea again. This hangover was brutal.

Stefan poured the unwanted smoothie into a tall glass and slammed it down in front of me. Then he sat down in the opposite chair and looked at me.

Did he know I was feeling like shit? Was he doing this on purpose to fuck with me?

I took another sip of my coffee.

"Your hands are shaking," he observed.

He was right. I was visibly trembling. Clearly, I needed to rest more after what had happened last night. Whatever it had been.

I desperately wanted to crawl right back into bed. Wrapping my hands more tightly around the coffee mug, I held onto it as if it was my lifeline. As I drank it down, one careful sip at a time, I realized that Stefan was watching me. He'd been pushing his own eggs around his plate without hardly eating them, glancing up at me every few seconds as if I was a bomb about to explode. Finally, he held out his toast.

"One bite," he said. "And then I'll leave you alone."

Leaning forward, I took the smallest bite possible and then chewed it up quickly, swallowing it down with a sip of coffee. My stomach seemed no worse for it. No better, either.

This felt like the Twilight Zone. Everything about this morning was unusual. His very presence, the meal he had made, his continued attention. Over the last month or so, we had become experts at ignoring each other. Now, I couldn't help wondering what had changed and if his asshole super-power was zeroing in on me during the moments when I was the most vulnerable. Because I was feeling pretty horrible right now and the last thing I wanted was for my lying, cheating, masterfully manipulative husband to take advantage of that.

I hobbled over to the coffeemaker and poured myself another cup, planning to return to my room where I could recover in peace.

"You look pale," Stefan said, a thick layer of faux-concern in his voice.

Ah. So I was right. Clearly, he was enjoying making me miserable.

"I feel fine," I lied, lifting my chin. I knew I probably looked like shit, but I wasn't going to admit how bad I was feeling so he could gloat about it. He obviously wanted to punish me for ignoring his dinner invitation last night and skipping out on family time with the Zorics.

"You don't look fine, kitty cat," he said.

The use of my nickname—the one that had become dear to me, that he had used in our most intimate moments —felt like a kick in the chest. Why was he using it now? What was he trying to do to me? If he wanted to make me more miserable, well, he was succeeding.

"You don't need to hover. I'm *fine*," I insisted, leaning heavily against the counter to steady myself.

"But you're not," he said, again laying on that obviously phony gentle tone. "You can barely stand."

It felt as if he could see right through me. Did he want me to admit I'd gone out with my friends last night when I shouldn't have, and that I was now suffering through the worst hangover of my life? Was I supposed to apologize, beg him for forgiveness, or simply break down in front of him for my own edification—or his amusement? And since when had he begun noticing that I existed again? The timing was suspect and I didn't trust him. Didn't trust that he wasn't trying to use my vulnerability to his advantage somehow.

"I have cramps," I finally blurted. "That's why I'm skipping yoga. I need a day of bed rest."

He looked at me as if he knew I was lying.

I didn't wait for him to say anything more. Instead, I headed back to my room with my coffee and climbed in bed, where I planned to spend the rest of the day. Recovering and wallowing. And hiding from my husband, who was clearly up to something behind my back, though I had no idea what it was.

The only thing I did know for sure was that I couldn't trust him.

CHAPTER 10

"**S**he's ali-iive!" Audrey squealed in her unmistakable New York accent, slamming into me outside my Intro to Psycholinguistics class in her trademark layers of black clothing and eyeliner.

I'd just walked out into the hall after staying late to speak with my favorite instructor, Professor Dhawan. She'd congratulated me on the strong first semester I was having and urged me to enroll in her Verbal Arts class in the spring.

"I...guess I am," I said, forcing a casual laugh as I disentangled myself from Audrey's aggressive hug. My hope had been that nobody would mention Friday night, but it looked like I wasn't going to get out of answering for whatever had happened.

"Where did you disappear off to?" Lila asked, appearing behind Audrey as we headed for the coffee kiosk in the lobby of Stuart Hall, where we always met up after our morning classes.

"I disappeared?" I said, feigning ignorance. Maybe if I played dumb, they'd tell me their side of the story—and I could figure out exactly what they'd seen, what I'd done publicly, before Gavin had somehow transported me from the 312 Club to Stefan's condo. It was now obvious that my girlfriends hadn't been the ones to see me home safely.

"Without a word," Audrey told me, shaking her head. "We were so worried. We called and texted but no answer."

I'd spent the majority of the weekend in my room, leaving only for quick trips to the kitchen to get coffee and food (after my stomach settled and could process something more than caffeine). Besides my strange interaction with Stefan on Saturday morning, he'd made himself scarce in the days following. Probably at the office or out with one of his model mistresses.

I was grateful for it. His sudden attention and intense scrutiny had made me uneasy.

"Did you lose your phone at 312?" Lila asked, her eyebrows knitting together in concern. "I'd just *die* if I lost mine. Especially at some club, where anyone could pick it up and see all my personal photos."

"I know exactly what kind of photos you're talking about, you dirty girl," Audrey teased as we got in the coffee line. Then she turned back to me, serious again. "Did someone steal it? There's an app that'll locate it for you. In the meantime, you should lock your account so nobody else can use it."

She was talking a mile a minute, as usual, but I managed to respond, "Yeah, um. It *was* lost, but I found it. The, uh, battery must've died at the club, and I thought I'd left it there. But when I called they didn't have it. Turns out it was at the bottom of my purse the whole time!"

It was a bad lie, a needlessly complicated one, but they seemed to accept it at face value.

"Oh my god, that same thing happened to me a few weeks ago," Lila said. "My phone died and I couldn't call myself and then I finally found it under my bed. Well. My friend's bed."

She and Audrey giggled.

The truth was, halfway through Saturday I had finally found the courage to turn my phone back on. After scrolling past the tons of texts I'd gotten from Lila, Audrey, Diane, and Gavin (which I was too embarrassed to read, afraid of what I'd find out about my drunken behavior), I opened Stefan's, bracing myself for an angry barrage of messages that he would have sent the night before when I hadn't shown up for dinner.

But there was only one from him, right around 7:30.

Where are you? he had asked. And that was it.

I'd been shocked to see that he hadn't followed up. That, combined with his oddly solicitous behavior on Saturday, still had me on edge. Stefan was acting differently. Strangely. And I didn't know why. I had no idea what his intentions were, when the other shoe would drop.

Compared to Stefan's radio silence, it had been nice to see the torrent of texts from my other friends. At least *they* seemed to care. And yet...besides the multiple "Where are you?" and "are u ok?" texts that I'd gotten on Friday night— and never responded to—no one had bothered to check in on me. For the rest of the weekend, I didn't get any more texts. Apparently once I was out of sight, I was out of mind. Some friends.

And here I had thought that school and my colleagues would be a substitute for the attention and love I had been missing in my private life.

It was my turn to order, so I asked for a tall mocha and then stood off to the side with my girlfriends as the barista whipped up our drinks.

Just then, Diane rushed up in a cloud of patchouli oil.

"Tori! You're safe! Where did you go on Friday? I've been on a personal media ban all weekend so I could meditate in harmony on midterms, but then I realized this morning that I never heard back from you."

"She lost her phone," Lila said breezily, slurping her frappuccino. "But actually, Tori, you never answered us. How *did* you get home? You seemed pretty wasted."

Now three pairs of eyes were focused on me as I tried to wrack my brain for the memory—any memory—of that night. But I was still drawing a blank. Except for the blurry hallucination of Stefan. There was no doubt in my mind: someone had drugged my drink.

"That's right," Diane said, peering at me curiously. "We did those shots with Gavin and then I went to go dance and then you were just *gone*. I figured maybe you'd left with someone."

Lila's mouth dropped open. "*Tori*," she hissed. "Did you go home with a sexy stranger?! Is that why you're being so coy? Tell me his name!"

"No," I protested. "I didn't—"

"Scandal!" Audrey crowed, taking a joyful swig of her espresso. "I bet he's friggin' hot."

"*Guys*. We're not here to judge anybody," Diane scolded, plucking Lila's frap out of her hand to steal a few sips. Then she smiled sweetly at me. "But you can tell us anything."

I was offended and horrified. Not only did my friends—who knew I was married—think I was the kind of person who'd just walk out of a club with a complete stranger (and try to keep it a secret later), but they didn't seem at all worried about how dangerous that could have been.

"I really didn't," I said, my voice tight. "I didn't leave with anyone."

"Huh," Lila said, tapping a neon fingernail on her cup as if she didn't quite believe me.

"To be honest, I don't remember anything that happened after those shots I took," I admitted, blushing hotly. "I have no idea how I got home. But I did make it home that night."

Diane's eyes widened. "Have you talked to Gavin? He was stuck to you like glue the whole time. He said he was babysitting since he's the one who got you that new fake ID —but he didn't seem worried at all when I asked about you later. In fact, he insisted you were fine."

Gavin.

I remembered being with Gavin on Friday night. Joking with him, flirting a little. The warmth between us. I even remembered briefly considering what it would be like to date him. Wondering if maybe, once my marriage was officially over, we could try it. If he'd wait for me.

Now I didn't know how to feel.

He showed up late to Latin class that afternoon, so I had to wait over an hour before I could finally talk to him. By the time the bell rang, I was practically vibrating with nervous energy. Surely he had an idea of what had happened to me that night. He'd been my self-appointed official babysitter. And he was the one who'd gotten me home, hadn't he?

"Gavin," I said, rushing over to grab his arm before he could leave class.

That was unusual. Usually he came to my desk and waited for me to pack up my things after Latin was over, so we could walk to the library together to study.

But then he turned and smiled at me, his usual, friendly, handsome smile, and I felt some of my worry ease. Gavin was a good guy. I liked him. I trusted him. He would tell me the truth.

"Tori. How are you feeling?" he asked, his voice kind and gentle.

"I'm okay," I told him carefully, pulling him off to the side a little. "But to be honest, most of Friday evening is a bit of a blank. Do you think you could...fill me in?"

Every time I had to admit my alcohol-fueled amnesia out loud, I felt a surge of embarrassment. I wasn't that kind of girl. The kind who got so drunk that she couldn't remember what happened later, who blacked out in the middle of a club. I was sure something had been slipped into my drink, but even so, I'd never been the kind of girl to put myself in situations where that could happen. I'd messed up. And I didn't want Gavin to think less of me.

Gavin frowned. "You don't remember what happened?"

I shook my head, my cheeks going hot.

He glanced around the emptying room, a stormy look crossing his face. "Your douchebag of a husband showed up," he said, dropping his voice low.

My brain was like a record skittering to a halt.

"Stefan? He was there?" I was in shock. How had he found me? He shouldn't have been able to track me with my phone turned off.

"Yeah," Gavin said, disgusted. "Let's talk outside, in the quad."

The pieces were falling into place now—not just my recollection of Stefan being at the club, but how he'd acted Saturday morning, how he'd seemed to know there was something wrong with me. Yet he hadn't said a word about it. Instead he'd sat there, smug and mostly silent, making backhanded comments about me being pale and trying to force food on me.

I felt the same nausea I'd felt that morning as I sank onto a bench, pulling my coat tighter around me.

And if Gavin was calling Stefan a douchebag, something must have happened between them. Oh no. "Wait, what did he do? Did he say something to you?"

Gavin shook his head. "You really don't remember." He sighed, and ran his hand through his hair. "Yeah, so everything was cool, you were dancing, having a few drinks, and then your *husband*," he practically spat the word, "shows up out of nowhere. Just barges in, acting like you're his property. We had a few words. He was all possessive, very aggro, and then he dragged you out of there. Like you didn't deserve to be out having a good time with your friends."

"And that's...that was all?" I asked.

He nodded. "Your husband has some anger management issues. And he obviously thinks he owns you. I know it's none of my business, but having gone through this same kind of thing with my mom, I gotta say...it's the kind of behavior that doesn't get better. I worry about you."

"Stefan's...complicated," I said. "He's not normally like that." But he was, wasn't he?

Something still wasn't right. I'd been drugged, I was sure of it, yet Gavin hadn't mentioned it at all.

He shrugged again. "If you say so," he said. "You know him better than I do."

I nodded numbly. I was only half listening, still struggling to make sense of it all. According to my own memory, I hadn't been having a good time in the least when Stefan had arrived. I distinctly remembered the nausea, the way the ground had rolled under my feet, the way I'd sunk to the floor as the room went black. How had Gavin not noticed?

"Did I seem..." I paused, not sure how to ask if I had acted like I'd been roofied. "Did I seem a little out of it?"

101

Gavin paused thoughtfully. "I guess you did seem a little off. I just thought you'd had too much to drink." He laughed. "I mean, but who hasn't had a night or two out where they couldn't remember what happened?"

Me. I'd never had a night like that and I never wanted to have one again.

"I don't think I was just drunk," I said slowly. "I think I might have been drugged."

His entire face changed, instantly stricken. "Jesus," he said. "Who the hell would..." he stopped, his words cutting off as if he was remembering something.

"What?"

"Nothing, it's just..." He paused. "No, that's crazy."

"What?" I demanded. "Tell me."

He took a deep breath. "It's just—if you think you were drugged..." he shook his head again. "I don't know. Do you remember seeing a big guy that night? Really tall?"

My stomach dropped. "Yes, I do. He was over six feet, black turtleneck, shaved head. I thought he was one of the bouncers."

Gavin looked me straight in the eye. "He didn't work there. He was the one who led Stefan to you. They left the club together, carrying you. I can't help wondering if...if Stefan and this guy had something to do with whatever you drank. I mean, dude was checking you out all night. Hovering not ten feet away from you at all times. I figured he just liked the way you looked, but...it's a pretty big coincidence."

My blood went cold.

"You think Stefan had me drugged?" I asked, my voice cracking.

"I don't know what to think, Tori," Gavin said. "But if you'd seen the way he was acting, how possessive and angry he was about the fact that we were just talking...I just wouldn't be surprised if he'd sent the big guy out that night to keep an eye on you. Maybe more than that."

I couldn't believe it. Stefan was a lot of things, had done a lot of despicable things, but I had a hard time imagining he'd send some thug to a club just to spy on me and drug me.

But Gavin's expression was so serious and so concerned that I felt my confidence waver. I *had* turned my phone off that night. What if Stefan really did have me followed once he'd realized that he couldn't track me? What if this wasn't even the first time he'd sent someone after me? Had I been drugged as punishment for flirting with Gavin?

"All I'm saying is, he didn't seem like the nicest guy," Gavin said. "And he's definitely got a jealous streak, and is extremely possessive of you. There's no way you can deny that."

"You're right," I admitted. Stefan *was* possessive. And he hadn't said anything about coming to the club that night or about how I had gotten home. Instead he had just watched me suffering from the aftermath of being drugged, and done nothing but taunt me.

I felt truly sick now.

And confused.

Gavin seemed so sure that Stefan had been the one to drug me, but I still couldn't help feeling like he was leaving something out.

"I'm sorry, Tori," Gavin said. "I don't know what else to say. Look, I'm not gonna harp on it, because it's your life and your decision to make. But if you ever have to get out, run away, I'll be here. I've seen it all before, I know how it is. So my couch is yours. In fact, I'll take the couch myself.

Just...you always have somewhere safe to go, with me. Okay?"

"Okay," I said. There was too much to process. Too much to wrap my head around.

"It's too cold out here," Gavin said, adjusting his scarf. "Do you want to grab lunch?"

I shook my head. "I have office hours with Dhawan. I'll catch up with you later."

But what I needed was some time to sort through this new information. Although Gavin had given me answers, I still felt just as much in the dark as I had on Saturday morning.

I had far more questions than answers now. How had Stefan found me in the first place? Had he sent that guy to spy on me? Was my husband ultimately responsible for my drugged state? Was it all part of his plan to get me home, or some kind of punishment for being out with Gavin, who he already had his suspicions about?

Maybe he'd actually rescued me from getting drugged by someone else at the club. But if that was the case, then why hadn't he said anything Saturday morning? Or any time since then?

Nothing made sense.

And it still felt like Gavin was keeping something from me, being cagey about what really happened. Like he wasn't telling me the whole truth.

There was no one I could trust.

TORI

CHAPTER 11

As I pushed my way past the students congregating in little groups outside the door of American Sign Language, my last class of the day, I heard Diane calling after me.

"Dinner and study group? I booked us one of the big rooms in Regenstein. Room 206."

I'd barely made it through ASL with my mind fully focused on what Gavin had told me earlier—that Stefan had been responsible for drugging me. I didn't know what to believe. I didn't know *who* to believe.

"I need to pass," I told her apologetically. "I've been dragging ass all day and there's no way I'll be able to focus. I could really use an early night in bed."

"Okay," Diane said, giving my shoulder a squeeze. "You know, meditation really helps me get centered the week before midterms when everything's all crazy. Maybe try the Zen-Me app? It's pretty great. Ooh, and maybe some echinacea!"

"Thanks," I said, meaning it. "I'll keep it in mind. See you tomorrow."

I still didn't feel a hundred percent recovered from Friday night, and my head was reeling with all the new information I'd gathered about Stefan's appearance in the club. It terrified me to know that, while under the influence, I could have easily been taken somewhere against my will, been violated or hurt badly, with absolutely no way to defend myself or even protest. I'd been totally helpless. And it was even more terrifying to think that my husband might be the one responsible for my incoherent and incapacitated state.

Hopefully some quiet time would give me the space I needed to sort it all out. Usually I loved the distraction of schoolwork and language, but tonight I just wanted to go home, put on my favorite pjs, and eat take-out on the couch.

But in the Uber on the way home, I couldn't stop replaying that night in my mind. And every time I did, a surge of fear and panic came over me.

By the time I opened the door to the condo, I felt like I'd been holding my breath all day. All I wanted was to relax, give myself a chance to recover and recuperate. But it was a hope that died immediately when I walked into the living room and found Stefan sitting on the couch.

"What are you doing here?" I blurted, too surprised at his presence to realize how rude the words sounded until they were out of my mouth. "Aren't you supposed to be at work?"

He glanced up from his phone and the moleskin notebook lying open on his lap.

"I believe this is still my condo," he said drily. Then he went back to whatever work he was doing.

Why had I thought I'd be safe at home? And why the hell was he even here? Knowing him, though, he had probably just stopped in for a quick break and a change of clothes. He'd probably head right back out in a few minutes and go meet one of his women on the side, if his behavior at the fundraiser was anything to go by.

I couldn't believe I was actually hoping that was the case—that my husband was about to go out and cheat on me some more—but after what Gavin had told me today, I was nervous about spending an evening with Stefan. I was actually afraid of him and what he was capable of.

Maybe confronting him was the best course of action. Maybe he'd actually give me some answers. Except he never gave me answers, did he? My husband was a certifiable expert in hiding things, lying by omission, and refusing to engage with me honestly and respectfully.

On top of that, I was all too aware that we were here alone. Stefan was bigger than me, a lot bigger, and it would be all too easy for him to harm me if I said the wrong thing and pissed him off. My mind conjured up images of his green eyes flashing angrily, the low growl of his voice when I made him angry, the way he'd gotten rough with me in the past. Shoving me against walls, ramming his tongue down my throat. His hands fisting in my hair as he groaned into my mouth. The thought of it made my lower belly go hot and tight.

God damn, I'd just gone there. Ridiculous that being stuck at home with my husband could make me this anxious and this turned on at the same time. I didn't want to think about it. I *wouldn't* think about it.

In my room I set down my school bag and armload of books, taking a minute to scroll through the various menus on my take-out app and see if anything looked good. I kept an ear out for the sound of Stefan leaving, expecting to hear it at any moment.

Instead, I heard a knock at my door.

I debated ignoring it, but I wasn't sure he'd just go away. And it was nice that he'd bothered to knock, considering that there wasn't a lock on my door—I appreciated that he was at least trying to show some courtesy toward me.

"Yes?" I said, swinging the door open and leaning against the frame.

Stefan stood there, his jacket off, his shirtsleeves rolled up, his top button undone and his tie gone. My pulse shouldn't have skipped at the sight of him, but it did. He looked incredibly handsome like this. Almost as handsome as he looked when he was completely put together.

"Gretna left us dinner," Stefan said.

I stared at him. Dinner? Us? We were eating together?

"It's Indian," he added. "I just turned on the oven to reheat it."

Without my permission, my mouth watered. I loved spicy curries, crispy hot samosas, and pillowy mounds of jasmine rice. It was the exact comfort food I'd been thinking of ordering to soothe myself tonight. Even now, I could smell the scent of it wafting into my bedroom.

The last thing I wanted to do was have dinner with my husband tonight, but I was too starving to make up an excuse and stay hidden in my room while he ate without me. So I followed him into the dining room. He had already set out the plates and utensils and when I sat down he went into the kitchen to bring the hot dishes out to the table.

I eyed everything—and Stefan—suspiciously. What was going on? Why wasn't he at work? And since when did he come home early enough to eat one of Gretna's meals with me?

He sat down across from me. For a moment, neither of us did anything but eye each other warily.

"Naan?" he asked. I nodded, and Stefan passed me the bread.

As I poured us each a glass of ice water from a crystal carafe, he carefully spooned rice, lentils, aloo gobi, and tikka masala onto my plate before serving himself. It was eerily quiet.

But the heavenly scent of exotic spices gave me a small sense of comfort, and with my first perfect bite of the soft, fragrant rice, I could feel my shoulders start to relax. Gretna usually leaned toward Italian and French cooking, but there was no denying that she was a master at Indian cuisine as well. As Stefan and I ate, however, I could feel the tension stretching out between us, the weight of all the unspoken words we hadn't said since Saturday.

I thought about what Gavin had told me about Stefan showing up at the club. About how he had been possessive and intense. The accusation that Stefan had put something in my drink, or that he'd ordered his emissary to do it. Suddenly, despite the delicious food, my mouth went dry. I took a long drink of water, trying to soothe my now-tight throat.

Had Stefan drugged me? What would he say if I looked him square in the eyes and asked if he'd been at the club the other night? If he'd stooped so low as to have me roofied in order to control me or punish me?

Glancing up at him, however, reminded me again how much bigger and stronger he was than me. With his shirt sleeves rolled up, I could see the taut muscles of his hands and arms. The bulge of his biceps were visible through his shirt, which stretched tight over his expansive chest.

He could easily dominate me.

The thought made me nervous and excited all over again. I had no self-control.

"How is it?" Stefan asked, gesturing at my plate.

"Good," I said, looking down to avoid his eyes. What was wrong with me? My husband was possibly a very dangerous man, but my body was reacting to him as if this was a seduction.

I didn't like thinking about it. Didn't like thinking about the power he had over me. The spell he had cast.

My appetite suddenly gone, I pushed my lentils around on my plate.

"How's school going?" he asked. "You get that Chicago landscape report turned in?"

I was so shocked, I almost dropped my fork at the question. It wasn't just that he was making an attempt to talk to me at all, or even that it was about school—something he knew I'd have no problem babbling on and on about—but that he remembered my big report and cared enough to see how it had gone. Or at least, he was pretending to care.

"I did," I said. "My group got an A."

"Hmm," he said. "You did well. Not that I'm surprised."

A rush of pride radiated through me, and I felt angry at my body for betraying me yet again. It was infuriating that he could so easily pretend that everything was fine—when he was fully aware of the danger I'd been in on Friday night. And what gave him the right to sit here and ask me about my school work? The last time we'd had any kind of normal conversation was before everything had gone to shit, before I'd realized what Stefan and Konstantin and the whole KZ Modeling enterprise was really up to. Were we going to pretend none of it had happened?

Was this his way of trying to get us back to some semblance of normalcy, or was he just lulling me into a sense of safety and complacency so he could hurt me again? I didn't trust him.

"Your other classes are going okay?" he asked. "Midterm exams are coming up, right?"

"Uh huh," I mumbled, staring down at my plate.

"Those late-night study sessions paying off?"

I cleared my throat. Was this a jab at my friendship with Gavin, or the amount of time I spent with my other school friends?

"Yep," I said, keeping my response short and curt. I continued pushing my uneaten food around my plate, unable to remember the last time I'd been so uncomfortable around someone.

"I'll bet Professor Dhawan is going to miss having you in class," he said.

I just nodded this time. My eyes had drifted upward of their own accord, following Stefan's strong arms to his capable hands and beautiful mouth.

There was something so sexy and magnetic about him that I was even turned on watching him eat, unable to tear my eyes away. He seemed to savor his food with a focused pleasure that reminded me of the intensity he'd brought to the bedroom.

My body still craved his. Wanted him desperately. Wanted him now.

It was sick and I knew it, but I couldn't help myself, the way I responded to his presence.

The room was still full of tension, but it had shifted. It wasn't just frustration or anger or fear. There was something more potent there. Repressed and highly charged sexual tension. It was so strong, I tightened my grip around my silverware as if I could squeeze it out of me.

Stefan's eyes followed the gesture, but his expression didn't change. If he was worried that I might do something with my knife, he didn't show it, but I doubted he ever worried when it came to me. Not when he was so fully aware of the power that he had over me.

I gave up on trying to eat and pushed my chair away from the table.

Whatever he was doing right now—with the food and the small talk and the feigning interest about my classes—it had to be an act. He wasn't really interested in hearing about my schoolwork. He wanted something from me. I just didn't know what.

He looked up at me and our eyes locked. My heart leapt in my chest. Those eyes of his. So green. So intense. I was equally aroused and frightened.

I quickly broke our gaze. "I need to go study."

"Such a hard worker," Stefan said. "Always got your nose in a book. Sometimes it's good to give yourself a night off, though. You know what I mean?"

He smiled.

"Yeah..." I said.

Narrowing my eyes, I picked up my plate. Was he fucking with me? Was this his way of trying to get me to admit something about Friday night, or about Gavin? Or was he trying to figure out if I knew that he'd caught me when I was out at the club—and had dragged me home when I was passed out? I felt like I was losing my mind. Like he was gaslighting me on purpose.

Bringing my dishes to the kitchen sink, I decided that I was done with this farce. If Stefan planned to stay in tonight, so he could corner me into awkward, stilted conversations and scheme against me all the while, then I would have to leave. There was no way I could stand to be in the same house with him anymore. Not like this. I needed space to think. To breathe.

My lingering confusion about Friday night made me too

uneasy and nervous to stay home while Stefan was here. Not that my body seemed to care about my concerns. I still wanted him. Wanted to finish unbuttoning his shirt, sliding down to my knees as I tugged down his pants. I missed the feel of his strong, sure hands on my bare skin. The feel of his body against mine.

I tried to push those feelings away.

I'd take myself out tonight. Find my own fun.

Heading into my bedroom, I went immediately for my closet. As I examined potential outfits, I pulled out my phone, intending to text Lila and Audrey and Diane to see if they wanted to go out with me, blow off a little steam.

Then I remembered that they'd all but abandoned me when I'd been drugged and incapacitated, that they'd delighted in the possibility that I'd gone home from the club with a stranger and cheated on my husband. Were they really the kind of people I wanted to spend a Monday night out with? Were they really the kind of people I wanted to spend any time with?

I knew I was blowing things out of proportion in my current state, but at this point, the only person I felt I could really trust was Gavin. I knew that he'd be happy to meet me anytime and anywhere, and would keep an even better eye on me after what I'd been through at 312. What was it he'd said, just this afternoon? That he was there for me. That I'd always have somewhere safe to go with him. I felt better just thinking about his warm brown eyes.

With a decisive tug, I yanked a tight, blush pink dress off a hanger and threw it on the bed. It was a gorgeous Herve Leger bodycon bandage dress that had a sultry vintage lounge singer flair. It hit at the knee, but showed off lots of cleavage and cupped my every curve.

I had to lose my bra and panties and do a ridiculous

wiggle-type dance just to get into it, but it was worth it. Tonight, I was going all out. I'd let down my hair, bust out the lipstick, and let myself have fun. There was no way I'd be able to walk into a club dressed like this and not have every eye turn toward me. I'd dance and flirt and forget all about Stefan.

And I'd definitely forget about the impact his sexy stare had had on me.

I brushed out my hair and gave it a shot of hairspray underneath to add volume, slipped on my stilettos, and gave my makeup a quick refresh. Then, standing in front of the closet mirror, I inspected my outfit one last time from head to toe. I wasn't one to brag, but between the bombshell hair, the second skin of a dress, and my nude lip/smoky eye combo, I looked hot.

With the lack of panties and the length of the skirt, I'd be revealing far too much if I dared even bend over, but it didn't matter. I had no plans to sit at all. I planned to spend the whole night on the dance floor, forgetting everything that had happened over the last few days. I'd lose myself in the crush of the crowd, in the pounding bass of music, in the adoring gaze of men who would clamor to buy me drinks. But this time, I'd stay sober. I'd stay in control.

I felt great. For the first time since Friday night, I felt like myself again. But better. Like a sexier, stronger version of myself.

I was ready to go out. Ready to have fun.

Grabbing my black Chanel bag and my phone, I headed out of my room, my thumb already scrolling for Gavin's number. I'd show him that I was someone worth waiting for.

But as my heels click-clacked on the marble tile of the foyer, I heard footsteps behind me.

Spinning around, I found Stefan standing inches away. My heart leapt to my throat as I let out a soft gasp.

His voice low and dangerous, he said, "Where, exactly, do you think you're going?"

TORI

CHAPTER 12

Stefan shoved me up against the wall, grabbing my wrist, and my purse hit the floor. With his other hand, he snatched my phone from my grip and tossed it on the entryway table beside him. He looked furious, the tension rolling off him, his green eyes flashing. I tried to pull away but he held fast, his gaze intense and hungry as it roamed my body.

"Let me go," I said, my heart slamming in my chest.

"I asked you where the hell you think you're going, dressed like that," he repeated, tugging my wrist for emphasis.

Goosebumps broke out all along my skin. It had been so long since he had touched me, since I had felt his skin against mine. Despite the underlying threat in his words, I wanted to melt into his touch. Dozens of warring emotions filled me.

"None of your business," I shot back.

I had to get away. I wasn't sure I could trust myself around him, not when he was looking at me like that, like he wanted to eat me, not when I couldn't deny that I wanted him just as bad. I needed to get out of the condo. I needed space. I needed to escape.

But he held on to me, his grip nearly bruising the soft skin of my forearm. I should have hated it, but I didn't. In fact, the tension that had built up between us throughout dinner threatened to overflow. To overpower me. I couldn't let that happen.

"*Let go,*" I ordered, more firmly this time.

He didn't. My protest died on my lips as he advanced on me, moving closer.

"I'll let you go as soon as you tell me where it is you're running off to," he said, his voice hard. "Because you're sure as hell not going to a study group in that dress."

It was pure torture, being this close to Stefan. Having his hands on me.

"I'm going out," I told him, sounding more sure of myself than I actually felt. "Didn't you just tell me that I should give myself a night off?"

"A night off from studying," he said, his voice hard. "Not a night on the town."

I lifted my chin, feeling rebellious and powerful. Something about the dress I was wearing—how sexy it made me feel—gave me the strength to stand up to him.

"I'm an adult. I'm going out. You can't stop me," I said, staring him straight in the eye.

I'd never really stood up to him like this before. The only other time had been when I'd moved into the guest room. It was a decision I still occasionally regretted, especially when I woke in the middle of the night, missing the feel of his body against mine, missing the arms that used to reach for me in the dark, the feel of his weight against me, his cock hard against my thigh or stiffening against the curve of my ass. He was like a fever dream that I couldn't quite shake.

But now I needed the fever to break. I needed to take a stand.

"I don't accept that," he said. "I need to know where you're going, and with whom."

My jaw fell open. There was no way I was going to comply with that. "I am leaving now," I said, pitching my voice low and steely, "and you are going to let go of me."

I said it like I meant it, even though I really didn't want him to.

What I wanted was for him to pull me tight against him. To bend me over the table right there and take me the way he always had—rough and intense and so hot I could hardly stand it.

"I'm your husband," he practically roared. "And I am entitled to know where you are at all times. I'm the only person who can keep you safe. Or are you still figuring that out?"

I wanted to believe that Stefan was acting this way because he was genuinely worried about my safety. His caveman ways might even be charming if he actually cared about me. But this was all about control. And I was more than a little afraid that he was the reason I wasn't safe.

I couldn't ignore Gavin's accusation that Stefan had been responsible for drugging me. I still didn't know if I believed it, but I wouldn't have been surprised to learn that it had been Stefan's attempt to make me think I wasn't safe going out on my own. That I would be in danger if my husband didn't know exactly where I was, every second of every day.

"Where. Are. You. Going," he ground out.

He was still holding onto me, waiting for an answer,

waiting for me to do what I always did—acquiesce to his demands. He fully expected that he would win this argument. But I refused to play along this time. And part of me was itching for a fight, to finally have it out with him.

I wanted to see the look on his face when I accused him of drugging me, when he realized that I was smarter than he gave me credit for, more worldly than the naïve, spoiled senator's daughter he assumed I was. Even if I was nothing more than his bird in her gilded cage, I wanted him to know that I saw through his act, and I wasn't going to let him get away with it.

But I also wanted to escape. To get out, go find Gavin, lose myself in dancing and loud, bass-thumping music and crowds of people where I could be anonymous. I was tired of fighting.

I didn't want to play Stefan's game any longer.

The escapist in me won out.

Wrenching myself out of his grip, I sidestepped him and turned back toward the door. But before I could even get my fingers around the door knob, he was blocking me. Standing there in front of the door like an immobile wall, arms crossed.

"Move," I demanded.

But instead of being reasonable, he grabbed my arm again, his fingers digging into my biceps. Hard. I tried to pull away again, but he wouldn't release me. Not this time. I thrashed against him, twisting my shoulders, but he spun me around and threw me against the door, his strong arms boxing me in.

My entire body was hot from his close proximity to me, his large figure overwhelming my small one. I could smell his cologne, that expensive spicy scent that he wore that had lingered on our sheets when we shared a bed. It still made my knees weak.

"You aren't going out," Stefan growled, his breath warm against my cheek. "You're too irresponsible. In fact, after what you let happen at that club on Friday, I'm never letting you go out again. You should be thanking me for keeping you safe."

For a moment, I was stunned silent. He'd gone there. There was no holding back now.

"How the hell do I know that you aren't the one who roofied me in the first place?" I said, my tone bordering on a yell. "Because it wouldn't surprise me."

"I'm the one who fucking saved you," he shouted back, breathing hard.

I clenched my jaw, staring him down. I didn't know what to believe. Stefan had just admitted that he knew what happened on Friday night. Was Gavin right about everything? About Stefan drugging me? Which words of Stefan's were true, and which were lies?

"Don't peg yourself as the hero," I said, my voice strained with anger. "You had me followed, by that huge guy all in black. You think I'm supposed to trust you? You obviously don't trust me. Why else would you be keeping tabs on me like that?"

Even as I argued, even as I reminded myself that Stefan was dangerous and manipulative, my body reacted in a way that I couldn't control. My skin was hot where he held onto me, my face felt flushed, and I had to press my legs together to combat the ache I felt there. It was an ache that never seemed to go away when he was near. An ache only he could satisfy. I wanted to hate him, but I couldn't.

"Don't you get it? I had you followed because you

matter," he said, his voice hoarse with emotion. "If anything happened to you..."

He shook his head, his eyes blazing with anger. I was just as angry, but beneath it was something else. Arousal. I was impossibly turned on being this close to him, feeling his fury, his passion, his concern. His body was so close that it took everything in me not to touch him.

His words echoed in my mind. I mattered to him. Deeply. That meant he cared.

It meant he felt something for me.

My heart pounded in my chest as I reached up a hand to touch his cheek, our eyes locking. He hadn't finished his sentence, but I didn't care. He'd said enough.

I pulled his face down toward me, closed my eyes, and kissed him, parting my lips just enough to invite him in deeper, moaning softly when his tongue found mine.

Stefan never hesitated, taking control of the kiss as if he had been waiting for it.

I knew this surrender would be my downfall, that this could destroy me, but I didn't care. How could I when he kissed me the way he did? When we fit so perfectly together?

I opened wider, letting his tongue thrust deeper, letting myself freefall.

Being with Stefan like this, the rest of world—all of our problems, all of our fights, all of our disagreements—seemed to fade into nothingness. All I could focus on was him and the way his tongue fucked my mouth, the way my core was turning to liquid, hot and needy.

His hands tangled in my hair, his fingers tightening there, forcing my head back so he could trace his tongue down my throat. It had been so long since he had touched me this way, tasted me this way, and now I was greedy for more. Greedy for everything.

I gasped as he bit me, gently and then less gently, his tongue soothing each mark that he was surely leaving on the sensitive skin of my neck. He was marking me, claiming me, and I couldn't get enough.

I arched against him, needing to feel more of him, needing his entire body to be pressed against mine. I wanted him to dominate me. To take me.

He pinned my arms to the wall above my head. I panted, gazing up at him hungrily.

"You're mine," he growled.

"Yes," I could barely gasp as his entire body trapped me against the wall. He rolled his hips against mine, his cock pressing into me, and I moaned with need. I was wet and ready for him, and had been all night, even if my mind had tried to deny the truth.

He looked down at the way my breasts were squeezed together and let out a low groan.

"You wore this slutty little dress for me, didn't you?" he asked, dragging his finger along the low neckline, making me shiver at his touch. "Tell me," he ordered.

"I wore it for you," I gasped, barely recognizing the sultry rasp of my own voice.

"This is all for me." He slid his hand down, cupping my breast harshly. "Say it."

"It's all for you," I confirmed, straining against my pinned wrists, wanting him to touch me more. Loving how rough he was being.

There was no one like him. No one else who knew what I wanted, who understood my desires the way that Stefan intuitively did.

He shoved the cap sleeves of my dress down, exposing

my taut nipples, which were tingling against the cool air and begging to be touched. Tasted. Bitten. Lowering his head, Stefan did exactly that, swirling his hot, wet tongue over the hard crest of each nipple before dragging his teeth along them, making me cry out with sheer bliss.

His hand slid lower, down to my hip, before curving around to cup my ass, pulling me even harder against his cock. There were too many clothes between us. I couldn't stand it.

"What are you wearing under this?" Stefan demanded, palming my ass.

I shook my head, wanting him to touch me, wanting him to fuck me. I was so aroused by him that I could barely speak.

"Tell me," he demanded.

"Nothing," I gasped as his hand slid lower to the hem of my dress.

"You dirty little whore," he murmured in my ear before whipping the fabric up and plunging his fingers inside me. "You're so wet for me."

"Yes," I cried out, too-hot and desperate now. I was pinned against the wall, my expensive pink dress bunched at my hips, my breasts and everything below the waist completely exposed to Stefan. I wanted him to finger me hard, but his hand stayed still, making me squirm.

"Does my kitty cat like that?" he said, his voice low and dangerous as he pumped once, twice, then stopped.

"Mm hmm." I was losing my mind. I needed more. "Please," I begged, opening my legs wider. "More. I need it."

His gaze pierced mine as he curled his fingers inside, just barely tapping my G-spot before pulling back. Heat flooded through me and I jerked against his hand, the touch too light, too teasing to provide any kind of relief. The smile he gave me was wicked. Dangerous.

"Again," he ordered.

I knew what he wanted. He wanted me to beg.

"Please," I moaned, thrusting against his hand. "Give it to me."

I was too far gone to even pretend that I didn't want it. He rewarded my shameless pleading by dipping his fingers deeper inside of me, his strokes fast and rough. I cried out as he fucked me with his hand, the sensation intense and perfect but still not enough.

"I want you," I murmured. "I want all of you."

I was gasping for air, my head thrashing back and forth against the wall as he used two, then three fingers, to tease me, slowing down on purpose just to drive me crazy.

"Please," I cried out, panting. "I need you."

"You need me?" He let go of my wrists finally and cupped my chin, forcing my face up toward him. "Tell me what you need me to do."

"I need you to fuck me," I practically sobbed, my hands squeezing his rock-hard biceps. "Please Stefan. Please fuck me."

It was his breaking point. His hands dropped away from me as he went for his belt, his pants hitting the floor as he shrugged out of his shirt. Finally, his cock—his long, hard, perfect cock—was free. He took it in his hand, rubbing it against my clit. I gasped at the pressure.

"Is this what you want? Say it," he demanded.

"Yes," I whispered. "Yes, please."

"Beg for it like a good wife."

"Fuck," I panted, humiliated at my naked desire but desperate to have him inside me. "Please fuck me. I need

124

your cock. I need you inside me, I need my husband inside me. Please. Fuck me, fuck me, fuck me."

With a roar he grabbed my knee and pinned my leg up against the wall, forcing my pussy wide open for him. Then he thrust inside me, so hard and deep that he stopped to let out a groan.

"Oh my god," I moaned, clenching around him. My head fell back against the wallpaper.

He was so deep, so big, so hard. It was everything I wanted. I was nearly blind from the sensations crashing through me.

His hips pinned me to the wall and his hands pulled my legs up around his waist, my ankles locking behind his back. It gave him even deeper access, and he pressed his head into my shoulder and began thrusting into me. He was relentless, every stroke pushing a cry from my lips. There was nothing but his cock, the intense feeling of him splitting my pussy wide open. It felt like coming home, and I shivered as he glided back and forth, fitting so perfectly inside me.

His hips drummed against mine as he fucked me hard against the wall, my ears filled with our groans of pleasure and the rhythmic thumping of our bodies hitting the wall over and over and over again. I heard myself gasping, and I clung tightly to his shoulders, my eyes shut tight as I let the pleasure roll through me in waves, building and heightening with every stroke.

He took me hard and I begged for more, my hands clawing down his back, my nails digging into his shoulders as his cock slid in and out of me, punishing me, pleasuring me. He forced my thighs apart, opening me even wider to him, pounding even deeper.

How I'd managed without this for so long, I would never know, but there was no going back now. He had claimed me, utterly and completely. With his mouth, his hands, his cock.

I was his.

He thrust inside me over and over again, never slowing, pumping strong and steady as my orgasm built, curling tight and hot in my belly.

"Make me come," I whispered, my fingers digging into his shoulders. "Stefan. Make me come."

And he did. When it hit me, it felt as if the entire world was exploding around me.

I couldn't stop myself from crying out as the pleasure slammed through me, the contractions of my pussy so fast and hard that it felt like an electric shock. Stefan pounded into me with a new fury, and I heard him say my name just before he found his own release, growling against the curve of my neck, the hot rush of his orgasm filling me up.

I closed my eyes, my jagged breathing in time with his, our hearts beating fast in our chests as we held onto each other.

It was everything I had ever wanted.

"Come," Stefan said, easing me back down to the floor and leading me toward our—no, his—bedroom. When we got there, he knelt, and I held onto his shoulders to steady myself as he slid off my tight, bunched-up dress, helping me step out of it. My legs were still weak, my body reeling with aftershocks. I watched him pull towels out of the closet, appreciating the taut muscles of his torso, the way his sweat-damp hair curled against his temples.

"You're a mess," I teased, knowing I probably looked just as unkempt, if not worse.

"Then we better get clean," he said.

Without another word, he lifted me in his arms like I weighed nothing and carried me into the bathroom, setting me on the bench. Then he brought in the towels and turned the shower on, letting the water get hot and steamy before leading me in.

I tried not to stare as the water rolled down his body but it had been so long since I'd seen him naked and he was truly a gorgeous sight to behold. Broad, strong shoulders, a narrow waist and that tight, perfect ass. I was sore from the way he had fucked me against the wall, but still I wanted him again. Immediately.

Instead, I let him hold me tight under the water, breathing out a deep sigh as the heat and the steam relaxed my muscles. It almost seemed to wash away all the weeks of anger and frustration, leaving me calm and satisfied and happy to be naked and wet with my husband.

"Are you warm enough?" Stefan asked.

I nodded, touched by his concern.

I reached for the shampoo bottle, but he stopped me with a gentle touch on my arm.

"Let me," he said, squeezing the shampoo into his own hands before rubbing them together to create a foamy lather. "Turn around."

I did, and he slid his hands into my wet hair, massaging the suds into my scalp. I closed my eyes, savoring the sensation. It felt so good to be touched by him this way. He had never been this tender before.

I felt my heart swell. Things were going to be different now, I could tell. Though I hadn't taken a real vacation or spent days away from home, my stepmother's advice had been dead on all the same. The time apart had really seemed to draw me and Stefan closer.

This might even become a real marriage. Exactly the fairy tale I had fantasized about the first time I saw him across the ballroom at my birthday party.

"That feel good?" he asked, whispering in my ear as he continued to massage my scalp.

I barely managed to nod, my entire body tingling as I lost myself in the luxury of being taken care of. It was almost as good as sex. Almost.

He finished washing my hair and began to rinse it

gently. But before he could start on the conditioner, I turned to face him. There was one thing I had to get off my chest.

"You really didn't drug me?" I asked, searching his eyes.

"I would never do that," he confirmed. "I swear it."

I paused, not wanting to pummel him with questions, but I had to know for sure.

"Then how did you get to me so quickly?"

He didn't bat an eye. "I got in a car the second my guy sent pictures of that asshole getting handsy with you."

"You were spying on me," I said.

"To keep you safe," he insisted. "I never would have come if you were okay. But you weren't. And thank god I showed up when I did. Your little friend is lucky there's no evidence pointing to him as the culprit."

"Gavin?" I asked, my heart sinking. "You're not saying you think it was him."

Had I been trusting the wrong person all along?

"I don't know who it was," Stefan said, his voice laced with disgust. "If I was positive he did it, he'd be dead right now. But I still don't trust that creep for a second. He was all over you."

I sensed he was holding back, that there was more to his contempt for Gavin than he was telling me, but it had to be jealousy making him talk this way. Admittedly, part of me liked it. The alpha male coming out full force, Stefan wanting to protect me and keep me all to himself.

"Honestly, it seems like it was a random stranger at the bar. It's not uncommon, though I fucking hate the fact. But that doesn't mean you'll be safe next time, kitty cat," Stefan said.

Despite his warning tone, his use of my nickname made my heart soar.

"I'll be more careful next time I go out," I said, choosing my words carefully. The last thing I wanted was to agree to be locked up at home. I'd still have my freedom, still hang out with my friends—I wasn't willing to let go of that. I'd just make better choices in the future.

Stefan cupped my face in his hands. "The thing is," he said, "this world you're involved in—our fathers' world—*my* world—it's dangerous. You have to let me take care of you."

"Okay," I said, liking the sound of it. But I hated the idea of being constantly spied on without my knowledge. "Are you having this guy follow me around all the time?" I asked.

"No. It was a last resort. Dmitri's a good guy, but he's not on call 24/7 to watch you."

I sighed with relief and leaned into his chest. "Can you just...please keep me informed when my bodyguard *is* going to be keeping an eye on me? I want to be able to trust you."

"I can do that," he agreed. "But you have to stop fighting me. I'm trying to protect you."

He poured some conditioner into his hands and began to massage my scalp again.

When he framed it like that, I didn't mind at all. Being protected by Stefan made me feel safe and secure.

After rinsing out the conditioner, Stefan soaped up his hands and began to rub soft, sensual circles against my skin, from my shoulders to my toes. I let my arousal wash over me, tilting my head back as the hot water flowed down my body.

I could see he was already hard again, but when I reached for his cock, he batted my hand away, kneeling on the floor instead. Roughly—just the way I liked it—he forced my legs apart.

"Hold on to something," he said, and before I could ask why, he was sliding his tongue along my slit.

I was wet and hot and more than ready for him. Gripping the shelves on the wall, I held on for dear life as he pleasured me with his mouth, his tongue lapping into me, making me even wetter, before following with a deep thrust of his thick fingers. First one, then two, and finally three. Even though I was still a little sore, it felt fucking amazing. I loved the way he stretched my body open for him. Like I belonged to him. Like I was his and his alone.

With one hand, I threaded my fingers through his wet hair, holding him steady so I could grind against his fingers as he teased my clit with the tip of his tongue. When he growled against my most sensitive spot, I could feel the vibrations sending shockwaves through me. My hand tightened against the back of his head with my impending release. I was so close, it was driving me crazy. The water was hot and steamy around me, but the only thing I felt was Stefan and his fingers and his mouth, pulling me toward the edge. My moans pitched higher and he moaned an affirmation against my pussy, and suddenly it felt like we were the only people in the world—just the two of us and the water and the heat and the pleasure. I never wanted it to end.

Except I wanted, I needed, that release. His mouth rolled over my clit again, sucking hard, and all I could do was cry out at the overwhelming sensations, the sound echoing through the bathroom as Stefan fucked me with his fingers and his mouth.

Throwing my head back, I arched my body, helpless to hold back any longer. My orgasm rippled through me, so deep and powerful that my entire body shook as I came. I was panting his name, mindless with ecstasy, coming so hard that I lost track of everything but my own pleasure.

Once my body stopped vibrating, Stefan turned the water off and grabbed towels for both of us, gently drying my body and then my hair before enveloping me in his arms and carrying me back to bed.

He was still hard, but when I reached for him again, he gently moved my hand away. I understood that this wasn't about his release, and let him tuck me in, the warm blanket coming up around both of us.

This was everything I had been waiting for. We were finally repairing the broken things between us.

I had told myself I was going to get over him, but now that I was wrapped in his arms again, I had to admit to myself that I hadn't even been close. The little girl part of me still thrilled at the word *husband* attached to this green-eyed god, this strong, protective, gorgeous man. He was mine. All mine. I was still in a dreamy haze over the orgasms he'd just given me, the way he'd been so rough and then so gentle, the way he held me now in our bed.

I snuggled deeper under the covers, pressing my naked body against his, completely lost in the perfection and bliss of the moment.

"It's good you've finally come around," Stefan said. "It's for the best."

"Come around?" I asked, not comprehending.

He nodded. "You've finally realized what your place is, and you're fulfilling your responsibilities. I expect you to have your things moved back to our room again tomorrow."

And just like that, he reminded me that I was an object. Just a trophy for his shelf, candy for his arm, a toy for his pleasure. I only mattered because I belonged to him—because I was his *belonging*. My purpose was to make him look good, to uphold the illusion that he and his father had created. And to fuck him when he commanded it. That was all. In short, I was no more to him than all the other women he thought he "owned" at the agency.

Rolling away from him, I muffled my tears, crying into a pillow. Even though Stefan was right there next to me, already drifting off, the room suddenly seemed cold and lonely. "Our room," he had called it. As though I was half of a couple.

When we both knew I wasn't anything at all.

TORI

CHAPTER 14

For the time being, my husband had won. I moved my things back into the master bedroom and forced myself to play nice during the few hours each day that he was actually at home. It was tough, but admittedly an improvement. Our marriage might still be one of convenience, but now that Stefan and I were having sex again, I allowed a glimmer of hope on the horizon. Things could still change. They could still get better. Who could say?

Part of me knew it was foolish to have such thoughts, but I was tired of locking myself up in the guest room, passively waiting for something to change. I hadn't at all forgotten about KZM's women, or my vow to help them, I just needed some time to figure out what to do next.

Later that week, I got a call from Emzee just after my Linguistic Landscapes class.

"What's up, lady?" I answered, plugging one ear against the noise in the crowded hallway.

"Not much. I have a few days off between photography gigs and I thought I'd nag my sister-in-law to join me for a ladies' night," she said. I could hear the smile in her voice.

"Oh my god I'd love to, but I have midterms coming up and it's crunch time," I told her truthfully. "I don't think I can swing it this week."

Honestly, I was desperate for some girl time after all the heartache I'd been through lately, even if I was sworn by Stefan (and bound by my own humiliation) not to discuss the specifics of my marriage, the KZM models, and everything else that had been going on.

"Aww Tori," she wheedled. "What if we just grab a lunch real quick? Someplace near campus, even. You still owe me for bailing on the family dinner. Talk about painful."

I cringed. "Guilty as charged," I admitted. "Sorry you had to deal with all that testosterone by yourself. I'm really sorry I couldn't make it."

"I survived. Don't sweat it. But you can make it up to me by saying yes to ladies' lunch. Unless you have back to back classes every day?"

"Tuesdays and Thursdays I'm free in the afternoon," I said. "Let's do this."

We made plans for lunch and I was glad to have a distraction to look forward to.

On Thursday morning, I let myself dress up. I tended to go a little more casual and basic for school because I didn't want to rub Stefan's wealth in the faces of my fellow students, and I liked blending in—but because I'd be meeting Emzee, who had her own similarly expansive wardrobe, I didn't feel guilty about wearing my nicer things. I slipped into a gorgeous Missoni sweater dress, a pair of knee-high designer boots, and accessorized with a super thick cashmere scarf that screamed cozy luxury. For a little glitz, I added the wristful of gold bracelets Stefan had gotten me for the fundraiser. I loved the festive sound of them clinking together. Hopefully it would cheer me up enough to get me through my morning classes and off to lunch with a smile.

When I walked into the sleek Asian fusion place in Hyde Park that Emzee had picked, my sister-in-law let out a low whistle at the sight of me.

"Look at you, you saucy little stunner! You really need to let me photograph you sometime," she said, giving me a hug and then two butterfly-light kisses, one on each cheek.

I blushed and waved the compliment away. "You look great, too," I told her.

It wasn't just her menswear-inspired vest and wool hat —though she always looked sophisticated and chic in her head-to-toe black outfits—it was the happy flush she was wearing.

"You're glowing," I told her, once we had ordered. "Tell me your secret."

This time she was the one who blushed, trying to hide it behind a sip of her drink.

"Well," she finally said, still fighting an uncontrollable smile, "I sort of met someone."

I clapped my hands together and let out a little whoop. This was exactly what I needed right now, and I was thrilled to listen to Emzee go on and on about the new flame in her life.

They'd met at a gallery, where Emzee had gone to check out the opening night of a new photography exhibit that had been getting a lot of pre-show buzz all over town.

"So I was gushing about the way the artist had captured the sort of rapacious hunger of the city—without showing even a single glimpse of literal food—and just the genius in that, where you barely realize what's missing even though you can just *feel* what the photos are all about—and he interrupted me and said, 'That's exactly what this exhibit is all about. You understand perfectly.'"

"Wow," I said. "You guys totally meshed."

"I *know*," Emzee said, nodding. "Turns out he hadn't had time to write up his artist's statement or the description cards for the photos, but he asked if I'd stay after the show and help him do it, which of course I said yes, and then he insisted on taking me to dinner to thank me, and later we ended up at his apartment and…" She blushed again. "He is *fiine*. And hung."

I laughed along with her. I'd never seen her so giddy. She continued dominating the conversation, telling me how brilliant he was, how he traveled as much as she did and loved all the same places, how he'd recently moved to Chicago from his former home base in Brooklyn.

"I didn't want to tell him who I was at first," she confessed as we ordered another round of spicy edamame and virgin mojitos. "Guys find out I'm a Zoric and they suddenly get all weird, like they think they can get something out of it. It's like I'm not even a person anymore."

I rested my chin on my fist, nodding, completely sympathetic. Even though I hadn't grown up with her family's reputation and wealth, I knew what it was like to be judged for your family's name. As a senator, my father had been famous in his own way, and people had always had certain expectations of me—not just who I should be, but also what I could do for them. There had been plenty of times I'd been fooled by a friend or a friend's parents or even a teacher who had expressed interest in my life, only to discover they wanted to use me to get close to my father (and his power) in some way.

"Does he know now?" I asked, reaching for a California roll.

Emzee nodded. "He didn't even care—he said he understood why I kept it from him!" She got a dreamy, starry-eyed look as she stared off into space. "When he slept over last week, I woke up to find he'd not only made me the most perfect goat cheese omelet, but he also hung my new curtains up over those crazy floor-to-ceiling windows in my living room and *walked my dog*. Can you believe that shit? I feel like I'm making this up! He's like...amazing."

I smiled at her. "He better be," I said. "You deserve nothing less."

"I think he's going to ask me to move in with him," Emzee confessed. "And I don't know, I think I want to. I feel like he could really be the one..."

"So what's holding you back?" I asked.

"I'm just so in love with my apartment. You know how hard it is to get a loft space in this town? And what if Munchkin doesn't like it? French bulldogs are totally prone to anxiety, and he gets destructive when he's upset. I just want to make sure it's the right thing, for both of us."

"Go with your gut," I told her. "You'll know when it's right. And if he's really the one, he won't mind waiting."

I sipped my drink, filled with both happiness and a little jealousy. At least whatever she had with this photographer, she'd know it was real. I couldn't say the same for my own marriage.

But even as Emzee continued to open up to me like we were really sisters, I couldn't help wondering how much she really knew about her family's business. If she was in the dark the way her brother Luka had been, or if she'd stumbled upon the truth at some point like me.

"You've been doing a lot of work for KZM lately, haven't you?" I asked, trying to go the diplomatic route.

She nodded. "I love branching out and doing my own

stuff, but yeah, it's good to have steady work through the agency, and my dad still lets me get creative with our models, so." She gave a shrug. "To be honest, commercial photography isn't really my thing. But it's helpful to have it on your resume when you're trying to build a name and a portfolio. Especially since all of the women we sign are so unbelievably beautiful."

"They are, aren't they?" I commented idly, swirling the ice in my glass. "I wonder if they ever feel uncomfortable about the jobs they're sent on…"

I watched Emzee's face, looking for any signs she might get defensive or bristle at the implication that any of the KZM models were being sent to do things that they might not like.

Instead, she just laughed.

"I guess I wouldn't blame them," she said. "There's a reason I stay behind the camera. I mean, if you think about it, modeling is weird. Prancing around in string bikinis, getting sprayed with baby oil in front of a huge fan, wearing nothing but a pair of sunglasses and a boa constrictor around your neck? Bleh. I'd totally feel like an object. And it's *hard*."

"Yeah…" I said, though her examples weren't at all what I'd been referring to.

"But I'm pretty sure they're used to it. Modeling's their dream, you know? And the agency treats them well. We take standard commission when they book a gig, but we also pay them a salary on top of that, and we help with immigration if that's something they want."

Either my sister-in-law was a really good actress, or she had completely bought into the bullshit PR campaign that the agency had been feeding her and everyone else. I couldn't really judge her for being naïve about the treat-

ment of the models, though. I myself had been just as ignorant up until recently, and that was on top of how little I'd
known about my own father's corruption. It was hard to see
the bad in people when they'd raised you, fed you, kept a
roof over your head, and said that they loved you.

Maybe Konstantin did love his kids. At least, maybe he
loved Emzee—enough to keep her in the dark, to protect her
from his corruption. But was it for her own good, or for his?

It didn't make me hate the guy any less, but I was glad
that Emzee seemed totally unaware of the seedy underbelly
her father was hiding. I didn't want to see her hurt. I cared
about her, deeply. She was like the sister I'd never had
growing up, but had always hoped for.

I also knew I couldn't possibly have these kinds of fun,
girl-talk-fueled dates with someone who was complicit in
human trafficking. Just imagining the horrors that the Zoric
family put their models through in order to pad their own
wallets made me sick.

For a moment, I fought my impulse to tell her the truth.
Because even though I would hate to destroy her image of
her father and her family, I also dreaded the idea of her
finding out the way that I had.

"So that's how I know that Munchkin's an excellent
judge of character," she finished saying. "But everyone
knows dogs can sense evil. That's probably why he hates my
dad."

Emzee giggled, but I had to force myself to laugh along
with her. She really had no idea.

In the end, I couldn't bring myself to say anything. I
wasn't going to be the one to ruin Emzee's life with the
truth. Not only that, but I'd be putting both myself and my
sister-in-law in danger. Stefan had said as much, and I was
well aware that Konstantin was a man to be feared.

"How about you guys?" Emzee asked, startling me out of my thoughts.

"Sorry?" I had lost the thread of conversation.

"You and my brother. Are things going any better with you guys?"

She'd caught me completely off guard. "I'm not sure what you mean," I said, playing dumb. "Did Stefan say something to you?"

"Yeah, right," Emzee scoffed. "Stefan's personal life is harder to get into than a locked iPhone. I figured there was trouble in paradise because he's been grumpy as hell for weeks. But he's been more like his usual self the past few days. I assume it had something to do with you."

She gave me a pointed look.

"I mean, I guess we've been getting along better," I said. "In some areas." I couldn't help but blush.

Emzee cackled with glee. "I knew it! He thinks he's so tough, but I can still read him."

I didn't know what to say. I couldn't imagine I had anything to do with his attitude at work, unless the sex had been as good for him as it was for me. Maybe he secretly craved the occasional tenderness of human connection in between all his rages and cold-hearted business deals. Maybe there was still a bit of human left beneath the monster I usually saw.

"I know he's a lot to deal with," Emzee went on. "He comes off all controlling and stubborn and impatient." She was thoughtful for a moment. "He wasn't always like this, though."

"You mean before your mom passed?" I asked. I tried to imagine Stefan as a sweet, playful little boy, before his world had been shattered by tragedy. A tragedy I understood well.

"Maybe. But I mean, he wasn't even this hard back in high school," she said. "When we were teenagers he'd drive me around with my friends and take me to the movies. He was one of my best friends, weird as that sounds now. Did he tell you he brought me to his senior prom?"

My jaw dropped. "No. *Stefan* did?"

"Yup. It was the best night of my high school life. Before that, I was the biggest nerd of the freshman class. But he treated me like I was the coolest girl in the room, and after that, so did everybody else."

"That's a great story," I said, my heart swelling. "I can't believe he did that."

"Yeah, that was him. And then right before he went to college...something changed."

"What happened?" I asked, taking another sip of my mojito.

"I don't know. He got cold. Maybe he was just preparing himself for the real world."

Emzee's words trailed off as she looked out the window. I imagined she was thinking of the way Stefan used to be. Missing that younger, happier version of her brother.

As we hugged goodbye outside the restaurant, I wondered about Stefan's secrets, wondered what kind of trauma or tragedy might have changed him into the man he was today.

Wondered if there was such a thing as a miracle that could change him back.

TORI

CHAPTER 15

When the valet pulled up with Emzee's cute black convertible, she turned to me.

"You want a ride back over to campus?" she asked.

She was struggling to keep her hat on her head as a gust of wind came up, her arms loaded down with bags, so I took her purse and the leftovers so she could duck into the car.

"Actually," I said, passing the bags back through the window, "I still have some time before my ASL class. I think I'll get Stefan something to eat and bring it over to him."

"Brilliant!" Emzee squealed. "Their food is so good, isn't it? He'll love that. My brother the workaholic, always laboring right through his lunch hour. Maybe I'll see you at the office?"

"Sure. Either way, let's hang out again soon," I said.

"Love it." With an air kiss, she rolled up the window and sped off.

But the excitement I felt at surprising my husband was quickly dampened when I remembered that I wasn't

143

supposed to go to the office without an explicit invitation. The last time I tried to bring Stefan lunch unannounced, it hadn't gone well.

Then again, my husband's rules about not showing up at KZM had probably been due to their behind-the-scenes activities—not whether I was allowed to visit. There was no way I'd get in trouble now that I knew the full scope of what was really going on at the agency.

Still, I was nervous regardless as I sat in the back of an Uber on my way over. What if he didn't want me at the office for other reasons? Maybe he was having an affair at work, or he engaged in "private interviews" with the models. I clutched the bag of take-out food, anxious.

"Thank you so much," I told the driver, sliding out of the car in front of the building.

I looked up at the huge skyscraper of glass and brick, taking a deep breath. The last time I'd been here, I had gotten turned around and accidentally overheard Konstantin Zoric yelling at Luka. The owner of KZM had admonished his youngest son for basically screwing "the help." That was when I'd first realized that the agency's talent were working as more than just models. It had shattered my entire world.

But Stefan was still Konstantin's favorite. If my husband was really the perfect son he was supposed to be, he'd know his father's rules. There was no way he'd be messing around with other women at work, in full view of everyone. Nothing went on at KZM that Konstantin didn't know about. I clung to that thought despite having no proof that it was valid. I had to believe that Stefan wasn't cheating.

The security guard at the front desk recognized me, and he waved me over to the bank of elevators without even making me sign in. When I got up to the 29th floor, the receptionist was equally warm.

"Mrs. Zoric," she said. "So good to see you again. He's in his office. Go right ahead."

It was almost too easy. My pulse was kicking as I tiptoed down the hall, turned the corner, and made my way to Stefan's office door.

To my relief, he swung open the door at my first knock and greeted me with a smirk.

"You know you're not supposed to be here, kitty cat." His voice was stern, but not angry.

"I know, but..." I held up the bag and smiled. "I thought you might be hungry."

"You are a goddess," he said, taking the bag gratefully and pulling me in for a slow, deep kiss. It took my breath away.

As he settled back into his desk chair, I closed the door behind me and made my way toward him. "I figured it was okay to come since Emzee invited me."

The last time I'd visited the agency's offices had also been on Emzee's invitation—but Stefan was well aware of what had changed recently regarding my knowledge about KZM, and neither of us said anything to acknowledge it.

"I'll let it slip this time," he said with a wink, letting his eyes travel the length of my body. "Especially considering you look good enough to eat, yourself."

As usual, I felt myself blushing under his lustful gaze. I liked his playful mood. After my long talk with Emzee at the restaurant, I also couldn't help wondering whether I actually *did* wield any sort of power over this man. He always seemed so self-assured, so completely in control. But I wanted him to let go of that. To lose himself, even if it was just for a short while.

Maybe I hadn't been wrong about things changing between us. Maybe there was something I could do to change things even more. Looking at my husband in his well-cut suit, feeling the executive power radiating from him, my thoughts went to a very, very naughty place.

Unaware, he untied the bag and started setting the take-out boxes on his desk.

"You know...there are benefits to me being here," I said. My voice was low and sultry. I barely recognized myself, but I loved it. I loved this risky, risqué side of me. The side that only Stefan seemed to bring out.

"Benefits?" he repeated, unfolding a napkin.

"Mm hmm," I purred. "You just eat your lunch now. Deal?"

He looked up at me and cocked an eyebrow. He seemed wary, but he said, "Deal."

With that, I let my coat and scarf slide to the floor and dropped to my knees.

Stefan had opened one of the boxes of sushi, but his chopsticks paused in mid-air as he watched me crawl toward him. His eyes were focused on me now, and the food wasn't the only thing he was eyeing with appreciation. And hunger.

I watched him watching me, saw the heat burning in his green eyes. I knew my sweater dress was hugging every curve, that my lips looked full and wet with the gloss I'd applied on the way over. I would have been lying if I didn't admit that part of me had been thinking of him when I got dressed this morning. That I had wanted him to see me looking like this.

"Don't mind me," I said, coming closer to him on my knees.

He ate a piece of sushi, his eyes never leaving mine,

looking both interested in my movements and incredibly turned on. I liked the idea that I was keeping him on his toes. That I was the one in charge right now—that he didn't know what was coming next.

But I could tell that he was ready to find out. One glance down at the bulge straining against his zipper indicated as much.

"Let me just help you with that," I murmured, sliding my hand across his lap, teasing him with a few soft strokes through his expensive Italian slacks.

Stefan let out a harsh breath, and with a wicked smile on my lips, I knelt between his legs and moved my hands to his knees. I felt his thigh muscles clench under my palms as I slid them back up to where his cock was hard and throbbing, the thick outline of it growing even bigger.

"Mmm," I moaned. I licked my lips and unbuttoned his pants, and then slowly, slowly dragged the zipper down. "I think I'm ready for dessert."

"Fuck," he said softly.

His cock—gloriously hard and thick—finally sprung free into my ready hand.

I squeezed gently and Stefan let out a groan, his own hand moving to the back of my head, his palm heavy there. I loved it, loved that he couldn't stop himself from reaching for me. His obvious excitement encouraged me to lean forward and lick a slow line from the base of his cock to the tip of its head, swirling my tongue around the swollen cap there.

I could tell by the way his fingers twisted in my hair—fisting so tightly that it bordered on pain—that he was very much enjoying having lunch delivered to his office today.

Although I hadn't had as much experience at oral as I would have liked, I wanted nothing more than to please him. I opened my mouth wide and took him all the way to the back of my throat, giving a long, hard suck. God, he felt good in my mouth, with my lips stretched around his thickness. I was going to do everything I could to draw out more harsh groans from his lips. The sound made me feel powerful. Made me instantly hot and wet.

Lightly cupping his balls with one hand, I gripped him firmly in the other, letting his cock slide out between my lips. Then I dragged my tongue along the underside like it was a popsicle, just like he'd taught me in the back of a private car the first time I learned how to give a blowjob. His fingers dug into my scalp tighter, tighter, tighter, and I began to stroke my hand in concert with the motion of my mouth as I bobbed my head back and forth, sucking him softly.

He swore, harshly and colorfully, and I couldn't help smiling as I increased the pressure of my lips and tongue, the speed of my movements. I sucked harder and faster, moaning a little as I fucked him with my mouth. I wanted to give him the same mindless pleasure he had given me against the wall, in our shower. I wanted to make him lose control.

My hand was wet as it slid in short, fast jerks over his velvety shaft, my tongue drawing patterns as I sucked him in and out of my mouth. I could tell he was close from the way he was panting, the way his dick was hard as a rock. All at once, both of his hands were in my hair and he was forcing my mouth down and up on his cock, thrusting roughly against my tongue, guiding me faster and faster into the rhythm he wanted.

"Take it," he groaned, his cock thumping the back of my throat, his movements getting erratic and harsh. "Take all of it." I took it, moaning around his length, loving that this was pleasure we were creating together, loving that he was taking control.

Suddenly he stiffened and suppressed a yell, and with that I felt him coming—that hot, thick liquid spilling into my open throat. I swallowed it all, enjoying every last drop, sucking him dry. When he was done, when his body fell limp and relaxed back into his chair, I licked my lips one last time and stood up, smiling down at him. He was spent, completely unable to say a word.

I'd never felt more powerful.

"Have a nice lunch," I told him, before striding out of his office.

I'd bet anything he was grateful that I—or he, actually—had come.

TORI

CHAPTER 16

As the days passed, Stefan and I found ourselves in a new sort of routine. It was almost like the early days of our relationship, where we had seemed to reach a place of understanding—although this time, we'd come to terms with our undeniable physical attraction to each other. I still hated what Stefan did and what he was tied to with KZ Modeling, but if I forced myself not to think about it, my life at home was much easier to bear. And my relationship with Stefan reflected that. We seemed to reach a place of harmony.

There was so much we couldn't speak about, so much we couldn't say to each other, but I found that it didn't matter for the time being. We found other things to talk about, other ways to communicate. The backdoor, shady dealings of KZM were still the elephant in the room, but we both became good at ignoring it.

It helped to remind myself that I would be getting a degree soon—a degree that would get me out of my dependence on anyone else. I was lucky to have schoolwork as a distraction, too, and I took comfort in knowing that with my education, I'd ultimately remove myself from the tangled web in which my father and the Zorics had entrapped me. I didn't know where Stefan factored into that web; how much he himself had woven or if he, at times, felt just as trapped as I did. There were times, when he was kind and gentle, that I thought he must be feeling just as disgusted with the situation as I was. And even when he was cruel, or relished his control and power over me, I wondered if he was lashing out because he, too, was helpless to stop his father.

I didn't know what to think and I didn't know what to feel. Nothing was simple anymore. Maybe it never had been. But was it so bad to try and enjoy the presence of my husband while I could? Because I did. And it seemed like he was enjoying me, too.

When we were together, I tried to focus on the good that was between us. On the little moments of peace and calm. Moments that seemed to grow and expand every day. Our new normal was based less on mutual suspicion and instead on a foundation of time spent.

Meanwhile, with midterm exams over and a little less stress on my shoulders, I let myself ease up on the study dates with my school friends. Most days after I got out of class, I'd come home and settle into the big comfy chair in the living room for hours, making sure I kept up with my homework while also taking some time to explore a little extracurricular reading.

I also signed up for an optional extra credit assignment a few hours each week. It required me to communicate in sign language over video chat with Deaf elementary school students and their parents. It was difficult, and I knew I signed painfully slow at time, but overall it was incredibly rewarding. I felt a lot less isolated after completing one of my ASL sessions.

Stefan seemed to be spending more time at the condo too, often bringing his work home with him early in the evening and tapping away on his laptop at the dining room table while I studied. It became a routine of ours. I grew accustomed to seeing him sitting there, and having dinner with him most nights. Sometimes I'd bring him a drink or a small snack I'd prepared while I was trying to make myself useful by helping Gretna in the kitchen.

It was on one of these nights—when I'd been madly refreshing my sign-in page on the UChicago website in between chopping vegetables—that my midterm grades officially posted to my student dashboard.

"Oh my god," I blurted, my voice shaking. "My test scores are in. I got straight As!"

I let out a little scream of victory, and before I knew what was happening, Stefan had run in and scooped me up in his arms, spinning me around in the middle of the kitchen as Gretna laughed gleefully and a stray tear rolled down my cheek.

"This calls for a celebration—Mr. Zoric, the good stuff," she commanded, pointing to the pantry where the wine was kept.

"My wife deserves nothing less," he agreed.

Dom Perignon, it turned out, was delicious. And here I had thought all champagne tasted exactly the same.

"I'm proud of you, kitty cat," he'd whispered in my ear that night, letting me ride him as long as I wanted. I came twice in succession, so hard I had to grit my teeth against the force of my orgasms.

I found that I liked waking up next to him, and sleeping next to him, even on the nights when we didn't have sex. There was something comforting about knowing he was there, that I could just reach my hand out and touch him if I wanted to.

Sometimes we talked about my program, though we both made sure to avoid mentioning Gavin. I honestly missed studying with him, our coffee breaks between classes, and his always-sunny mood, but I'd told him I was taking some time to myself and he'd been supportive.

Stefan brought up Emzee one night, saying her new boyfriend had stopped by the office that day. I was dying to know what he thought of the guy that Emzee was head over heels for.

"What's he like?" I asked. "Emzee's crazy about him. I'm excited to meet him, too."

"I doubt you'll get the chance," he said. "They'll probably be broken up before spring."

"Really?" I was shocked. "Your sister made it sound like he was...pretty perfect."

Stefan scoffed. "You don't know photographers. Always flying all over the world, heads filling up with new projects left and right. They're flighty. You can't trust them," he said.

"You do know that your sister is a photographer, right?" I teased him.

"Exactly," he responded. "And you just proved my point. In fact, she'll probably get sick of him first. She changes boyfriends like she changes outfits. My little sister's got game."

We laughed together, and I felt the knot in my chest ease.

From the kitchen, Gretna sang out, "This dinner is about to change your life!"

My mouth watered. Whatever she'd been working on for the past few hours, it smelled amazing. The entire condo had slowly filled with the scent of rich tomato sauce made with fresh herbs, crushed garlic, a pastry baking in the oven, and a plethora of other delights.

"I don't know what Gretna's been up to in there," Stefan said, "but I'm done waiting to find out. I'll get the plates and utensils, you grab the wine and the glasses."

I nodded and we split off to get the table set in record time. After we sat down—on the edge of our seats—Gretna carefully brought in the heavy platter. I couldn't help but gasp.

"Is that a..." Stefan's voice trailed off, his brow creasing.

At first, I didn't know what I was looking at. I had expected one of her expertly homemade ravioli or gnocchi dishes. Instead, the thing she was carrying into the dining room looked more like a huge pot pie. It had a smooth, doom-shaped shell and was the size of a basketball. It smelled like a dream, but the visual gave no indication of what was inside.

"What is it?" I had to ask.

"It's called a *timpano*," she told me proudly, setting it in the center of the table.

"Timpano...that sounds so familiar..." I said.

"It's an assembly of pasta with onions and cheeses and sausages and meatballs," Gretna explained. "But it's all baked in a shell of pasta. It's everything good about Italian food."

As Gretna said goodnight and headed out the door, leaving me and Stefan to our dinner, I was momentarily distracted by the sight of my husband shrugging out of his suit jacket and rolling up his sleeves. I liked that I was one of the few people that saw him this way—tie loosened, top button undone, forearms exposed. Something about it was intimate, unguarded. I also couldn't help relishing the fact that he looked very, very sexy when he took off his clothes.

And then, right as he cut into the drum-like pastry and the scent of Italian spices and sausage rose up into the air, it hit me. "Oh my god! *Timpano*! It's the centerpiece of *Big Night*!"

Stefan's face lit up with recognition, and his cutting hand froze. "Stanley Tucci? Mid-90s movie? Two brothers trying to save their failing restaurant?"

"Yes!" I crowed. "The chef brother was Tony Shalhoub! That dinner party scene is such a revelation. Course after course, and these people are practically swooning with every bite."

"You feel like you're actually sitting at the table with them." Nodding, he leaned forward in his chair. "And then the scene with them eating their eggs the morning after—that stabbed me right in the heart."

"Yeah," I sighed. "It's pretty much the best food movie of all time."

"It's definitely one of the greats," Stefan agreed. Then he looked at me appraisingly. "I've never met anyone else who appreciates that movie as much as I do. It's so underrated."

I shrugged, pleased and surprised that we had this semi-obscure movie love in common.

Stefan cut two slices of the dish and plated them for us. After pouring a glass of wine for each of us, we took our first bites.

"Mmm," I practically moaned. "This must be as good as the one in the movie."

"'To eat good food is to be close to God,'" he said in an Italian accent, holding up his hand, fingers pressed together.

"I love that quote," I said, before loading up my fork with another heavenly bite.

"Words of wisdom," Stefan said.

As I chewed, I tried to remember some of my other favorite lines. It had been years since I saw it last, but I'd watched it many times. It was one of my go-to comfort movies.

"Sometimes spaghetti likes to be alone," I said, giving my best Stanley Tucci impression and dissolving into giggles.

"Bite your teeth into the ass of life!" Stefan threw in, and then we were both laughing. "What a great movie."

"And this is the star of the show," I said, pointing my fork at the serving dish. "I've never had a timpano before, but I always wondered if it would be as good as it looked in the movie."

"Well?" he asked, gesturing. "Is it?"

I took another bite, closing my eyes as I chewed. "'People should come just for the food,'" I said, quoting the movie once again.

"I know," he quoted right back at me. "But they don't."

I opened my eyes and found that he was looking at me. We both smiled.

The truth was, I'd loved that movie not just because it was all about food and eating, but because it was about family and connection. Two brothers working together, trying to create a perfect evening, a perfect meal, in hopes that it might save their restaurant and solve all their problems. In the end, they don't succeed at their original goal—but in the process, they come to realize how important family really is.

I couldn't help taking this new, shared connection between me and Stefan as a sign.

Feeling emboldened by this new common ground, and like I'd finally gotten my husband to let his guard down, I figured this moment was the best opportunity I'd have at getting him to talk to me about what was going on at KZM. It was now or never.

I took a sip of wine to give myself some courage.

"I want to talk about the agency," I told him.

His easygoing smile and relaxed demeanor instantly vanished, his expression gone wary.

"I have a few questions," I went on. "And I hope you'll answer them, if you can."

I held my breath, waiting for Stefan's response. Finally he nodded—one short, curt nod.

"Come at me," he said. "I'll try my best."

Starting slow, I asked, "I want to know how it started. Not just the agency, but everything that goes along with it. The..." I didn't know how to say it now that we were having a civil conversation. "The illegal aspect of it," was what I finally settled on.

Stefan didn't answer for a long time, taking a slow drink of wine as he considered.

"Are you sure you want to know about this, kitty cat?" he asked me.

Even though I got a little thrill at the use of his nickname for me, I knew that it was also a warning. A reminder about curious cats and the dangers that could befall them.

"Whatever it is, I can handle it," I said, glad that my voice didn't waver.

Stefan nodded. "When my father emigrated here from Serbia, he had a job waiting for him, something to do with importing. He won't talk about what kind of work it was, so I'm not sure if he was already into shady dealings, but if I had to guess I'd say it was probably illegal."

"So when did he start the agency?" I asked.

"The first job lasted a few years, but he had some kind of "professional disagreement" with his boss—probably over something my father did—and he left to start his own business. You think he talks about the talent like they're a product, and that's because—to him—they are. He learned about sales and commissions through that first job. The models are just another version of goods, as far as he's concerned."

He looked up at me to gauge my reaction. I nodded. "I get it. Not that I agree with it."

"Yeah. So I have no idea when the agency started offering...additional services. It could have been since day one. Or it could have happened later—I can't imagine my mother turning a blind eye, and she was smart enough to have figured it out. Maybe it was after she passed."

Stefan was quiet for a moment, and I inched my chair closer to him.

"Either way, I've been aware of it since I was old enough to understand such things. Probably around the time I was eleven or twelve."

"Wow," I whispered. That meant KZM had been involved in human trafficking for at least fifteen years. Maybe closer to two decades.

He paused.

"To be clear: we are absolutely a full-scale modeling agency," he said. "That's the work I'm mostly involved in. Finding talent, booking them modeling jobs, managing them, contracts."

I could sense that he was choosing his words carefully, that there were things he still wasn't saying, but I was grateful (and surprised) that he was being open with me at all. So even though I wanted to know more, I didn't push. It would only shut him down. I was sure of it.

Stefan continued talking shop. He seemed to enjoy discussing how the agency worked, and what his job entailed. It was obvious that he took pride in fostering the careers of KZM's talent and he said nothing about the sex work that went on—almost as if he was willfully pretending it didn't exist. I'd bet anything that was how he acted at the office, as well.

But if Stefan was telling me the truth—and KZ Modeling truly was a legitimate operation—then why carry on with the seedy side of the business? It was clear the agency had the potential to run on its own, without Konstantin's illegal hustling and backdoor dealings. I could really see the company thriving solely as a modeling agency. Especially given the success and industry reputation that KZM had built up over the last few decades.

And I couldn't help wondering—why couldn't Stefan see it, too?

STEFAN

CHAPTER 17

"This conversation is over," I told Tori, leveling a hot gaze in her direction.

Our discussion was getting too close to one I couldn't be having. Tori's curiosity—her endless need to know the truth—was putting both of us at risk. I couldn't allow that. Couldn't allow her to get any closer to my secrets. For her good and for my own as well.

But I also knew that she was stubborn and persistent. Now that I had agreed to talk about the agency, she was going to keep asking questions until she knew everything. Until she became a liability. Something that would have to be dealt with, and god help her then.

I had to distract her.

"But—" she started to protest.

"Go to the bedroom, take off all your clothes, and wait for me," I commanded.

I saw her desire warring with her need for answers.

"Go now and I'll let you come twice," I told her, knowing she wanted it. Knowing she craved me. "I won't say it again."

We both knew that she liked it when I talked to her this way—when I ordered her around, when I told her what to do. Still, she hesitated, the wine glass held tightly in her hand.

"Do we have a deal, kitty cat?" I asked, pitching my voice low.

I also knew that she loved it when I called her by that pet name. It drove her wild.

Her face was flushed, and she set her glass back on the table.

"Deal," she breathed.

Without another word, she pushed back her chair and all but ran to the bedroom.

I downed the rest of my wine, imagining my wife getting more and more turned on as the anticipation built inside of her. I knew that when I went down the hall and walked through that door, she'd be naked and spread across our bed, her pussy wet and more than ready for me.

The sight of her was even more of a turn-on than I'd imagined. She was staring up at the ceiling, her chest heaving with the rapid breaths she was taking, her pale hair fanned across the bedspread. Her cunt looked like a glistening dessert, waiting for me to wrap my mouth around it.

"You look good enough to eat," I told her from the doorway.

I sauntered over to her, forced her thighs even farther apart, and gave her a long, slow lick. Just to drive her crazy. Just to make her beg. And she did.

Lapping at her slit with the flat of my tongue, I steadily worked my way into a hard, fast rhythm. When her moans got frantic and high-pitched, I slipped two fingers inside of her, picking up where my tongue had left off. She was close, I could tell by the way her hips were bucking wildly.

The way she was thrashing her head back and forth on the bed.

There was nothing like the feeling of getting her off, knowing I was completely in control. I had all the power. It was my favorite kind of high. Tori was right on the edge, so wet, her breaths harsh and fast. Knowing exactly how to finish her off, I leaned down and sucked her clit into my mouth, still pumping my fingers. I felt her thighs press tight against the sides of my head, her fingers twisting in my hair.

"Oh my god," she was saying, over and over again.

"Come in my mouth," I said, pausing just long enough to say the words. "Come for me."

My wife knew how to follow an order. I smirked to think that some of the neighbors might be able to hear her moans, that they'd know exactly who'd made her scream like that.

"Please," she panted after that first orgasm, her nails raking my shoulders. "I need you."

I stripped off my clothes and climbed over her on the bed, plunging my cock into her, fucking her hard and steady until she cried out with her release again.

After that it was my turn.

"Get on your hands and knees," I demanded.

Tori crawled to the center of the bed and did as I asked, her back arching so her ass was in the air, her knees spread as far apart as possible, her perfect tits hanging like round, ripe fruit.

Taking her from behind, I kept one hand fisted in her hair, tugging her head back, and the other gripped tight on that perfect ass. I could have come in seconds, but instead I slowed my pace. I wanted Tori to feel every inch of me. Gliding back and forth. Deep. Relentless.

"I'm coming," she whimpered, as if asking for

permission.

I pushed her face down into the pillow, knowing this new angle would allow me to penetrate even deeper, hitting her G-spot. Then I started thrusting faster, letting the bedspring do half the work, watching her ass bounce as I slammed into her again and again.

"Fuck, fuck, fuck," she was moaning, the words punctuated by her cries of ecstasy.

I made her come. I could feel her tighten and release around my cock, her entire body trembling with the orgasm I'd given her. She started to catch her breath, but I didn't let up.

Because I was just getting started.

Pulling her on top of me so she could ride, I took her once more, her legs spread wide as I fucked her. I loved every minute of it. Loved being with her this way. Pushing her body to the limit, watching her eyes glaze with desire, her pupils dilating from pure animal lust. In many ways she was still a virgin, and I was her teacher, opening up a new side of her, a new world.

My fingers pinched her taut nipples and toyed with her wet, slippery clit. She tilted her head back and murmured my name, getting lost in the sensations as she rocked her hips. Her pussy fit me perfectly, but I had to stay focused. My mission was clear.

I was going to fuck her until she didn't know where she ended and I began. Fuck her until she forgot how to speak, let alone ask questions about the dark secrets polluting my business and our lives. I knew she would fall back on the bed once I was done with her, feeling nothing but pure release. Mindless with the pleasure I had given her, she would be exhausted and satisfied and unable to ask any more questions.

If only it would be the same for me.

After we were both finished, I lay on my back, the sweat cooling on my body as I listened to Tori's deep breathing. She always slept like a baby next to me, even when she was stressed. I'd managed to distract us both with a few intense rounds of serious fucking, but now, in the aftermath, I was reminded of all the reasons why I'd had to distract her in the first place.

She was getting too close to the truth. Too interested. Too curious.

My secrets needed to remain secrets, especially from someone like her.

I was a mess of confusion, and furious about it. Logically, I knew that I needed to keep Tori as far away from me and those secrets as possible. That meant pushing her away at every available opportunity. But instead, over the past few weeks, we'd developed a newfound closeness.

I hated to admit it, but if I was honest with myself, it was comforting.

Still, I knew it had been foolish on my part, foolish and dangerous—and I'd been making excuses for my actions each step of the way. Telling myself that this intimacy, this connection between us, was just a way to make living together easier. That with less friction at home, I'd be less distracted at work. That Tori would be less likely to try running to the cops. In a sense, the new place that our relationship had gotten to was all my fault.

I hadn't been wrong, though. I'd never tell Tori—not that she'd believe me anyway—but the condo had felt cold and sterile when she'd been sleeping in the guest room, when we'd been living like roommates. It hadn't felt like a home at all.

Which was ridiculous, because I knew that this

marriage was a farce. That our relationship was a conse-
quence of the machinations between our fathers. It wasn't a
marriage at all—it was an arrangement, a chess move. Tori
was intended to be my wife in name only.

But when she was here, eating dinner across from me,
studying in her favorite chair while I worked, chatting with
Gretna in the kitchen, bringing me snacks, sleeping next to
me in bed, it all felt real. It felt like a partnership. Like a
marriage.

Even though it definitely wasn't.

I was a lone wolf in this, and I needed to keep it that
way. Especially right now. Especially with so much at risk,
with all the pieces finally moving into place.

It was dangerous that I cared about Tori, but even worse
that I trusted her. I hadn't trusted anyone in years. It was
what had kept me and my plans intact. It was how I'd
survived. Yet somehow, Tori was breaking down each of my
carefully constructed walls, one by one.

Was it possible I was falling for her?

But no—before I could even seriously entertain the idea,
I pushed it away. There was no way I was going to let
myself sit here and dwell on it.

One thing was certain: no matter how much I longed to
confide in her, to release some of those pent-up secrets
weighing down on me, I knew I couldn't. There were some
secrets that couldn't be shared. No matter how badly I
wanted a confidante who was on my side. To tell her the
truth—to share everything I'd worked so hard and so long to
keep under wraps—would spell certain danger for her. And
possibly much, much worse for me.

Because knowing everything that I did about KZM...
even a Zoric could end up gone without a trace. Like all the
other people my father had made disappear.

TORI

CHAPTER 18

Balancing a stack of mail and a bag of Chinese take-out in one hand, backpack weighing me down with texts, my purse and keys in the other, I managed to unlock the front door of the condo and burst into the foyer, all but collapsing on the marble tiles. I took a deep breath, smiling with relief at the fact that I was home at last. Then I set the food on the entry table, along with the mail, and bent to unlace my boots, letting the stress of the day roll off of me.

"Stefan?" I called out. No response.

I wasn't sure if he'd be home this early or not, but I was looking forward to a cozy night in together. It had been one disaster after another at school—first I'd struggled with conjugations in Latin (Me! Vice president of my high school Latin club! Official Latin tutor of my study group!), and with my mind still stewing on that failure, I'd confidently given the answer to a verbal pop quiz in my Slavic languages class...in Latin.

Though my answer had technically been correct, it had

taken a few seconds of the class laughing at me before I'd realized my reply had been in the wrong tongue entirely. My professor had smiled and told me to try again, but at that point I could feel my face burning and I knew nobody even heard me correct myself.

Still, despite the fact that it had been embarrassing in the moment, I'd gotten through it. I knew I'd be able to come home that evening and tell Stefan about it, and we'd both laugh. He still teased me about the day I'd been engaging in conversational Russian in front of the class and had told my partner I was afraid of *khuy*—thinking I was using the correct word for needles. It turned out modern slang words for "penis" evolved faster than my textbook had.

I could hear shuffling in the other room, and I knew it wasn't Gretna since she had the night off.

"Stefan?"

As I stepped into the living room, swinging the heavy bag of lo mein, kung pao, and egg rolls, a man in head-to-toe charcoal grey turned away from the art hanging on the walls and toward me. It wasn't my husband. Instead of Stefan's handsome, confident, familiar face, all I saw was the stern visage of his father and the grim expression he wore. Konstantin.

He was like a bad omen brought to life, and my good mood immediately vanished. Dread washed over me, and I suddenly had the urge to run out back out the door and hide out in a nearby coffee shop until I knew Stefan was back.

But I refused to let this man chase me away. Even if I feared him.

"Mr. Zoric. We weren't expecting you. Are you enjoying the art?" I asked pleasantly.

All of the paintings in the condo were the work of Stefan's mother Danica—Konstantin's wife—and I wondered if seeing her art here had affected the man at all, had reminded him of his dearly departed. Though Konstantin tended to either ignore me or size me up like a piece of meat, perhaps we'd finally talk like two humans. It wouldn't change the fact that I knew he was a bad man, one who did despicable things, but I could at least play nice until Stefan got home.

"My wife painted what was inside her head," Konstantin said, unsmiling. "She was a troubled woman. I prefer art that is nice to look at."

Inside, I bristled. Stefan loved these paintings. They'd grown on me as well. They had a modern edge, with thick paint, dark colors, and stormy skies, but they were also gorgeous. The longer you looked at them, the more you saw the hints of beauty hiding in the shadows. Danica had painted patches of wildflowers. Birds. Fingers of sunlight breaking through a forest canopy.

"They do say beauty is in the eye of the beholder," I said, trying to keep things neutral. "I guess sometimes you just have to look a little harder."

"What would you know about having to look for beauty?" he sneered. "You've always had it right outside your window, growing up in a life of luxury and ease. You didn't have to immigrate to this country from a land of hardship, unlike some of us."

His words stung. "I may have been privileged—"

But he didn't let me finish. Konstantin was on a roll. "Oh no, little girl. You don't get to tell me. I worked my ass off my entire life to secure visions of beauty. I wasn't born into it. Nobody handed it to me. I did it the hard way. My way."

As he'd ranted and railed at me, I'd subconsciously backed further and further away from him. Now I was almost up against a literal wall, my adrenaline spiking.

How dare he stand there and try to shame me for the way I'd been raised, when his own good fortune had been built from the exploitation and subjugation of others. And he had the audacity to stand here and talk himself up, as if he'd actually done the hard work himself—instead of manipulating, coercing, and threatening people to get where he was now.

"Where's my son?" he barked. "I came here to see him, not stand around wasting time with his wife's pointless small talk."

"I'm not sure exactly where he is at the moment," I said, my fake smile slipping. "But he should be home soon. I can call him for you—"

"You think I didn't try that? He's not answering!" Konstantin shot back.

"He's probably just out somewhere having a meeting," I said placatingly. "With his phone off. I'm sure we'll hear from him as soon as he gets out."

"No. He has no meetings." My father-in-law was shaking his head, but he looked at me and in his narrowed gaze I saw loathing and rage. "He's too distracted lately. Never where he's supposed to be. Never picking up his phone. And I know it's because of *you*."

"Excuse me? You think *I'm* the distraction?"

His finger pointed in my face. "You're the reason he can't focus. You're the reason he's not on top of his game anymore. The second he married you, everything started going to shit."

Konstantin took a step closer. My heart was pounding, but I'd had enough.

169

"I'm sure you'd love to place the blame on me," I said, dropping my voice to a steely register, "but maybe he's starting to realize how much better life can be when KZM isn't dictating every minute of his schedule. Maybe he's starting to realize he can breathe easier outside of the KZ family. You know, where people actually have ethics. And obey the law."

Before I could even blink, Konstantin was on me, his hand around my throat, my body slammed up against the wall. I gasped in shock and fear.

It was exactly the kind of thing I normally enjoyed my husband doing—and in a flash my mind replayed the memory of Stefan throwing me into the wall the other day, similarly aggressive—but this was completely different.

With Stefan, I had wanted it, wanted him. His forceful behavior was an act of passion, not a threat, and he knew exactly how far to push me. He never caused me any actual pain. Instead, he walked the fine line between dominance and restraint, the air between us charged with an undeniable sexual chemistry, so intense that I had no hope of resisting it. But this?

This wasn't that.

This was terrifying. This was dangerous. I was clawing at Konstantin's hand, my breaths becoming labored and difficult as he practically choked me with the tightness of his grip.

"Talk to me like that again, and I'll slap you so hard you won't be able to speak," he growled at me.

I felt my blood go cold as he held me against the wall, his fingers thick and hard against my throat. His cologne was overpowering, his body like a wall, and the more I struggled, the harder it was to get a breath. I was panicking. If only I could close my eyes and disappear, completely disconnect from this moment, from my body. Even though he wasn't a tall man, he was strong, and he'd pinned me to the wall high enough that I was standing on my tiptoes. But I couldn't find solid ground beneath me, the soles of my shoes scrambling against the glossy hardwood of the living room floor.

"I'll ask you one more time," Konstantin ground out, his face coming closer, his sour breath making me flinch. "Where. Is. Stefan?"

I wanted to spit in his face. Wanted to knee him in the crotch and run. Wanted to scream. Wanted to escape.

But I knew I couldn't do any of that. If I spit at him, he'd hurt me worse. If I managed to knee him in the balls, he'd probably double over for a second but still be able to grab me before I got out of the apartment. If I screamed, he'd tighten his grip on me.

There was no escape.

"I don't know," I croaked, shaking my head.

It was the truth, but I could tell that he didn't believe me.

"You lying little whore," he said. "You think you're different, don't you? You think you're better than the women I hire, the women I sell? You're the same. You might be a kept woman here, but there's no difference between you and the whores who spread their legs when I tell them to." With each word, his fingers tightened around my neck. "We could just as easily keep you in a cage as in a penthouse," he said.

I couldn't breathe. My fingers came up again to scrape at his hands. I was desperate for air, desperate for freedom. He laughed at my efforts, my attempts to free myself from his clutches. The world around me began to go dark at the edges—my lungs desperate for oxygen, my vision blurring. All I saw was Konstantin and his cold, leering face.

But before everything went black, I heard the door to the condo slam open.

TORI

CHAPTER 19

"**G**et the fuck away from her."

It was Stefan. Konstantin released me, and I nearly collapsed to the floor, my weak legs giving out beneath me. Never had I been more grateful or relieved to see my husband's cruelly beautiful face. I was still gasping for air as Stefan barreled into the room and got right up in his father's face.

"What are you doing here?" he demanded.

Konstantin smiled, as if Stefan had merely walked in on him having a conversation with me instead of shoving me against a wall with his hand wrapped around my throat. My vision had cleared and I was able to get back on my feet, but I moved as far away from the Zoric men as I could. Rubbing my throat where it was sore, I was certain I'd see bruises there in the morning.

"Your wife and I were just having a friendly little chat," Konstantin lied through his teeth. "So glad you showed up when you did."

Had Stefan seen what his father was doing to me? Konstantin had let me go so quickly, the moment he'd heard

Stefan's voice from the foyer, that it was hard to know if Stefan had seen his father's hands around my throat, the way I'd been struggling to breathe.

Maybe all he'd noticed from the adjoining room was how intimidatingly close Konstantin was to my body, how he'd been towering over me. But the anger in my husband's narrowed green eyes made it clear that regardless of what he'd seen from the other room—or thought he'd seen—he still wasn't buying any of the bullshit his father was selling.

"How the hell did you get in here?" Stefan demanded.

Konstantin scoffed, "You think I don't have keys to all of your apartments? I'm the one who paid for these properties. The only reason you have this life is because of *me*. You'd both do well to remember that."

Fury flashed in Stefan's gaze. That gaze I had seen soften when he looked at me, that could reflect such kindness and humor. It was flat and cold now—reflecting only rage. And yet something was holding him back. I could tell he wanted to say more, do more, by the way he clenched his jaw, his hands in tight fists at his sides. But he was fighting to stay calm.

I knew exactly how he must be feeling, but there wasn't anything either of us could do right now. It was clear we were all trapped in Konstantin' sick, twisted world. He had all the power.

Was there any way out?

"You need to leave," Stefan told his father.

"We need to talk," Konstantin replied.

"We'll talk later," Stefan said, his voice hard with anger. "It's time for you to go."

Konstantin gave a shrug and dusted off his fine wool coat, as if annoyed that in his effort to intimidate and strangle me, he had gotten it mussed. I could still feel his fingers squeezing around my throat and flinched when he turned in my direction.

"Good evening, Victoria," he said mockingly. "I'm sure I'll be pleasuring you with my presence again soon."

That was the last straw. As he turned to go, Stefan was right there, right in his face. Konstantin was plenty bigger than me, but he was practically dwarfed by the size of his tall, thickly muscled, broad-shouldered son. I could tell by the way Konstantin was appraising Stefan that he realized it as well. It might have been the first time in his life he'd looked at his son that way—as an actual opponent—as one man assesses another in the heat of a conflict.

I saw Konstantin's arrogant expression falter for a split second, though he didn't budge, still maintaining a façade of control. Stefan moved to block me from his father, and pointed at the door.

"Get out. And if you ever lay a hand on her again, I'll fucking kill you."

It was the same thing he'd said to his brother Luka. A combination of pride and relief spread through me. Stefan would keep me safe. No matter what, I could trust that. If he would stand up to his own family, heedless of the consequences, then I knew that he would do anything in his power to protect me.

Konstantin said nothing, but I saw his expression shift, go cold and calculating—and that scared me more than anything he'd just done to me. Because despite the fact that Konstantin had been forced to back down just now, recognizing that Stefan could overwhelm him physically if it came down to it, I knew that Konstantin was the kind of man who wouldn't forget the slight. Wouldn't forget the way Stefan had undermined him. I'd bet anything that my father-in-law would find a way to get even later.

Knowing he was temporarily bested did nothing to secure our future safety from him.

"Please go," I murmured, purposefully letting the fear come into my voice.

Maybe pleading with the man would make him feel like he'd won the argument, like he'd gotten his power back. Make him forget that he wanted to make Stefan pay.

"I'll show myself out," Konstantin said, smirking as if it was his own disrespect toward Stefan that was spurring his exit.

"You do that," Stefan said.

Without another word, Konstantin pushed past both of us and left the condo, slamming the door behind him. I finally let out the breath I was holding.

Stefan strode to the door to turn the lock and bolt the door. Then he whipped out his phone and dialed a number.

"I need a locksmith to come to my condo first thing tomorrow and change all the locks on the front door," he said to the person on the other side of the call. "I don't care what it costs, just get someone over here with the best fucking lock money can buy and only two sets of keys."

He hung up the phone and turned to face me.

I sagged against the wall, my knees weak, my throat still aching. A river of unshed tears gathered behind my eyes. But I wouldn't cry. I wouldn't allow myself to break.

Stefan came toward me.

"Did he hurt you, kitty cat?" he asked.

I didn't know what to say, too choked up with the lingering fear and trauma, so I didn't say anything. No doubt Stefan would be able to see the bruises forming on my throat.

"Come here," he ordered, but in a gentle voice.

I did as I was told, walking toward him. Most of me felt

numb at this point, the shock kicking in, but my heart was still hammering in my chest.

"What happened?" Stefan asked, his hand coming up to cup my face, forcing me to look at him. "What did he do?"

I didn't know if I could speak.

Stefan seemed to sense that I was having trouble forming the words, so he led me over to the sofa and pulled me onto his lap, cradling me in his strong arms.

"I'm not going to let anybody hurt you," he said. "Tell me what went down."

Finally, I managed to say the words. "He was here when I got home. He wanted to know where you were," I said, my words slow and halting.

I looked up at Stefan's face. It was impassive, as it always was, but there was a softness in his green eyes. I realized I truly did feel safe with him. I felt protected.

"Go on," he urged.

"I said I didn't know, and that you were probably at a meeting. I offered to call you." I paused, hesitating before I could say what had happened next. Because I knew that I should have kept my mouth shut. That talking back to my father-in-law, provoking him, had been a huge mistake. The consequences wouldn't just fall on me, either—I'd dragged Stefan into it as well.

"And then what?" Stefan coaxed.

"He knows that I know about the models," I said. "He accused me of distracting you. He said everything went to shit after we got married." My chest got tight, my lip starting to quiver.

"That's not true," Stefan said. "He knows nothing."

I shook my head, forcing back my tears. "He's right, though. I am a distraction."

"Tori, listen to me." He tilted my chin up, staring into

my eyes, and then dropped a soft kiss full on my lips. "The way you distract me...it has nothing to do with my performance at work. What I do at KZM, that's completely separate from us. My father's just looking for a scapegoat. You're not to blame. You understand?"

I slowly nodded. "I tried to tell him that. And then I said..." I had to look away, feeling ashamed over how hotheaded I'd been. How I'd so obviously put us both in danger. "I said maybe you were realizing your life was better outside of the family. Where people obey the law. That's when he...pushed me."

I could see Stefan's jaw tense.

"What else?" he asked.

"He put his hand on my throat and he—" I took a deep breath, trying to steady the tremble in my voice. "He choked me. He told me I wasn't any different from the women at the agency." My tears were falling now, and there was nothing I could do to stop them. "And that he could keep me in a cage as easily as I was kept in this penthouse."

Stefan's grip on me tightened as sobs wracked my body. The floodgates were open, my emotions hurtling through me as I relived all the fear and agony I'd experienced.

"You're safe now," he murmured, over and over again. "Shh. I've got you."

When I was done crying, Stefan's shirt soaked with my tears, he tilted my head back to examine my neck. I nearly flinched as his fingers brushed the soft skin at my throat, but his touch was gentle, so gentle as he caressed the place where his father had brutalized me.

"My beautiful girl," he whispered, dipping his head down to place his lips softly against my throat, kissing away the pain that his father had left. "You've been through hell and back today. But you got through it. You're so strong."

I closed my eyes as he kissed me again, losing myself to the tender sensations his touch created. In his arms, I was safe.

"Where else are you hurting?" he asked.

"My arms," I whispered. "My shoulders." I could still feel Konstantin's rough hands as he'd thrown me back against the wall, as if I'd been burned by a hot iron.

Stefan helped me tug my sweater over my head, easing down the straps of my camisole and my bra, his mouth moving to drop kisses along my biceps, my shoulders, my collarbone.

He was touching me everywhere his father had touched me, as if trying to erase him. He was a hero. My hero. I had never wanted to believe it, but it was true. I was beyond grateful he had come home right when he did. My husband had saved me.

"What else hurts?" he asked.

Locking eyes with him, I pushed my bra and camisole down to my waist, exposing my torso, my bare breasts. Then I placed his hand over my heart. "This," I said. "This hurts."

"I can make it better," he said, his voice coming out husky.

I let out a sigh as he kissed the hollow between my breasts, his warm breath calming the rapid beating of my heart. My nipples were getting tight now, too, and I dug my fingers into Stefan's hair and held his head against my chest, letting myself breathe him in.

"Take me to bed," I whispered.

With one fluid movement, Stefan stood with me in his arms. I felt as light as feathers, nuzzling his neck as he carried me into the bedroom and lay me down on the bed. On *our* bed.

Then he slowly, carefully finished undressing me. With

every article of clothing he removed, he soothed my skin with more kisses. This was different from our usual love-making. Something completely new. And I wanted to give him everything. Give my entire self to him.

When I was fully naked, I leaned back, loving the sight of my husband stripping off his clothes before crawling onto the bed with me. His hands stroked my body, taking extra care every place I had been violated, lavishing my throat with kisses, overriding the hurt I'd suffered. By the time he knelt between my legs, kissing my thighs, my mound, my wet, swollen lips, I could barely remember what had happened less than an hour before. All I knew was the plea-sure that Stefan was giving me.

He licked my clit, sliding a finger inside of me as he sucked at me with his firm lips and tongue. I was already so turned on that I was afraid I'd come too fast, so I gently eased him away from me and placed my hands on either side of his face.

"I want you inside me," I said.

I could see that Stefan was hard, so hard. I spread my legs for him, needing to feel him fill me up. But he didn't. Instead, he turned me over on my belly, my face pressed into a pillow.

He had taken me like this once before and I had loved it, loved the tight friction of his cock, the way his hand had slid under my hips to pinch my clit as he'd fucked me from behind, so I waited, eager for him to slide into my pussy, to take me hard and fast. When his hand slid up my inner thigh, spreading my legs wide for him, I moaned in anticipa-tion. But instead of touching me where I wanted him to, where I expected him to, his hand moved higher.

Spreading my cheeks, his finger traced the seam of my ass.

I shivered at the unexpected sensation.

"You're mine," Stefan said, his finger stroking my asshole. "Say it," he ordered.

"I'm yours," I said, my voice shaking a little, my body taut and on the edge. What was he doing? And why did it feel so good? Every nerve ending was alive beneath his touch, and I could feel tingles like electric shocks reaching straight to my clit.

He pulled his finger away and I felt him slide off the bed, then heard a drawer opening, the snick of a cap flipping open and then snapping closed. Then his weight came toward me again, and he was pulling my legs apart further, exposing my ass to him again.

"What are you doing?" I asked, trying to keep the nerves out of my voice. I wanted this, wanted to experience something new with him, but it was all so unfamiliar to me.

"I'm going to take your ass," Stefan said. "And I'm going to do it slow. Then faster, if you like."

"Okay." A shiver ran through me, my pussy clenching with desire. "Will it hurt?"

"I'm not going to hurt you," he said. "We'll take it at your pace. If you say stop, I stop. All you have to do is relax."

I looked over my shoulder at him and nodded. "I'm ready."

First he slid one lubricated finger into my ass, but he stopped partway when I gasped.

I could feel myself tightening up around his finger, and I tried to focus on relaxing, as he'd instructed. "More," I said. "I can take it."

He shifted slightly, the rest of his finger sliding in, and as he pumped gently once, twice, a third time, a tremble of pleasure rippled through me from deep inside. It was totally unexpected, and it made me cry out. It felt different, but good. Really good.

"I'm fine. Keep going," I told him, my voice husky with desire.

He slowly pulled his finger back, just a little, and then plunged back in. I hissed a breath, then let out a moan. It was unbelievable, and so sensual. I could feel every tiny movement of his finger. It was like nothing I'd ever felt before.

"Give me more," I pleaded. "It feels good."

So softly, stopping only to add more lube before picking up where he left off, he continued fingering my ass, easing me into it before he finally began to move faster. My nipples were rock hard, tingling where they pressed against the bed, my pussy wetter than it had ever been. His finger pumped back and forth, lighting up the tight bundle of nerves there. When I started grinding my hips into the bed, he added another finger, stretching me even further. I'd never experienced anything like it. Soon I was begging for more, begging to be filled by him.

Without warning, he withdrew his fingers and I nearly wept from the sudden loss. I was desperate for relief, but also anxious. This was something I had never imagined doing.

"You're mine," he said, and I felt him settle his body behind me, felt the bed shift as he straddled me, his knees on either side of me. He pulled my hips up off the bed, spreading my ass wide, opening me up to him.

I knew what was coming next, but I was still surprised when I felt the head of his cock press hard against my well-lubed ass. I gripped the bedspread in my fists, bracing myself for what he would do to me. My eyes were shut tight, my ass up in the air. I was ready for him.

Carefully, he slid his cock into my ass, groaning with the slow, agonizing friction.

I moaned along with him. It was so intimate, like nothing I had ever experienced. I loved how close I felt to Stefan, having this intense physical connection. He pushed deeper, inch by inch, and I pressed back to meet him, willing my muscles to relax as he fully entered me.

"You're mine," he said again, lust straining his voice. "You belong to me."

He was on the edge already, just as I was. I could tell his control was at its breaking point. I loved that my body did this to him. That I drove him wild the same way he did for me.

"I'm yours," I said. "Don't stop, please."

I was begging now, and I didn't care. I needed him to fuck me. I needed him to fill me up. He began to thrust, gently at first, his cock stroking back and forth inside my ass. As I ground into him, meeting every stroke, he started moving faster, deeper. My entire body was shaking. I moaned with the pleasure that spread through me, from my head to my toes.

"Oh my god," I panted as he slammed into me, my fingers twisting in the sheets as he fucked my ass harder. It was good, so good I had to bite down on the bedspread. I could hardly see straight.

"Take me," I moaned. "Take my ass."

As he fucked me, one hand came around my hip to toy at my aching clit. The dual sensations were almost too much to bear, and I felt myself hurtling toward an orgasm. I could sense that Stefan was close too, as he began thrusting even harder and faster, his groans mingling with my cries of pleasure that were only barely muffled by the bedspread.

"You're mine," he kept saying. "You're all mine now. No one else's. Never anyone else's."

"I'm yours, Stefan," I said. "All yours."

It was hotter than I ever could have imagined.

He stroked my clit more roughly, pinching it, and with that searing, white-hot sensation, I came hard. Gasping with the shockwaves, my body shook as Stefan slammed his cock deep into my ass one last time. I felt him come along with me, heard his groan as he filled me with his hot release. We were moaning together, our cries a symphony.

Afterward, we collapsed onto the bed, trying to catch our breath. Stefan rolled onto his back, pulling me onto his chest. Our bodies were hot, exhausted, and completely satisfied.

I knew in that moment that his claiming of me had been complete.

I was his.

TORI

CHAPTER 20

There was a coffee shop called Kahve Moon a few blocks away from campus that I'd taken to haunting lately; a small, warm space lovingly decorated by the Turkish couple who had owned it for years. Brass planters overflowed with succulents and tiny ferns, the floor was painted wood, and each table had a colored glass candle holder in its center.

As I looked up from my textbook, I saw Reyyan, the wife, approaching with my coffee, her long skirt swishing over the floor with every careful step. Turkish coffee was made from beans ground into a fine powder, and was dark and strong, stronger even than espresso. I loved it. By now, Reyyan knew that I preferred mine with an obscene amount of sugar and just a little milk, though the milk was a thoroughly American accompaniment. She was a master barista.

"Just as you like it," she said, smiling as she placed the delicate cup with ornate silver handle, called a *kahye finjani*, on the table. "Let me know when you need a refill."

"Thank you," I murmured over my notebook, inhaling the rich scent. "It's perfect."

"Need any help with your verb tenses today?" she asked.

I'd been dabbling in Turkish on the side, trying to see if I had any affinity for it. There was a course offered at UChicago that broadly covered Turkic languages, but I'd have to give up ASL next semester to fit it in. I was still on the fence.

"I'm all good for now," I said, gesturing at the stack of books beside me. "But soon."

Reyyan nodded and went back behind the counter, busying herself with another customer. Brewing Turkish coffee was more of a ritual than a process, gorgeous to watch, but I reminded myself I had to buckle down today and get caught up with my coursework.

Regardless of how happy I usually was to study at home, Stefan was becoming more and more of a distraction at the same time that my classes started getting more difficult. He was a sexy, gorgeous, orgasm-giving distraction, but a distraction nonetheless. I'd never pass my finals if I didn't find a new place to camp out and hit the books.

I knew I had an open invitation to rejoin my study group whenever I wanted, and of course Harper Memorial was always open to me, but after everything that had happened at the club with my girlfriends, and the new distance I'd established between myself and Gavin, I wasn't as obsessive about spending all my free time with my classmates as I'd initially been. We were friendly at school and texted often, but I had told them that I'd found a new home base off campus. Sometimes my hippie friend Diane would meet me there, but mostly I was solo.

With Kahve Moon, I'd found the perfect place to study.

Hot, fresh, super-strong coffee that was within walking distance of campus, a quiet and cozy atmosphere, and friendly owners who were more than happy to speak to me in Turkish and correct my grammar when I got confused. There was nothing like total immersion to help get the hang of a new language, and I started spending practically every afternoon there, chatting with Reyyan and Kadir in Turkish and drinking as much caffeine as my body could handle. It was my home away from home.

Flipping to a fresh page in my notebook, I started copying questions from the study guide in my psycholinguistics text. I was so caught up that I didn't even notice that someone was standing right next to my textbook-strewn table until she cleared her throat.

Distracted and confused, I looked up and tried to figure out if I knew this woman. "Can I help you?" I asked.

She was tall and lovely to look at in that remote, other-worldly way. Her eyes were wide-set, her hair was a waterfall of black, and she had gorgeously bushy brows.

"Sorry to bother you," she said, dropping into the seat across from me.

I looked around the café. There were plenty of empty tables.

"Have we...met?" I asked, tugging a book out from underneath her Vuitton hand bag.

Though I didn't think I knew her, she looked vaguely familiar—the kind of Eastern European gorgeous that was KZM's hallmark. And her accent seemed to jive with that suspicion.

She was dressed expensively. Her designer coat was draped across the back of her chair, her snug black sweater looked to be cashmere, and her heels were black and extremely high.

"No. But I know your husband well. Stefan, yes?"

I felt my stomach drop, and tried to prepare myself for the worst. I should have known one of Stefan's mistresses might seek me out eventually. I'd finally convinced myself that he wasn't sleeping with the models, was just a workaholic, but maybe it had been wishful thinking.

Still, it was disconcerting that she'd found me so easily. First Stefan's bodyguard, now this woman. How long until Konstantin started having me followed, too? Maybe he already was.

"Yes, Stefan is my husband," I said, feeling more than a little unnerved.

After everything that had happened over the past few weeks—the drugging at the club and the horrible incident with my father-in-law—I was very aware that my life wasn't as safe as it used to be. Stefan had warned me, told me that finding out about the dark, seedy underbelly of the KZ Modeling empire meant that I was a part of his world now. But now that world had hunted me down, right in broad daylight.

"I'm Irina," the woman said, holding her hand out.

She was smiling at me, her expression warm and open. She didn't seem dangerous, nor distraught in any way. I relaxed a little and shook her hand, but still I braced myself for what she had to say. Maybe she'd say she was pregnant. Maybe she'd ask me to leave Stefan.

But Irina just nodded, her face still lit up with that mega-watt smile.

"Will you please tell him that everything worked out?" she asked me. "He is, I think, a good man. A very good man. You are a lucky woman."

I stared at her.

"I don't understand," I said, still waiting to hear the word "pregnant" or "relationship."

"I cannot get word to him anymore," she continued. "That is why I seek you out. Please tell him for me?"

I tried to process her words. She wanted me to tell Stefan that everything had worked out, so he wouldn't worry. What had worked out? What had he helped her with?

Somehow, I nodded.

"I'll tell him," I said.

"Thank you." Irina took my hand in hers and squeezed it gratefully. "So much."

Before I could say another word, she got up, took her Louis Vuitton bag and her designer coat, and strode out of the coffee shop on her slick spike heels, disappearing into the cold Chicago air and leaving me gaping in her high-fashion wake.

I just sat there trying to process what had happened.

Stefan, a good man? It seemed like a bit of a stretch to me. He had definitely been easier to deal with lately, and there was no doubt that he was an extremely handsome and powerful man, but good? I couldn't imagine it.

Yet clearly Irina felt indebted to him. He had done something to help this woman. Something that was so important that she had sought me out in order to pass him a message regarding her welfare. What the hell could he have done to help her? And why would he bother helping in the first place? My husband had never shown an altruistic side.

Maybe there was a good and noble heart hiding inside the human that hid inside the monster, a soft spot beneath the cold and ruthless front that Stefan put up every day. How many layers deep was he? His sister had said that he'd been different once, too. That when they were younger he hadn't been as hard, hadn't been as mean. That something big had happened to change him into the man he was today.

Did that mean he could change back?

I felt a twinge of hope. Maybe he really could be the man I wanted him to be. The man I had first thought he was, the man he'd been on the night we first met.

And maybe I could help him be that man.

I thought back to what my stepmother Michelle had told me shortly after my wedding. About how when you married a busy, important person, it was your job to make their lives easier. She'd said people like my father and Stefan were under so much pressure on a regular basis that they needed someone to come home to who could be the calm in their storm.

Maybe if I did that for Stefan, and tried to be the kind of wife that Michelle had told me I should be, he would be able to become the man I needed him to be. The man I hoped he still was. But first, I needed to know more about Irina and the reason behind her cryptic message. And there was only one way to find that out.

I'd have to confront my husband.

TORI

CHAPTER 21

By the time I arrived back at the condo I was practically vibrating with a combination of caffeine and anticipation. Unfortunately, Stefan wasn't home yet. I couldn't stop imagining how our conversation would go. How he'd react, and what he would say, when I dropped the bomb and told him about the "friend" of his who'd come to see me at the coffee shop that afternoon.

He had finally started opening up to me about KZ Modeling recently. Not necessarily the details regarding the agency's shady dealings, but about his role in handling the legitimate side of the business. I hoped it was a sign that he was beginning to trust me more, and that he'd continue to grow increasingly comfortable about confiding in me. Especially when it came to Irina and what she'd meant by saying that everything had worked out.

I wanted answers now, and I wanted him to give them to me.

Sitting around and waiting for him to walk in the door was a surefire way for me to drive myself absolutely batty with nerves, so I busied myself by heating up the dinner that Gretna had made for us that evening.

When I entered the kitchen, I found it was still warm and redolent of *coq au vin*, a rich French poultry dish made with red wine, mushrooms, cognac and pancetta. It was one of Gretna's specialties, and the perfect meal for a cold autumn evening, full of carrots, sautéed onions, and garlic. But I could barely manage to appreciate her efforts as I pulled the large pan back out of the oven, our dinner now piping hot and ready to be served. I was getting frantic.

Where was he? Every minute that ticked by made me squirm.

My phone vibrated with a text and I bolted toward it, slamming my shin painfully into the coffee table as I lunged for my cell. But it wasn't Stefan. It was Gavin.

How's my favorite Latin tutor hanging in there? he had texted, along with a winking emoji. *Our study room at Regenstein just isn't the same without you.*

Before I could respond, another text popped up. *WE MISS YOOOOOOOU!!* It was from Lila. After that, a series of heart, flower, and book emojis appeared from Diane's number.

I couldn't help smiling. *That's ex-Latin tutor to you, Gavin,* I replied. *And I miss you all, too. Just trying to play catchup on my assignments at home. This semester's whooping my ass.*

OMG me 2, Audrey texted. *Midterms were not kind. I need to seriously ROCK my finals.*

After reassuring them all that I'd be back as soon as possible, I went back to the kitchen to warm up the dinner rolls that Gretna had made. The crusty homemade bread smelled so good, I couldn't help dipping one of the rolls in the wine sauce and eating it as an appetizer.

I was just setting the table in the dining room when I heard a key turn in the lock. Dropping the silverware in my hand, I ran to meet my husband.

Stefan was taking off his shoes in the foyer, and I could barely stand to wait for him to shrug out of his coat and put his laptop bag down.

"I need to tell you something," I blurted, just as he was unbuttoning his shirt cuff and rolling it up. "I met Irina."

He froze. He'd been looking down at his sleeve, but when he lifted his head, I was startled by what I saw.

I honestly hadn't expected much of a reaction. Stefan was excellent at hiding his emotions. At hiding everything. I figured he'd be surprised that I'd met someone from his private circle, but the expression on his face was one of shock, and...what almost looked like fear.

"Irina?" he said slowly. "I'm not sure who that is."

He was obviously lying, but I wasn't going to play that game. I kept my gaze focused on his face—needing, wanting the truth.

"You know her," I told him. "She showed up at the coffee house where I've been studying all week and told me she wanted me to give you a message. Though I guess if you're the wrong Stefan, I shouldn't tell you what it is."

I gazed levelly at him, noting the way his mouth twitched. He knew he was caught.

"Tell me what the message is," he finally said.

Nodding my head, I relayed it. "She wanted you to know that everything worked out. She said she couldn't get word to you anymore, but she was very grateful. She also said that you're a good man. And that I was a lucky woman."

"Hmm," is all he said in response.

I watched his face very closely as I said, "Is this—did you have a relationship with her?"

There. That got a reaction from him.

"We've been over this before," Stefan said, blatantly annoyed. "As difficult as it is for you to believe this, I haven't been unfaithful."

But he wouldn't look me in the eye.

If he hadn't been cheating on me, what was he trying to hide?

"Is that dinner I smell?" he said, attempting to change the subject.

As he walked out of the foyer and into the living room, I trailed behind him, refusing to play along, to just let the whole thing drop.

"Who is she?" I prodded. "And what's the meaning of that message I was supposed to give you? What did you do for her?"

"I don't know what you're talking about," Stefan said, sitting down at the table when he reached the dining room and settling his features back into their usual icy solemnity.

Why the obfuscation? He knew exactly what I was talking about. Asking me what the message was had clearly shown me his hand. On top of that, I had seen the mix of emotions that had played out on his face, even if it had lasted only a few seconds. He was involved with her, somehow. There was no denying it.

"Don't lie to me," I told him. "I know you know who Irina is. What's this all about?"

"It's not your concern," he said. His stock reply. "Now sit and eat."

I didn't budge from the doorway.

"It *is* my concern. You're my fucking husband! Irina approached *me.* She found me, Stefan. How many more

194

women are going to bring me strange messages for you? How many more are going to give me secret information to deliver?"

"It won't happen again," he said. "And you're going to let it drop. Now."

"How does this not put me in even more danger than I'm already in?" I asked. "Everyone is spying on me."

"You're being paranoid."

"Says the man who told me himself that this world is dangerous and that I had to let him take care of me?" I goaded. "Well, you're doing a bang-up job of that, aren't you?"

Rather than engage with my fury, Stefan ignored it, setting a steaming hot roll on his bread and butter plate and then one on mine. "Can you pass the butter, please?"

He was gaslighting me. Again. But I wasn't going to just stand there and let it slide.

"If I'm *yours and no one else's*," I said, throwing his own recent words back in his face, "then doesn't that mean that you're also mine? Doesn't that mean I'm entitled to know what the fuck you're doing with these mysterious women all the time?"

I was breathing hard, furious and running low on patience, but Stefan was just gazing at me impassively. He casually poured himself a glass of water. It only infuriated me more.

"Why won't you talk to me?" I pushed.

Stefan stood and ran a hand through his hair. "You're obviously not ready to sit down for dinner," he said. "Just let me know when you are. I'll be in my office until then."

Having completely blown me off, he picked up his glass and walked out of the room.

I stared after him, ready to blow a fuse. His behavior

was maddening. And I hated when he walked away from me. Hated it more than anything when he ignored me like this, completely disregarding my questions and feelings, as if running away from his wife when things got tough was a perfectly acceptable method of conflict resolution.

Following Stefan back through the foyer, down the hall, and into his office, I said, "Tell me. Tell me and I'll never ask about her again."

"What do you want me to say?" he asked, glancing up from his desk chair.

"I don't want you to say anything. I want you to tell me the truth," I said.

"There's nothing to tell."

He turned back toward the desk, opening his laptop.

"Why are you acting like this? I don't understand why you won't confide in me. I already know so much. I'm already in danger. Why not just lay it all out on the table?"

"We're not having this discussion right now," he said, tapping away at his computer.

Folding my arms, I said, "Then when are we having it? The secrets and the lying and the women are too much. I can't take any more."

"Remember what curiosity did to the cat," he reminded me. "We're done here."

I was livid. But fine. If that was how he wanted to play the game, I was more than ready to play. It was time to pull out the big guns.

"You lied to me before, didn't you?" I practically spat. "She *is* your mistress. Did she terminate a pregnancy? Is that what "all worked out"?

He froze, his shoulders tensing as if I had thrown something at him.

"Tori—"

"And I bet you paid for it," I went on. "That's why she was so grateful."

I wasn't completely convinced what I was saying was true—not at all convinced, actually—but I was trying to get a rise out of him. Get him to react. Back him into a corner, so he'd have to tell me something true in order to prove that my accusations were false.

"You think you know everything, but the reality is, you're completely in the dark."

He stood up from his chair, closing the gap between us, his eyes blazing with anger.

"So enlighten me," I said, as calmly and slowly as I could manage.

"You know nothing about what's really going on here. Not everything is as it seems."

"Then *talk to me*. I'm on your team."

I wanted to give him another chance. Wanted him to understand that I could help him, that I was here for him if only he'd let me be.

"I'll say this one more time. It's not. Your. Concern," he said through gritted teeth.

And then he stood, and in two strides, he was in front of me. Without warning, he grabbed the front of my sweater, fisting the fabric in his fingers and pulling me hard against him. His mouth came crashing down on mine. Brutal. Intense. Perfect.

He kissed me as if he owned me, and I couldn't resist. I never could resist him.

As I kissed him back, I put my whole heart and soul into it. I wanted to show him that I was on his side, that we wanted the same things. He had to realize that he could trust me—that he could tell me the truth. About Irina. About KZM. About everything. I could be exactly the wife he wanted me to be, if only he would let me in.

"Stefan," I moaned.

His mouth plundered mine, cutting off my words, his hands rough on my body. I knew he was winning, that our conversation was effectively over for the time being. And I also knew that there was a good chance he was doing this on purpose.

Did he kiss me this way to distract me, to hide the truth from me? Maybe the brutal way he treated me in bed wasn't what it seemed, either. Maybe his crudeness was a disguise for passion, a way to avoid the inherent risks of intimacy, a way to keep his true feelings buried. Knowing what I did about Stefan, it all made sense. That he would keep something vulnerable and tender protected by a coarse exterior. Did he feel more for me than I realized?

He had just told me that not everything was as it seemed. Was he only alluding to the situation with Irina, with all the models, or did he mean his behavior in the bedroom as well?

I didn't know what to think or how to feel as his hands gripped the back of my head, his fingers tight in my hair, forcing my head back as his tongue fucked my mouth. His hips were pressed hard against mine, and I could feel his cock, hard and throbbing against my hip.

There was no denying he wanted me—and I wanted him too. I couldn't pretend otherwise. The connection we had was so strong, the sex we had was so affirming, that I didn't know if I'd ever be able to say no to him. I was already wet as we grappled against the doorway of his office, ready and willing to do whatever he commanded of me. But even though I couldn't control the way my body felt toward him, I could still hear the voice in my head telling me that he was using sex as a way to hide something.

That all of this was an act, part of his master plan.

But regardless of his ulterior motives, I wouldn't stop kissing him.

Scooping my ass into his hands, he lifted me against him, my legs wrapping around his waist. As I moaned softly into his mouth, losing myself in his kisses, he began walking us down the hall and toward the bedroom.

"I need you, Tori," he growled.

Never had I heard him say those words to me before. I was incredibly turned on, but I also felt powerful. If he could admit that he needed me sexually, maybe it was only a matter of time before he realized that he needed me in other ways. Emotionally, yes, but also as an intellectual partner. A life partner.

But as he carried me over the threshold into our room, throwing me down on the bed with anger and force, I knew that I couldn't just let him get away with this. As much as I wanted to lose myself in pleasure, to let him dominate my body, to take out all my stress and anger and betrayal on his cock, I had to get him to tell me about Irina. About all the women like her.

It wasn't easy to focus with the way he hungrily made his way up my body, pressing hot, hard, biting kisses against my skin as he began to tug my clothes off me. My body screamed out for his touch, for the release I knew would be coming if I let him continue. He pulled my jeans down to my ankles and shoved my sweater up and over my head, leaving it there so it covered my face and left me in the dark, as if I was blindfolded.

I panted, unable to see him, only to feel his mouth, his skin, the heat of his breath. My nipples were aching from the kisses he left there, nipping and licking through the sheer lace of my bra with his tongue. I thrashed beneath him as he pinned my wrists over my head, wanting him so badly that I could barely maintain focus on the questions still burning in my mind.

That was how I knew I needed him to stop. Because if I let him continue to distract me with sex, then I'd never know the truth. I'd never learn who my husband really was, and what he was truly capable of.

And there was no way I could live with that.

TORI

CHAPTER 22

S tefan finished pulling my jeans off, leaving me in my lacy thong underwear, and then tugged off the sweater that had been covering my face and my skimpy bra. Even though my body didn't want him to stop, I knew as I lay there panting that I had to stop this before it went too far—and I was too mindless with pleasure to get the answers I needed. We'd gone down this path far too often. It had taken my husband no time at all to figure out that all he had to do to stop me from asking dangerous questions and pushing him for information was to kiss me until I swooned and then carry me off to bed.

But this contact with Irina had changed everything. Whatever was going on, it was clearly much more complicated than I had initially realized. And I couldn't let Stefan keep me in the dark any longer. This was my *life*. This was our life.

It wasn't just about KZM and these women and what the extent of my husband's involvement with both of those things were. I needed to know if I could trust him. If he really was a good man. The ambiguity was just too much.

So as much as I wanted to give in to him, as much as I reveled in the thought of total surrender, I pulled my wrists from his grasp, put a hand on his chest, and said, "Wait."

He pulled back immediately. I was still pinned beneath him, and he was still in control. But he cared about me, too. This wasn't just about what he wanted in the heat of the moment.

"Are you okay? Am I hurting you?"

I shook my head no, and he gently cupped my cheek.

"I just...I need some answers first," I told him, even as my hips arched up against him.

He climbed off me and I felt my heart sink. I scrambled to my knees and grabbed his shirt, pulling him back before he could get off the bed.

"Give me something, Stefan," I begged him. "I've given myself to you over and over. Please, just..." I struggled to find the words. "Give me something I can hold onto in return."

He looked at me, and I saw the conflict warring in his eyes. And then his features softened in a way I'd never seen before. His hand came up to cup my face again, his thumb stroking my cheek so gently it made me shiver.

"Hold onto this, Tori," he said.

Then he leaned down and kissed me. Once, twice, three times, so soft it made my chest ache, the touch of his lips against mine more tender than it had ever been.

I let out a shuddering breath and our eyes locked.

"Stefan," I whispered. "I—"

He swept his lips over my own, this kiss more passionate, and when I opened my mouth to let him in deeper his tongue stroked perfectly against mine, the taste of him like a drug I couldn't get enough of. He had never kissed me so tenderly, had never touched me like this before—like he was trying to hold onto me. His hand moved from my cheek to the back of my head, his fingers weaving into my hair, forcing my head back so I could take more of his tongue. He was taking his time, drawing quiet moans out of me, making the whole world disappear. It was as if he was kissing the very essence of my soul.

I curled my hands tightly into his shirt, pulling him closer. This was what I wanted. This was what I needed. I couldn't believe he could be this way with me. Already, I felt closer to him. I never wanted him to stop touching me.

Slowly, languidly, he slid his hands down my back, then around my waist, up toward my breasts. They fit perfectly in his hands. He palmed them gently before circling my nipples with his thumbs, teasing them until they were hard and aching. Then he lowered his head and took one into his mouth. The sensations were overwhelming. I could feel myself shivering. He dragged his teeth along the hard ridge of one nipple and then the other, lavishing them with a focused intensity that had me panting. As he sucked one nipple, his fingers would tweak and twist the other. The combination of pleasure and just the right amount of pain had my hips arching off the bed, the rest of my body begging for the same attention.

I was wet and aching for him, desperate for his touch, for his cock, but he seemed to be in no rush. He was going to take his time with me tonight and there was nothing I could do about it.

Finally, his hands slid down my hips, finding my thong. Then he hooked his fingers into the waistband and my whole body tensed with anticipation, expecting him to revert to his usual routine—driven by rough, pure, animal lust—and rip it right off of me.

But he hesitated. I was confused for a split second until

the realization dawned on me that what was happening between us now was different than it had ever been.

My pulse quickened as Stefan slid my panties off slowly, carefully, delicately. I arched my back and closed my eyes, savoring it. He was doing exactly what he had said—giving me something to hold on to. Something to trust.

I felt his passion, his desire, his care with every kiss, every touch, every stroke.

I loved that he was still fully dressed, except for his bare feet. He leaned over me, gripping my hips with his warm, strong hands, and dragging me forward so my ass was right at the edge of the bed. Then he spread my legs wide, opening me up. I could feel how hot and wet I was in the cool air of our bedroom. I was ready. I wanted his cock inside of me. I wanted him to take me fast and hard, but instead he pushed my knees wider and pressed hot, burning kisses along the insides of my ankles before moving up my calves, then over my knees, slowly but deliberately trailing closer and closer toward my pussy.

I was gasping for air, my breaths turning short and shallow. He didn't quicken his pace.

The tension was so much that when he finally kissed the soft skin on my inner thigh, I nearly jumped out of my skin. I was so eager for his mouth. For his tongue.

"More," I begged him, feeling weak with desire. "Please."

He gave my inner thigh a nip with his teeth, enough to make me cry out with the shock of it, and then he plunged his tongue into my pussy. I sighed with the pleasure of it, the way his tongue filled me, and then he pulled back.

"Don't stop," I said. "You're teasing me."

I heard him laugh and then I felt his tongue return, lapping up my wetness. Long, slow licks, up and then back down, until I was squirming on the bed. I wanted him so bad. I could hardly contain the needy moans spilling out of me. His tongue was so soft against my tender, sensitive lips that I thought it would drive me crazy. My toes curled against the floor, my desire making me dizzy. Just when I thought I couldn't stand it anymore, he finally thrust his tongue deep inside of me again.

Cursing at the sensation, I lost control of myself, thrusting toward him, wanting more. He gave me what I needed, fucking me with his strong tongue, his teeth capturing my clit and finding the perfect amount of pressure, the heat of his breath adding to the sensations.

"Yes," I moaned, loving the way his tongue was pumping into me. "Fuck, yes, yes."

I lost myself in the mind-bending pleasure as he held my legs apart, making the taut muscles of my inner thighs ache deliciously, spreading me wide so he could taste me. So he could take me fully with his mouth.

"I'm almost there," I told him. "Come here."

Reaching out a hand, I expected Stefan to get off his knees and climb onto the bed, fit his body against mine, plunge his hard cock into my waiting pussy and fuck me until I could barely see straight. Instead, the thrusting of his tongue got faster, making my soft cries grow louder and more desperate. He wasn't going to stop. He was going to keep tonguing me until he made me come. The thought of it pushed me over the edge, and my orgasm shattered through me, my entire body shaking with the intensity of my release.

Still murmuring his name, I came back to earth.

"You ready for more, kitty cat?" he asked, a wicked smile on his lips.

And then he kissed my aching inner thigh and started all over again with his tongue.

This time, he added his fingers, two and then three of them, filling me up. It felt so good, so tight, the friction sending hot sparks of pleasure through me. As I thrust against his hand, he brought me quickly to the brink again, stretching my pussy wide with his pumping fingers as his tongue teased my clit. It was almost more than I could bear, but I never wanted him to stop. I never wanted this to end.

His fingers fucked me harder and harder, his tongue lavishing my sensitive clit with hard, wet strokes. This time I threw my head back and screamed as I came, unable to control the way my body reacted to his touch. The waves of this orgasm seemed to go on and on and on. I struggled to catch my breath.

Still, I needed more from him. More of him.

"I want to be with you," I said, still panting on the bed. "I want to feel you inside me."

"I want to be with you, too," he said.

My body humming with anticipation, I watched as he stood and quickly shed his clothes. I would never tire of seeing him naked, of taking in the flawless view of his strong, powerful body and perfect, hard cock. He was more than ready for me and I could see his chest heaving with desire. He wanted me as much as I wanted him. It was everything I wanted—everything I had hoped for and more. He was perfect and he was all mine.

Finally he climbed onto the bed with me, crawling up my body, my legs still spread wide open, waiting for him. Wanting him. Needing him. I was so wet, so ready, that it only took one smooth thrust for him to bury himself deep inside of me, so deep that I couldn't tell where I ended and he began. We were one in that moment, our bodies joined.

And it was more than that. More than just sex.

I had asked for something to hold onto. This was it. This was what I had been craving.

Stefan couldn't tell me in words how he felt, but he could show me with his actions. With his body. As he began to fuck me, taking his time, his strokes long and languid, I knew that he was telling me how much I meant to him. How important I was to him. There was something between us—something powerful and perfect and right. Maybe it was better that he was showing me this way, because I didn't know if there were any words that could describe how I felt, either. Maybe he felt the same.

He spread my legs wider, going even deeper with each stroke of his hard cock. He had never been this deep inside me before, practically splitting me apart. It was like a revelation. I never wanted it to end. Our bodies were slick, his breathing labored, my own words gone. I could only moan my pleasure, could only drag my nails down his chest as he lifted my legs and rested my ankles on his shoulders so he could go even deeper. Impossibly deep. My body was his, an instrument of pleasure for both of us, and one that only he knew how to play. I knew in that moment that there would never be anyone like him. Not now. Not ever. No one would ever be able to make me feel the way Stefan did.

He rocked into me, his hips slamming against me as he began to speed up. I could sense that he was losing control, that he was close to climaxing. My own orgasm was building inexorably inside of me and I could feel my toes curling against his shoulders. My fingernails bit into his shoulders, but Stefan didn't even seem to register the pain, all of his attention focused on fucking me, on pushing me closer and closer toward my release.

I didn't know how much more of this pleasure I could take, but then suddenly, Stefan fisted his hand in my hair, bringing my lips to his in a searing kiss that I felt in every cell of my body.

"Tori," he whispered.

The connection pushed me right over the edge.

My scream of pleasure was muffled by his mouth as my pussy clenched around his thrusting cock. Still, he didn't stop, thrusting harder and faster as I came, his hips pumping furiously until he was moaning his own release, spilling his hot come inside of me, his body shaking with the power of his orgasm.

When it was over, when our bodies had stilled, when our hearts began to slow to their normal pace, Stefan collapsed on the bed next to me, his body hot against mine. Without a word, he pulled me close and it wasn't long before both of us were falling fast toward sleep.

As I was drifting off, I realized something with perfect clarity. That even if he couldn't say the words, there was something between us that neither one of us could ignore.

TORI

CHAPTER 23

"Please reach out if there's anything else I can do to help before finals, yes?" Professor Dhawan said, the encouraging smile on her face giving her a saintly appearance. "I've seen firsthand how bright you are, and I hate to see stress get in the way of your learning experience."

"I will," I said, clutching my exam. "Thank you so much."

As I left Dhawan's office, I felt a fresh surge of determination to pull my grades back up. After bombing my most recent Intro to Psycholinguistics test, which had shocked both me and my professor, I'd scheduled an appointment with Dhawan to go over the questions I'd missed. It wasn't that the information wasn't sticking—but that I was so behind in my coursework, I hadn't had time to catch up on all the reading assignments that would have prepared me for the test.

When I'd woken up in bed this morning, I'd wanted nothing more than to spend all day fantasizing about the new turn in my marriage. About what it had become, and what it was still becoming. Though my husband had already left for work, I could still smell the scent of his cologne on his pillow, clean and masculine, and I could have easily lolled around all morning, replaying the intimate night we'd had in minute detail.

But I knew I couldn't do that. I had to focus.

So I'd dragged myself into the shower and gotten ready for school, all with a big smile on my face. I had practically skipped across campus to the Social Sciences building, my body still tingling from where Stefan had touched me. And licked me. And stroked me. He was almost like a heady drug and I was completely, utterly addicted to everything about him.

Receiving our graded tests back in Psycholinguistics had sent me crashing back down to Earth, though. I'd known I was slipping behind with my assignments, but the C- in red ink across the top of the test booklet was like a sock to the gut. It was still a passing grade, but my whole grade point average was now in danger, and I could lose my partial scholarship. I felt sick.

Instead of spiraling into panic, though, I'd stayed after class to ask Dhawan if we could talk more about the exam. She'd agreed to meet me later that afternoon, and I'd visited her during office hours to go over the test questions together.

I was in no danger of failing any of my classes, but it was clear to me that I wasn't fully engaged in the program the way I wanted to be—the way I needed to be. Studying linguistics at UChicago had been my dream—was still my dream—and I hated the thought that I'd been basically sleepwalking through my courses. It was a disservice to both me and my colleagues. I'd have to put my nose to the grindstone and stop letting distractions get in my way. Between skipping study group with my friends and my complicated relationship with Stefan, I'd let myself fall way too far behind.

That wasn't me. I wasn't someone who felt comfortable with mediocrity, with the bare minimum, especially when it came to something that I hoped to dedicate my life to.

The only place I wanted to be was at the top of my class.

Now that things were in a much better place between Stefan and me, I hoped I'd be able to concentrate on acing my classes again, and absorbing as much knowledge as I possibly could.

As I headed to my next class, I sent Stefan a quick text telling him that I was going to be home late because I'd be studying at school.

I'll be waiting for you then, he responded. *Deal?*

He was really coming around. I couldn't help smiling at his text.

Deal, I typed back.

I skipped lunch in order to go to Harper and take copious notes from my psycholinguistics text, and after that I was on cloud nine for the rest of my classes that day. I was already getting a handle on things. My mood was so evident that a few of my classmates even asked if I'd gotten any good news recently, since I looked so happy.

"Just having a good day," I told them cheerfully.

Even though it was nearly winter and frigid outside, I barely felt the cold as I headed to the Regenstein Library where my study group was meeting. The place was open until 11 at night, but I planned to be out before then, even though my friends seemed to thrive on all-nighters.

As I pushed open the door, I had a brief moment of doubt that made my pulse speed up and my smile falter. Despite the texts I'd continued to exchange with Gavin and my girlfriends, what if coming back to study group out of nowhere like this was weird? After all, I'd basically ditched them after the incident at the club and had begun spending all my time studying at home or at Kahve alone. I might have permanently thrown off the balance.

Part of me debated turning around and heading to my coffee shop, to Reyyan and her expertly brewed Turkish roast. Where I could hide out at my corner table and bury myself in my textbooks. But I convinced myself I was being ridiculous.

Taking a last deep breath outside of Room 206, the usual location of our sessions, I opened the door and stepped inside.

"Aggghhhh she's back!" Lila squealed.

I couldn't help laughing as Diane launched herself into me for a quick hug.

"I see you guys in class every day," I said. "It's not like I've been M.I.A."

"But we all miss your intellect," Audrey pointed out. "Especially Gavin."

Glancing over at him, I couldn't help noticing the faintest blush tinging his cheeks.

He gave me a nod, trying to suppress those dimples. "Glad you could make it. Your epistemology insights are always much appreciated."

"Thanks," I said, feeling like I had never left.

There was no sign that they had felt abandoned or ignored during my brief absence, and for that I was beyond grateful.

As we got into our notes, I realized I'd forgotten how easy it was to be around them, how well we all jived when it came to our shared passion for languages and learning. They were incredibly helpful catching me up, sharing their notes and going over the study guides, especially Gavin. I'd missed his kind patience, the way he was always so attentive toward me.

The girls got up and left one at a time until the study room was down to just me and Gavin alone. Realizing how late it had gotten, I blurted, "Shit, it's almost ten already."

But as I stood from my chair, I felt so lightheaded that I had to sit right back down.

"You okay?" Gavin asked.

I rubbed my temples. "Yeah, just dizzy. I guess I haven't eaten all day."

"Well that's no good. You gotta keep fuel in the tank if you want the engine to run," he said. "Let me take you to grab a quick bite."

I'd been more or less avoiding Gavin ever since Stefan had made it clear that he didn't trust him. I still wasn't entirely sure how I felt, but at that moment, I had a hard time imagining Gavin being anything but completely trustworthy. He had been a good friend to me, and I was going to be leaning hard on him and the others to get through the upcoming tests that our instructors had promised would be a challenge to even the most dedicated students.

"I'm fine," I told him. "I'll just grab a protein bar from the food court."

"Sorry, but I can't walk out of here with a clear conscience knowing I let you starve yourself in the name of your education." Gavin gave me a look, and I held up my hands.

"It wasn't on purpose," I insisted. "I was running late this morning so I didn't have time for breakfast, and then I spent my lunch break studying in Harper. After class I came straight here, and once we started working, I got caught up."

"I believe you," Gavin said, shaking his head. "I've never met anyone else who's as obsessed with language as you are. You're the kind of girl who'd forget to eat dinner one second but then tell me where the word 'famished' comes from the next."

"From the Middle English *famen*, which means 'to starve,'" I said without thinking.

Gavin laughed. "I rest my case."

He helped me back to my feet. "Come on," he told me. "There's a great pizza place right down the street, and I don't wanna be the sad guy sitting in the corner, eating a whole deep dish by himself. We'll be in and out of there in thirty minutes, tops."

"Okay," I said. "As long as we're quick."

Beyond the fact that I was starving, I figured it would have been rude to say no after all the help Gavin had given me. Besides, I liked his company, and there was no guarantee that Stefan would be home for dinner considering the fact that I'd already told him I'd be out late.

I let Gavin lead the way out of the library, allowing him to carry my bookbag as we made our way through the stacks and out the door.

The pizza place Gavin brought me to was called McGee's, but since it was ten o'clock at night and adjacent to a college campus, the restaurant was completely packed and more than a little rowdy. We had to elbow our way through a crowd of people just to get to the counter to order and then we had to sit elbow to elbow at the counter because all the tables were taken.

"Sorry about the crowd," Gavin said, flashing an apologetic smile. "I've never seen it like this in here before. I guess I'm usually here during lunch, when everyone's still in class."

"It's okay," I told him, my voice straining to be heard over the commotion. "I'm sure the pizza will be worth it! Must be good if it's this busy, right?"

"The best," Gavin agreed.

Our pizza arrived and we dug into it, elbowing each other in the process. I couldn't help giggling a little. My thigh was pressed up against Gavin's, his arm jostling mine as he reached for his soda. When the waitress squeezed by behind me, I leaned forward with my hot, melty slice, realizing too late that I'd spilled half the toppings all over his jacket.

"God, I'm so sorry," I apologized. I tried to dab up the oil and cheese with my napkin, but I ended up nearly elbowing him in the face in the process.

"No worries," he said, gesturing at a blob of melted cheese and black olive. "This just means I'll have a snack for later."

We both laughed.

It was nice just sitting here with Gavin, laughing and joking and having a good time. Even the proximity of our bodies felt comfortable, despite the fact that I could feel the heat radiating from his leg into mine.

As I reached for a second slice, he twisted a little on his stool to face me.

"You have..." He gestured toward my face, but I had my pizza in one hand and a beverage in the other.

Before I could free my hands, Gavin reached out and tucked a wisp of loose hair behind my ear. His touch was soft, gentle, and as his fingers brushed my cheek, his gaze caught mine. He wore a look I knew well.

It was the same way Stefan looked at me when his guard was down.

At the same moment I realized it, Gavin leaned in to kiss me.

I didn't know what to do. I'd wanted this before, when I'd wondered if Gavin would be a better match for me than my arranged spouse. Without even consciously realizing it, I found my eyes fluttering closed.

As soon as our mouths touched, with the softest brush of dry lips, I knew that it wasn't what I wanted anymore.

I pulled back gently, not wanting to make a scene, especially in the crowded restaurant.

"I'm sorry," I told him. "I can't. I'm married. You know that. We—we can't do this."

Even though I was trying to smile, he looked like I'd just doused him in cold water.

"I don't care. This wasn't the plan when I first...god damn it." He stopped and shook his head. It seemed like he wanted to confess something, but he stopped struggling for words and switched gears. "I feel things for you, Tori. And if you feel things too, we can work this out."

I wasn't used to this: having two men that wanted me. I was completely out of my depth, but even though I didn't want to hurt Gavin, I knew that I was committed to Stefan.

Looking into Gavin's eyes again, I rested a hand on his arm.

This was all my fault. I'd flirted with him like crazy at the club that night, and then continued to encourage him in the text messages we'd exchanged while I'd been figuring out where things stood with Stefan. It hadn't been intentional—I'd been genuinely confused about my feelings—but there was no excuse for the fact that I'd put my friend in the middle of my marriage, made him think that maybe we had a chance when we didn't. At least, not anymore.

"The truth is...I do feel things," I confessed. "For Stefan. I love my husband."

It was the first time I had said those words out loud. I felt a rush of conflicting emotions. I felt scared and lonely, but also empowered. Confident. Because now I knew what I wanted.

And what I wanted wasn't here.

I watched the hopeful light in Gavin's eyes fade.

"I'm sorry," I told him gently, giving his shoulder a final squeeze.

Carefully, I turned and slid off my stool and then made my way through the crowd of people eating and laughing around us. Now that I knew how I felt, I was desperate to leave. I shouldn't be here, with Gavin. I should be at home, with my husband.

I should be telling him how I felt.

STEFAN

CHAPTER 24

I paced the living room, waiting for Tori to come home. Even though I had promised I would tell her when she was being followed, at times like these I was glad I'd become good at keeping secrets. Especially from her.

Though I'd considered pulling Dmitri out now that my wife and I had grown closer, in the end I'd decided to keep the security detail on her. It wasn't that I didn't trust Tori—I just didn't trust other people with her.

It was too dangerous out there, especially now that she was part of my world. I felt better knowing she was being watched considering the people I associated with through my work, and that went double for the people who associated with my father. The business we were involved in wasn't one synonymous with safety.

And then there was my father himself. He had shown what kind of man he was when he'd crossed a line with Tori the other night. I wasn't going to take any chances now. I wasn't going to let history repeat itself. Nobody was going to lay a hand on my wife.

Still, I felt a small twinge of guilt for not being

completely forthright with Tori. I knew she would be upset if she found out. But ensuring her safety was well worth her anger.

It was almost eleven, but I told myself I didn't need to worry. After all, she had texted earlier to let me know she would be home late, and I knew her favorite library on campus was open all night long. It was completely conceivable that she was still studying, or catching up with the school friends she hadn't been seeing as much lately. On top of that, Dmitri had been keeping tabs on her all day and the last I'd heard, she was still with her study group.

Suddenly, my phone started vibrating with a barrage of incoming texts. As I scrolled through the photos downloading onto my screen, I felt a shock of adrenaline. Then dismay. And then outrage. The pictures Dmitri was sending were of Tori—and Gavin. They were at a crowded restaurant, but their bodies were so close they could have been fucking. Their heads were leaning close, their lips a breath apart. Tori's eyes were closed, Gavin's hand on her arm.

I couldn't believe what I was seeing, and I didn't know what to think. I was completely caught off-guard. I had thought the two of us were finally getting somewhere. We had been communicating—and connecting—like never before. Not just in the bedroom, but out of it as well. And now here she was, cheating on me behind my back? With this smug asshole?

My hand curled into a fist seeing his face again. I knew it was inevitable that he'd make his way back into Tori's life, considering they were good friends and classmates. But something about him was off, and it wasn't just the way he couldn't keep his dick in his pants around my wife, or the fact that he'd been with her at the club the night she'd been drugged. He was hiding something. I didn't know what it was, or what he might be lying about, but there was something about him that I didn't trust.

I texted Dmitri back, demanding more updates. His response was that Tori had gotten in a cab and was heading home. Without Gavin. Dmitri, being the professional he was, had then sent me a picture of Gavin standing on the street by himself looking dejected.

It did little to calm my fury.

I continued pacing around the condo, knowing she'd be home any minute, my anger growing stronger with each passing moment. By the time I heard her key turn in the lock, I was practically vibrating with fury. I stormed into the foyer, flipping the bright light on overhead.

"Where the fuck have you been?" I demanded.

She had one chance to come clean. To tell me the truth. But just one.

"I was studying," she said, but her eyes shifted down, avoiding my gaze.

"Don't give me that bullshit," I seethed. "I know where you've been. And I know *who* you've been with."

Looking up at me, she glared. "Because you've been tracking me through my phone? Because you don't trust me?"

"Why should I trust you when you just lied to me?"

She folded her arms. "If you were tracking my phone, you'd know I spent most of the day at the library. Studying."

"We both know that's not all you were doing," I ground out, as visions of her and Gavin kissing flashed through my mind.

"Fine!" she said. "I stopped for pizza before I came home. I didn't eat all day. If I was doing something inappropriate, don't you think I would have turned my phone off?"

"You're going to stand there and tell me kissing another

man isn't appropriate?" I sneered. I pulled out my phone and showed her the pictures Dmitri had texted me.

Gasping, she ripped the phone out of my grasp.

"You still have someone following me?" she said, before slamming my phone down so hard on the entry table that she had probably shattered the screen. "You said you'd tell me when I was being watched. You lied to me! I can't believe you."

Shaking her head with disgust, she pushed past me, heading for the bedroom.

I reached out to grab her, but she rounded on me, shoving her finger into my chest.

"You're such an asshole," she said, shoving me backward. "You look at this one moment, this one instance, and decide it's everything. Aren't you the one who's always telling me that 'not everything is what it seems'? You're a fucking hypocrite, Stefan."

"Me?" I couldn't believe what I was hearing. "You're kissing some asshole and I'm the hypocrite? We're still married, or did you forget that small detail?"

"How could I forget?" Tori demanded. "You never let me forget what this is, and what I mean to you. How I'm something you own."

"That's not what this is," I tried to say, but she wasn't done.

"Gavin did kiss me tonight," she said, her voice turning to steel. "But I pushed him away right after. Which you would have known if you'd just fucking asked instead of standing there accusing me like this."

Despite her explanation, I felt like I had been punched in the gut.

"You expect me to believe that?" I said. "You've been hanging all over him this entire semester. And you've spent every waking minute with him ever since school started."

"He's my classmate!" she shot back.

I scoffed. "You can't expect me to believe that. He was at the club with you that night. He made a claim for you then, did you know that? Said he wouldn't have to drug you to get you into bed with him."

Her eyes went wide. "He said that?"

"It's obvious he's into you. He's made no secret of that, and still you hang out with him. Why should I believe that you would turn him down now that he's finally made his move?"

"Because I'm in love with you, you idiot!" Tori shouted at me.

The words hung between us like an invisible wall.

I was blown away.

I had never dared to believe that Tori could love me. Especially with all the secrets I had—all the ones she knew, and all the ones I was still keeping from her. But she did. And I could tell from the look in her eyes that she meant it. That she truly did love me. Despite everything. Or maybe even because of it.

I speechless.

We both just stood there for a moment, staring at each other, both of us breathing hard. I didn't know what to say.

Tori's eyes filled with tears and I could tell that she was taking my silence as a rejection, when I was really just struggling to process how quickly everything had just changed between us. Now that she had said the words out loud, now that she had confessed her feelings and the enormity of them, I realized what a fool I had been.

I should have trusted her. All this time, I should have trusted her with my secrets. With everything I had been keeping from her. Everything I had been afraid to share with her.

She started backing away from me, and I grabbed her by the arms and pulled her close.

"Tori."

Now was the time to be honest with her. To tell her everything. To share my life with her completely.

She was looking up at me, blinking back her tears, trying to be strong. Just like always. My wife was so strong. I gazed into her eyes, overwhelmed by everything I felt, unable to believe that this was truly real. That someone like her could truly love me.

But she did. I knew she did.

I leaned down and I kissed her. I kissed her with everything I had pent up inside. For a moment, she was stiff in my arms, but then she wrapped her arms around my neck and kissed me back. It was a kiss full of passion and love. Of everything I wanted. Everything I needed.

My hands skimmed her shoulders, her neck, then came up to cup the sides of her face gently. I kissed her more deeply, wanting to show her exactly how I felt. But I knew it wouldn't be enough. I couldn't just show her.

It took everything in my power to stop kissing her, but I did, slowly pulling back so I could look at her strong, beautiful face. She looked up at me, the question evident in her eyes. Finally, the words found their way out of my mouth.

"I love you too," I told her.

TORI

CHAPTER 25

They were only three words, but they had changed everything. Now that Stefan and I had fully and honestly admitted our feelings for one another, there was a palpable shift between us. I could hardly believe it. I had broken down his walls. He had finally let me in.

Every kiss felt more charged than ever. Deeper, more affirming, more connected. Even his touch was more intense, his hands both tender and undeniably electric against my skin. It was as if the second Stefan had let down his guard, he'd allowed himself to become more passionate. Everything was more. We'd had this invisible barrier between us all this time, but suddenly, with these words of love, I could sense that it was gone.

There was no going back now—only forward. Together.

As I lost myself in his kiss, I could feel his love radiating throughout every inch of my body. I never wanted it to stop. And I wasn't just turned on by the look in Stefan's gaze, the way he was holding me so tight. In his arms, I knew with certainty that my husband wanted me, he loved me, and he was claiming me as his—and his alone.

Adrenaline was still racing through my system from our fight, and Stefan's jealousy about Gavin had made me hotter than I'd ever thought possible. The way his green eyes had flashed with passion and rage had aroused me even as I was yelling at him. Who knew that Stefan's possessiveness would be an added bonus to our sex life?

It almost made me glad that he had been spying on me. That my dinner with Gavin had pushed Stefan over the edge, pushed him to confess how he truly felt about me. He might never have revealed that he loved me if he hadn't been motivated by the sight of that almost-kiss.

Not only that, but I knew without a doubt that my safety had been the reason for the bodyguard. Just one more way my husband was trying to protect me. I couldn't really be mad that he'd wanted to keep an eye on me. If anything, I could see now that it had brought us closer together. Had shown me the true motivation behind his possessiveness and control issues.

And now that I knew Stefan had been acting out of love, out of desire, it was even hotter to be with him. I wanted to give myself to him completely. Not just my body, but my heart as well. I couldn't deny my feelings for Stefan, and with this new honesty between us, I wouldn't have to any more. I could tell him I loved him whenever I wanted. And so I did. Between kisses, I whispered the words, wanting to hear them back, shivering with pleasure when he did.

I could even see the love he felt for me in his eyes. I had never imagined I would feel such passion for one person, or that my feelings would be returned in kind.

My heart raced as Stefan led me toward the bedroom. His touch was gentle, his hands at my waist, in no rush to undress me. But I wanted him badly. I wanted him now.

I also wanted to be sure that he fully understood that I was his, that I was ready to submit to him—to be his and his alone. There had to be a way I could show him that. Not just with my words, but with my actions. With my body.

Pulling back from his kiss, I gave him a wicked smile. Curiosity and excitement lit his face as I began tugging his shirt out of his pants, unbuckling his belt. I could feel his cock straining against the zipper and my mouth practically watered. I knew what I was going to do to him, and I could hardly wait.

But despite my excitement and my eagerness to please him, my hands still shook as I unbuttoned his pants and pulled the zipper down. I was overwhelmed with emotion for him and with my desire to bring him pleasure, but I was still new to this. I knew how naïve and inexperienced I must seem compared to the other more experienced women he had been with.

I hoped he would see it as a turn on. As proof that I was his. That I was ready and willing to bend to his will, give myself to him completely and totally.

Pulling his cock out, I sank to my knees and locked eyes with him as he slid his clothes to our bedroom floor. He was hot and hard in my grip and I couldn't wait to show him how I felt. With my hands. My mouth. My tongue.

Stefan groaned as I dragged my tongue over the head of his cock, tasting him. His fingers tangled in my hair, holding me tight against him as I wrapped my wet lips around his shaft. I started sucking, softly at first. Loving the way he began to guide me up and down his cock, showing me the rhythm he wanted. The rhythm he needed.

I took him as deep as I could, opening my mouth wide, relaxing my throat to take all of him as far back as possible. His grip became hard and rough and I absolutely loved it as he began to thrust inside my mouth. The thought of what he was doing to me, what I was doing to him, drove me wild. I could feel how wet I was already. I moaned a little, knowing he would feel the vibrations in his cock, that it would turn him on even more.

Clutching his hips to keep myself balanced, I looked up at him again. I wanted him to enjoy the sight of my wide blue eyes and the view of his cock pumping in and out of my mouth as I kneeled in front of him.

There was nothing but passion, desire, and love in his gaze. The muscles in his jaw were tense and I knew I was doing everything right. I smiled around his cock, loving the control I had over him. Loving how I could tease him and tempt him with my mouth. With my body.

I swirled my tongue up his length and over the soft skin of his head, and then added my hand, pumping his shaft with long, tight strokes that followed the movement of my mouth. I made his cock wet, just like he'd taught me, knowing that my pussy was just as soaked and ready for him. I wanted him so badly, but I wasn't ready to stop pleasuring him yet.

Before I knew what was happening, though, Stefan was pulling me up, dragging me back to my feet in front of him. I wanted to protest, but his mouth crashed onto mine, silencing any words I might have spoken. As he kissed me, his hands started tugging off my clothes and the shirt he was still wearing. I loved the way his hot, unclothed body felt against mine, the hard muscles beneath my hands as he stripped me bare, the smooth slide of his skin beneath my palms. Still, I wasn't done with him. The moment we were both naked, I began to kneel in front of him again, needing his cock in my mouth. Needing to taste him more.

But before I could, I was tossed onto the bed like I

weighed nothing at all. Stefan followed me down onto the sheets, but instead of positioning his cock at my entrance, he settled himself between my legs, his mouth kissing up between my thighs.

I cried out as he licked my pussy, the wetness and heat almost too much for me to handle. He gripped my ass in his hands, holding me in place while he fucked me with his tongue, thrusting it hard inside of me, nearly making me come right away. It felt so good and so intense, but I wanted more. I tried to pull him up toward me, clawing at his shoulders, but when he started to move, it was to position himself beside me, his mouth never leaving my pussy.

Turning my head, I could see his cock near my shoulder, and I rolled to my side and reached for it, eager to take him in my mouth again. He shifted closer to me, readjusting, his head still pressed between my thighs as I finally closed my lips around his cock again. I felt his groan as I took him deep, the sound of his pleasure vibrating through my entire body. He was lapping at my clit at the same time I was bobbing my head back and forth over his length, sucking wetly, hungry for his cock. We both wanted to give pleasure as much as we wanted to receive it, and the connection was more intense than I could have ever imagined.

I ground my hips against him, wanting his tongue even deeper inside of me while I stroked and sucked at his shaft, my hands moving hard and fast up and down, following the motion of my mouth. I took him deeper than I ever had before, and all of my insecurities about being inexperienced fell away as he began thrusting against my tongue, finding the rhythm he wanted. I could feel his head thumping against the back of my throat, feel how hard he was inside my mouth, and I loved every moment of it. I could feel him going wild, could taste his pre-cum, and it was all I could do to hold back as I felt my own orgasm start to rise inside of me.

He was licking and stroking me hard and fast, adding his fingers to stretch my pussy wide. I was mindless with desire, writhing desperately as he brought me to the edge, just as I was doing for him. We were both moaning, thrusting, losing control as we gave and received in tandem. It was so erotic that I could hardly stand it.

Finally, he curled his fingers inside of me, knowing exactly how to find my G-spot. As his tongue rolled over my clit, I exploded with one of the most powerful orgasms I'd ever experienced. It hit me in waves, each one stronger than the last, and I felt tears gathering behind my closed eyes as I moaned in ecstasy.

I had popped his cock out of my mouth when I came, and I was still grinding my pussy against his face as I rode out the aftershocks, my hand tight on his wet cock. My jaw was sore, my lips swollen, but my mouth was ready to take him again.

Instead, Stefan flipped me onto my back first. My body was still trembling, but he spread my legs without hesitating and plunged his cock deep inside of me.

"Yes," I panted. "You feel so good."

He kissed me as he fucked me, his tongue matching the rhythm of his thrusts. I cupped his face, wanting to be even closer to him. Wanting to touch every inch of him, inside and out.

My body was open wide to him, allowing him to go deep—so deep—inside of me. I wanted him to go hard, to be rough with me the way he always was, but that wasn't what he wanted. Not tonight. Instead, his strokes were long and languid as he took his time, kissing my lips, my throat, my breasts, his cock moving slowly in and out of my body. He kept my hips pinned to the bed so even if I wanted him to move faster, even if I wanted him to take me harder, there was nothing I could do about it.

His hot gaze met mine, and I saw all the love and passion that he had been afraid to speak of. Until now. My body tightened in response and I could feel another orgasm gathering inside of me. Stefan could see that I was close, his lips curving into a smile as his hand slid between our bodies, his fingers finding my clit. He teased me there, still thrusting oh so slowly—painfully, agonizingly slowly. Making sure I felt every inch of him. This was a different, new kind of torture. I hated it and loved it at the same time. I never wanted him to stop, yet I was desperate for relief. Greedy for it.

"Please," I begged him. "Harder."

I knew that he liked it when I begged. When I was at his mercy. His eyes flashed with victory as he pressed hard against my clit, his fingers pinching and holding me there, providing the perfect combination of pleasure and pain. A combination of sensations I had learned to love because of him. A combination of sensations I knew I'd never be able to live without.

As he tortured my clit, his thrusts went deeper, my moans pitching higher and faster. He began to pump into me stronger, gaining speed, leaving me breathless.

"Come for me, Tori," he said, and in that instant I came hard, the orgasm cresting over me, my body arching hard against the mattress. I could feel my pussy clenching tight around Stefan's cock as I cried out, my nails digging into his back with the force of my climax.

When I returned to earth, I realized that he was still moving inside of me, completely in control of his own pleasure. I couldn't allow that. Not after the two mind-bending orgasms he had just given me. I wanted to dominate him the way he had dominated me. Wanted to force the pleasure out of him as he had done to me.

Shoving him hard on his chest, I pushed until he had rolled onto his back and I was on top. He had let me ride him before, knew how much I loved this position, but this time would be different. Tonight I wanted to show Stefan what I had learned from him—how to give pleasure the way he liked. How to tease and torment and satisfy.

I began to ride him, leaning back, spreading my thighs even further apart, knowing that in this position he had a full view of my bouncing breasts and his cock buried inside me. I took him deep, so incredibly deep, and his fingers slid up my thighs and then dug into my hips, as if he thought he would be able to control me, even with me on top. I was eager to prove him wrong. This time, I wanted him to be the one begging.

I began to move slowly, leaning forward to press my palms against his chest for balance, arching my hips against his, drawing him deeper and deeper into me as I fucked him. My knees dug into the bed beside his hips, my clit rubbing deliciously against his body as I lifted myself up and down on his hard, gorgeous cock. The muscles in his neck stood out as his head fell back against the bed, his eyes closed as he let me take control.

He was the sexiest man I'd ever seen, his muscles tensing as I rode him, his stomach contracting with each thrust, giving me an incredible view of his six pack. His hands slid up to cup my breasts, his fingers teasing my hard nipples, sending hot sparks of pleasure through me. I knew I had to be careful or I would come again too quickly. This was about him.

I rode him even more slowly, but it only turned me on more. I tried speeding up then, and I could tell by his groans that it was exactly what he wanted, that he was starting to lose control. It wasn't long before I was wet enough to speed up even more, savoring the tight friction, unable to resist the rhythm my body craved. The rhythm my body needed.

His fingers pinched my nipple hard and I gasped. I rode him harder and faster, my moans pitching higher, chasing my own orgasm. His hands dragged back down to my hips and he was urging me on, his own hips rising up to meet me, slamming against me, making my whole body shake with the power of his thrusts. Even though I had intended to take him to the edge, it was Stefan who was dragging me over it. The way he always did.

Without warning, he sat up so we were facing each other, and I could feel him even deeper inside me as he positioned my legs so they wrapped around his torso. He grabbed my hips again, rolling me back and forth over his cock in short, fast circles, steady as he fucked me, our faces inches apart so I could see the desire in his eyes. We were so close. So connected. And I loved it.

I was filled with so many emotions and so much pleasure that the entire world seemed to shatter as my orgasm hit me. This time, I felt Stefan coming with me, thrusting impossibly deep inside of me, filling me with his hot release. I gasped, collapsing against his chest as we held onto one other, whispering those words again and again as we rode out the waves of pleasure.

"I love you," he whispered between jagged breaths.

And I loved him. Completely. Utterly. Unmistakably.

I would never look back.

CHAPTER 26

"I want to tell you about Anja," Stefan said.

We were stretched out in bed together, and my head was heavy against his chest, where I'd been listening to his racing heartbeat slow back down to its normal pace.

"You mean Irina?" I asked.

At last I could breathe easier. He was finally going to tell me what he'd done for her. What she'd meant by the message she had asked me to deliver to him the other day at the café.

"No," he said. "Anja. Anja Borjan."

Stefan's hand was in my hair, his other arm wrapped around my waist, keeping me close.

Confused, I raised my head and looked up at him. I expected him to be half asleep after the marathon sex we'd just had, maybe to the point of being mixed up regarding the woman he was telling me about. But he was wide awake, his green eyes focused intently on the ceiling.

"Okay," I said softly. I couldn't help fearing the worst. "What do you want to tell me about her?"

Whatever it was, we'd get through it. If he was making the effort to be honest with me, it meant he wanted us to work out. To be together, despite anything that had happened in the past.

He didn't say anything for a long time and I started to worry that he'd changed his mind. That he was going to return to the quiet, closed off version of himself that I had lived with for so long. At last, he let out a long sigh and looked down at me.

"Who is Anja?" I asked, keeping my voice gentle and accepting.

"She's a woman...from my past," he said.

I nodded, feeling relieved. This wasn't his mistress. It was someone from a long time ago. But clearly someone that had a hold on him, still. Someone who meant something to him.

"You can talk about her," I urged him. "I'm listening."

I wanted him to be honest with me. Open with me. I wanted to know all his secrets, even if they were hurtful or dangerous. It wasn't like I expected him to have never loved anyone else.

"I knew her when I was younger," he went on. "I was a teenager. We met just before I turned eighteen."

Thinking back, I remembered what Emzee had told me. About how different Stefan had been in high school. How she thought something had happened to him to make him change. Was this woman Anja the reason for the way he was now? Hard, controlling, fiercely guarded to the point of cageyness? I propped myself up on my elbow, rolling to my side, and placed a hand over his heart. I could tell he was struggling for the right words, but that he wanted to keep talking.

"How did you two meet?" I asked.

"She was one of KZM's models," he confessed. "I met her at a show in Paris. I knew that she was working for my father, the way all the models work for him. The...jobs on the side."

"Sure," I murmured, letting him know I was following his words without judging.

"You have to understand—I thought, back then, that they were doing it because they wanted to. I had no idea they were being forced. I didn't judge them for it, but I never stopped to think—I just assumed it was another job to them. Another way to make money."

He shook his head, obviously angry at his naïveté.

"You were young," I said, soothingly.

"I had my head up my own ass," he scoffed. "And I wasn't an innocent seventeen, either. I should have known."

I felt a twinge of sympathy for a seventeen-year-old Stefan. It must have been a terrible thing for him to discover.

"You couldn't have known," I told him. "Not the way your—the way the company runs."

Placing the blame on Konstantin, though fair, wasn't the way to help Stefan right now. As much as I would have enjoyed it. As far as I was concerned, his father was pure evil.

Stefan took a breath and then continued. "I started seeing Anja, casually at first but then it got more regular. A few months into it, I realized I was in love. She was the first person I was with who seemed interested in the rest of the world, who was ambitious and tough like me. She had nerves of steel. It wasn't just that, though. We had fun. Actually...she was a lot like you."

"I'll take that as a compliment," I said. The way he was talking about her, I couldn't feel jealous. Because despite how great she sounded, I could tell by the tone of his voice that things between them were long over. And I guessed that something had gone terribly wrong.

Turning his eyes back to me, Stefan tucked a strand of hair behind my ear and smiled. He took a deep breath and said, "Me, being the fine young idiot that I was, decided I wanted to marry her. But when I told her that, she said my father would never allow it. And I didn't believe her. I thought—foolishly—that love could conquer all. That he would understand."

Bitterness had crept into his voice, and my heart sank. I knew exactly where the story was going, and it was nowhere good.

"What did he do?" I said.

Stefan looked away. "A few days after I proposed to Anja, she was gone. Disappeared without a trace. When I went to my father for help, he told me he'd had her deported. I was devastated."

I wrapped my arms around Stefan, feeling his pain as if it were my own. All I could think about was this bright, optimistic young version of my husband, still so new to the world, his first relationship—his first love—torn out of his hands by his vile, criminal father. He'd been even younger than I was now.

"I'm so sorry," I whispered. "Did you go after her?"

"My father made me swear I wouldn't, but I tried." He cleared his throat, as if to break up the emotion that was making it hard for him to speak. "It didn't matter, though. I never saw or heard from her again."

My heart broke for Stefan. For the man he had been. No wonder he had become hardened after losing someone he cared about when he was so young.

He was looking up at the ceiling again. "I've been

searching for her ever since," he said. "Trying to figure out where my father sent her. Wanting to make sure she's safe." He shook his head. "It's been eight years and I've never found a trace. Sometimes I think she's..."

But he couldn't say the word. His hand tightened into a fist. I could feel his frustration. His anger. And I could understand it. It was cruel what his father had done. Beyond cruel.

"I want to believe that my father wouldn't have done anything to her. That she might be in hiding, but that she's still safe. Still *alive*. But after all this time, I can't be sure. She's eluded every private investigator I've hired. I've called in every resource, spared no expense. There's been no sign of her."

I suddenly remembered our honeymoon. The way Stefan's colleague Marco had shown up at one of our dinner reservations in Austria. At first, they'd discussed KZM's marketing plans, hiring new models for a runway show, the kinds of things that would practically put me to sleep. But when I'd returned to the table from the restroom, I'd overheard them discussing something much different. Stefan had been angry, and Marco had looked apologetic and upset. I walked up just in time to catch the end of a conversation that I knew I wasn't supposed to be privy to. Stefan had been looking for someone. Searching for someone.

"That's who you were looking for," I said. "On our honeymoon, that night with Marco. You were searching for her. For Anja."

Stefan nodded. "I'm still looking. I refuse to give up, even though she hasn't been seen once in all these years. I refuse to let my father win."

I was filled with sympathy for Stefan. Almost a decade

of searching, of hoping, of not knowing if the woman he'd loved was safe, or even still alive.

"I can't believe your father did this," I said, my own words filled with anger.

And yet I could believe it. I believed every word. Stefan's story only proved what I already thought of Konstantin—that he was a bad man who deserved to be locked up, put away where he couldn't hurt anyone ever again.

Stefan said, "I decided then and there, the moment he told me that he'd sent Anja away, that I would never be like him."

I was glad to hear it, even though I now knew that Stefan was nothing like his father. The two could not have been more opposite. Konstantin was cruel and hard and monstrous. Stefan was capable of great love, as he had shown me tonight. It was amazing he could still open his heart up to someone after how damaged he had become as a result of Anja's disappearance. All thanks to his father's cruelty. I didn't know if I would have been able to do the same.

"You're not like your father at all," I told him. "You never will be."

He didn't respond, but closed his eyes for a brief moment.

"I want to undo everything my father has done. Erase him, erase what KZ Modeling stands for," he said, opening his eyes to look at me, his gaze burning with clarity. With focus. "I've spent almost a decade of my life working my ass off to get my father to trust me. To involve me in running the family business. So that I know enough about how the agency works—how the prostitution ring works—to turn him over to the feds. It's the only way I can even begin to fix all the damage he's caused. All the lives he's destroyed."

"You're going to shut it all down," I said, the pieces coming together.

Stefan nodded. "But my father doesn't trust anyone. Even me. Not completely, anyway. He still remembers Anja, how I cared for her. He doesn't think I can play ball the way he does."

The conversation I'd had with Stefan on the night we first met came back to me. Stefan had point blank told me that his father was old school. That he wouldn't hand over the agency to someone he didn't trust, someone who hadn't settled down. It all made sense, the way I'd gotten caught up in this mess.

"You agreed to this marriage so you could take him down," I said. "Not just to take over the company. But to obliterate it."

"Exactly," Stefan agreed. "It was my plan all along."

I sat up, my mind still reeling with all the implications. "What about my father? How is he involved?"

There was still bad blood between us. We hadn't spoken since the fight we'd had at his office, the day I'd told him he wasn't my father anymore.

"I shouldn't tell you," Stefan said. "This is between me and my father."

"No it's not," I said. "It's so much bigger than that, and you know it. Tell me."

But waiting for Stefan's response, I couldn't help holding my breath. I needed to know the truth, but whatever he told me about my father would change my opinion of him forever.

Stefan took a deep breath and then sat up, leaning back against the headboard.

"Your father," he began, "is deeply involved with KZM's illegal business dealings."

It wasn't a surprise, but I still felt my stomach drop. Still felt the shock of betrayal.

He went on, "Not only is he one of the company's most profitable clients himself, but he also gets kickbacks for referring other wealthy, high-powered men to the backdoor side of the agency. And he refers a lot of them."

I felt as if the wind had been knocked out of me. I had braced myself to hear something bad, but I hadn't expected it to be this bad. Hearing that my father used KZ Modeling as a client made me sick—and my heart went out to my step-mother, Michelle. I couldn't help wondering if she knew. She'd always told me there were trade-offs to being a trophy wife. Was that because she knew firsthand the kind of indignities I might have to face? Had she spent her entire marriage to my father turning a blind eye to his indiscretions? Or had she been in the dark as much as I had been? Maybe it was something in between. Knowing that he wasn't faithful, but never imagining that he had aligned himself with an illegal sex trafficking ring.

The more I thought about it, the more I began to realize the implications.

"This information would destroy my father's career," I said out loud, understanding dawning on me. "Not just politically, either. He'd be in jail. Maybe for the rest of his life."

Stefan nodded. "You can see why both of our fathers approved of this match," he said. "Marrying you gave my father a reason to protect your father's secret. And in turn, being connected to your father publicly gives KZ Modeling legitimacy. If there were any rumors about KZM being an illegal front, they'd be much more easily dismissed thanks to having a highly respected U.S. senator connected to the Zoric family. Our marriage protects both of them."

"And puts us in the middle of their tangled web," I said bitterly.

It was a lot to take in. A lot to realize how deeply my father was involved.

We sat there together in silence, Stefan giving me time to absorb all the information and the harsh reality of our situation.

"What about Irina?" I asked, thinking of the beautiful woman who had come to my table at the coffee shop. "Why was she thanking you? Was that related to all of this?"

"I've been trying to help the models as much as I can," he said slowly. "It's complicated. Sometimes, if I can, I book them as a client—under a fake name—just to give them a night off from their work. I get a hotel room, order up a hot meal from room service, listen to them talk. I try to help them make plans to escape. Sometimes it works."

I nodded. "That explains all the nights you come home so late. Or not at all."

Stefan took my hand. "I don't sleep with them," he said firmly. "I'm not like my father, and I don't use women like that.

"Irina was one of the models I was able to help get away. I've done that with a few women—I wish it were more, but it's too risky. There was a woman in Hungary, do you remember Oksana? She's one of the women I helped."

"I remember." And I remembered clearly. At the time, I had found her devotion to Stefan suspicious and worrying. Now I understood it. I understood, too, why Irina had called Stefan a "good man." All the sneaking around, the cagey-ness, the secrets and lies—all this time, my husband had been trying to save as many of these exploited women as possible.

"How many women have you helped?" I asked.

He shook his head. "Not enough. But the organization is so big. So massive. My father's reach—and your father's influence—are a powerful shield. They're well-protected, they have allies, and there's only so much I can do without putting my bigger plans at risk."

"So what are those plans?" I wanted to know. "What's the end goal?"

"My dream is to eventually go straight," he said. "Make KZ Modeling a real talent agency and nothing more. It doesn't need to be a sex slave ring. In fact, we could have gone straight years ago, from the beginning, if not for my father's greed and megalomania. He wanted too much. Money, power, women, connections. And control. Always control. He's willing to do anything to get that." He looked at me, his eyes blazing.

I was overwhelmed as I thought of everything Stefan had gone through all these years. I couldn't believe he'd done all this on his own, that he'd been carrying the burden on his shoulders with no one to talk to.

"You should have told me," I said, my voice thick with tears.

He'd protected his brother and his sister, while doing everything he could to combat his father's monstrous behavior and practices. Always wearing that mask, keeping up that façade, just so he could continue to work for his father, continue gaining his trust, while at the same time secretly attempting to dismantle the very company he was expected to inherit.

No wonder Stefan had become so hard, so closed off.

How could he not be, after everything he had seen? After everything he had gone through, the lie he'd had to live?

"I couldn't risk getting you involved," he said. "I wanted to keep you safe. Tracking you, hiring that bodyguard, they were never about keeping you in a cage. They were about making sure my father never took you the way he took Anja. Never used you as leverage against me."

His hand came up to cup my cheek, his thumb brushing my tears away.

It all made sense now. His behavior. His need to know where I was at all times. No wonder he had been so furious when I would disappear, when he couldn't find me, when I was out with people he didn't know.

I would never put him through that worry again. Especially now that I knew the truth.

"I thought you were cheating on me," I confessed. "I thought you were seeing other women, hiding a mistress from me..."

Stefan shook his head. "It's only been you," he said.

"All this time?" I asked. I had to be sure. I had to know the truth, once and for all.

He kissed me, slow and soft, and then pulled away to look me in the eye.

"Ever since our wedding, from the moment we said I do, its only ever been you," he said.

TORI

CHAPTER 27

When I woke up the next morning, I lay there for a long time, replaying the events of last night in my head. I was alone. It was a Saturday, so I didn't have any classes to rush off to, but Stefan might have gone into the office for the day. The condo seemed quiet. Hushed. Empty.

At first I was afraid that our night together had been a dream, or worse—that it had all been real, but that Stefan would be different in the light of day. That he'd go back to his old self, acting as if nothing had passed between us, as if he'd never opened up to me and told me his secrets. Never told me that he loved me.

Had it really all happened? Had we torn down all the walls that had stood between us? Was our marriage real now? Was it true? Or would I get out of bed, walk into the kitchen, and find the same Stefan that I had been living with for all these months? A man that was as shut down and closed off and dangerous as his father?

I couldn't stand the thought of it, but when I caught the unmistakable scent of fresh-brewed coffee, I decided it was

244

best to face him now, as soon as possible, and find out right away just how much things had really changed.

Cautiously, I wrapped my soft, luxurious robe around myself and then padded out of the bedroom, straining my ears for sounds of life in the apartment. The smoky smell of bacon in the hallway hit me immediately. Inhaling deeply, my mouth watering, I headed to the kitchen.

Rounding the doorway, I was shocked to find Stefan at the stove. The last time he'd tried to make me breakfast, I'd been too ill from my night at the club to appreciate it. But now, I couldn't imagine anything I wanted more than to be cared for, and cooked for, by my husband.

"Who are you and what have you done with my husband?" I teased.

"I told Gretna to take the day off," he said, turning to smile at me. "It's just us."

The food wasn't the only reason my mouth was watering. Stefan was naked from the waist up, his jeans hugging his great ass and powerful thighs. I stood there silently for a moment, taking it all in. His gorgeous broad shoulders, his strong back, the way his muscles tensed and bunched as he tended to the pans on the stove. He was gorgeous. Beyond gorgeous.

I was starving now, but not for breakfast.

"Did you sleep well, beautiful?" he asked, his voice warm and full of promises.

"I did," I replied, realizing by the way he was acting that everything last night had been real.

The Stefan I had spent all night talking to—and making love with—was still here.

I was so full of love I could barely see straight.

"Breakfast is just about ready," he said, draping a kitchen towel over his shoulder.

It didn't seem possible, but it made him look even sexier and more appealing than he had mere moments ago.

Then he poured a coffee into my favorite mug, added a splash of my coconut creamer, and handed the cup to me. I thanked him, unable to help the blush that spread across my cheeks. A blush that only made him smile more widely at me.

"Why don't you have a seat and I'll bring you a plate?" he said, gesturing toward the table.

I settled into a chair, watching him finish up. It wasn't easy to keep my hands to myself, when what I really wanted to do was join him at the stove, loop my arms around his waist and rest my cheek against the warm skin on his back. Then I'd slip my hands around to his front, unzip his jeans, spin him around to face me and beg him to take me right there on the counter. Who needed breakfast, anyway? I knew I'd be able to satisfy his hunger in other ways.

In fact, I couldn't wait to spend the rest of the weekend getting to know him better—in every possible way. And on every possible surface of our home.

Instead, I watched him carry our plates to the table and settle down in the chair beside me. There was a pile of crisp bacon, fried eggs, perfectly cooked crepes stuffed with strawberries and topped with whipped cream, and orange juice that might have been fresh squeezed.

"This all looks amazing," I said, in awe at his efforts. "Thank you."

"You are so welcome," he said.

But even as we began to eat, I was still having a hard time believing that this was all actually happening and even though I knew it was stupid, I surreptitiously pinched myself. But apparently not surreptitiously enough, because before I knew it, Stefan was laughing.

"Are you seriously pinching yourself?" he asked. "Don't you know that's my job?"

I laughed along with him and let him pull me into his lap, where he dropped kisses down my neck as his pinched my sides, my hips, and my ass.

"Stop tickling me!" I panted between giggles, squirming in his arms.

He pulled his hands back, kissing me on the tip of my nose. "I couldn't help myself. Please forgive me."

"Apology accepted," I said, finally sliding back into my own chair. I was still laughing a little as he picked up a piece of bacon and fed me a bite.

"Crispy enough for you?" he asked.

I nodded. "It's perfect." I had no idea he had ever paid such close attention to my breakfast choices, but clearly he had. I wouldn't eat bacon any other way.

After that, he insisted on feeding me a few more bites of it, his eyes glazing with lust as I made sure to moan my satisfaction.

I loved it. I loved having his hands all over me, having him play with me. Touching, teasing, feeding me. How was I ever going to get through breakfast without tossing my napkin down and sliding under the table to show him exactly how glad I was to be married to him?

"Since when did you learn to cook like this?" I asked, pointing at the golden-brown pile of tightly rolled crepes. They were light, buttery, and the slightest bit crispy. "Crepes are hard."

"You'll find I have many hidden talents," he said, winking at me.

"I have no doubt," I said, flirting back. "I can't wait to discover the rest of them."

I dragged my tongue down the curve of my spoon as I said that, enjoying the way his eyes followed the movement.

"I have a few ideas of what you could do with that tongue of yours," he said.

I went hot, a flush spreading over my skin as his eyes seemed to burn through my robe.

This was exactly the fun, sexy flirtatious Stefan I had hoped for on my honeymoon. Months later, we finally seemed to have the kind of marriage we both had secretly craved.

"You're playing with fire, kitty cat," Stefan warned as I picked up a ripe, red strawberry from the bowl of fruit and popped it in my mouth.

"I think you like it when I play with fire," I teased him.

His eyes were burning with intense heat as he picked up another strawberry and held it in front of my mouth. I parted my lips and he placed it on my tongue. Closing my mouth around his finger, I made sure to drag my tongue along it as he slowly withdrew his hand.

"You're good at that," Stefan said, his voice thick with lust.

"I'm learning," I told him, smirking.

I wanted to make him break. Wanted to make him push his chair back and pull me into his arms. Wanted him to carry me back to the bedroom where he would rip off my robe and feast on me the same way we were feasting on this breakfast.

Somehow, we made it through the rest of our meal without tearing each other's clothes off.

The moment he pushed his plate away, however, I was more than ready to take our little back and forth flirtation to the bedroom. Looping my arms around his neck, I crawled onto his lap, enjoying the feel of his hot, bare skin against my hands, my robe gaping open as I straddled him. As we kissed I could feel his desire, hard and throbbing behind the seam of his jeans, and I wanted him more than I wanted my next breath.

But I had also come to a decision since last night—a decision he wasn't going to like right away. Luckily, I was more than willing to use my powers of persuasion to convince him to see things my way.

"I want to help you," I told him as I dropped kisses along his jawline.

"Mm hmm," he murmured, his hands busy with the tie of my robe, his fingers already pushing past the fabric to stroke my soft, hot skin.

It took all my concentration to focus on the task at hand.

"The women," I gasped as his hands cupped my breasts. "I want to help you save them."

He pulled back and gripped my upper arms, holding my body still.

"No," he said, his expression serious. "Absolutely not. You can help by keeping your head down. By staying out of all of this."

"But I want to help," I protested, sliding my hands down his chest, making for his zipper, knowing that I could convince him if I touched him.

As if he could sense exactly what I was planning, Stefan slid his hands down to my wrists and then pulled them behind me, pinning my arms behind my back. The gesture pushed my breasts forward, a movement I could tell he instantly regretted. And one that I could use to my advantage.

"Please," I begged, arching my back, tempting him with my nearly bared breasts.

"No," he said firmly, keeping his eyes on my face.

Fine. If he wasn't going to look, there were other ways I could tempt him. Wriggling forward, I pressed my pussy against his hard cock. Even through his jeans, he could probably feel how hot and wet I was for him. His jaw tensed and I bit back a wicked smile. He might be holding me, but I still had some control. I rocked against him, using my hips to torment him.

"Think of all the ways I can be an asset to you," I purred, my lips close to his ear, my body pressed up against his.

He groaned, his eyes closed.

"No," he said, but he wasn't fighting me.

"You know I can help." I licked his earlobe into my mouth. "Between all my newly polished language skills and the fact that I'm a woman myself, I can do things that you can't do. Learn things you can't. No one suspects I'm anything other than a trophy wife."

I could tell he didn't like the idea, but I could also tell he loved what I was doing to his cock. Not only could I feel him hot and hard against me, but I knew that if he didn't like it, he could have pushed me off of his lap at any moment. Instead he was straining against me, clearly eager for more.

I kissed his throat, dragging my teeth along his hot skin.

"It's not just your father who deserves justice," I told him, my voice husky with emotion. "But mine, too."

Because in the end, that's what I really wanted. For the men who had done this—who had tried to destroy and control not just our lives, but the lives of countless other women over the years—to be brought to justice. To pay. I wanted them to be punished for what they had done.

"We can do it," I told Stefan. "We can do it together."

Stefan released my arms and captured my mouth in a

fierce kiss, his mouth tangling with mine as he pulled me tight against his cock. I wrapped my legs around his waist as he stood, heading toward the door.

"Say yes," I begged him, my arms around his neck.

"I'll think about it," he promised.

And then he carried me into the bedroom, where he proceeded to make me forget about anything but him and his body and the pleasure he could bring me.

STEFAN

CHAPTER 28

I hung up the phone after a long call with a designer watch brand rep and tried to remember what I'd spent the last forty minutes talking about. Glancing at my notes, I saw I'd scribbled the words "modern luxury," "faces —James Bond-type," "classy/exotic," and "multi-function timepieces with sophisticated edge." That was all I had to go on. But at least it was a start. Matching the right KZM models to our clients' project needs was my specialty.

It hadn't been easy to come into work on Monday and focus after the weekend I'd had. Not just because of the sex, either. Opening up to Tori had changed everything in my life. She was no longer simply the woman I fantasized about fucking and had married out of necessity. Now that I'd finally come to terms with—and admitted—my love for her, had confided in her, she was my partner. In every way. I had never imagined it could be like this.

But as I sat in my office, taking in the view of Chicago from my floor-to-ceiling windows, I knew I had to confront the reality of our situation. Of what I had agreed to. Because Tori had told me she wanted to help...and I couldn't deny that I was tempted to take her up on her offer. She was right; she would be a valuable asset.

Yet I also knew that allowing Tori to participate in my plans to bring down my father and the shady side of KZM would mean putting her in harm's way. I couldn't allow that. Worse, I was well aware that if we weren't careful, my father would do to Tori what he'd done to Anja. He'd make her disappear. And I couldn't bear the thought. Not after all we had been through.

Everything about this situation seemed impossible. It didn't help that whenever I thought of her, my head immediately filled with images of all the filthy things I had done to her. The things I still wanted to do to her. I couldn't concentrate.

I wished I could take her on another honeymoon. A real one, where we did nothing but stay in bed and explore each other bodies. Each other's fantasies.

She was so hot. So responsive. Tori might not be a virgin anymore, but she still approached every sexual experience like a beginner. Everything we did, everything I taught her, was exciting and new to her. I'd never been so turned on by a woman before. And without any secrets between us, our newfound intimacy had heightened everything. We'd practically set the sheets on fire this past weekend, stopping only long enough to eat and talk.

And every time we had talked, Tori had done her best to convince me that she needed to be a part of my plan to see justice served, and to dismantle the sex trafficking aspect of KZM.

She had found numerous ways to be very, very persuasive with her argument.

My mind was replaying some of the more intense persuasive moments when the door to my office slammed open and my father stormed in, in a furious rage. His face was red, his normally impeccable tie askew, and he was clutching a fistful of papers in his hand.

"What the fuck?" he yelled. "Is this?"

I stood from my chair, lifting my hands to appease him. I had no idea what I was in for, but it was far from the first time I'd been subjected to my father's rages—he was volatile and unpredictable. He'd been this way my entire life. Given my familiarity with his temper, I forced my face into a conciliatory, neutral expression. It never served me to stoop to his level or to show any sign of emotion—especially weakness or fear. My father was like a bomb, but you never knew what would set him off. It was best to say as little as possible when he was like this.

"What's the problem?" I asked.

"*This* is the problem." Konstantin slammed the crumpled fistful of papers down on my desk. "What do you know about this?"

As I leaned down to smooth out the pages, I saw that they were photographs. They were so grainy that I could barely make out the details, but I recognized the general features of the faces I was looking at. It was Tori. And that fucking asshole Gavin. Her classmate.

I slid the pictures around on my desk, fanning them out, keeping my expression passive.

"To be honest, I can hardly tell what I'm looking at," I said.

"Then look harder."

My father's face grew redder, and he pushed one of the photos toward me, rotating it so I could get a better look. It was Tori and Gavin sitting side by side, almost on the same chair.

For a moment, I thought they were the same pictures

Dmitri had sent from the pizza parlor—the ones that had shown Gavin leaning forward to kiss my wife—but upon closer inspection, it was clear that these were completely different. Tori and Gavin were in a library. The reason they were so close was because they were huddled around a textbook. Studying.

I stared at the photos, playing innocent, but inside I was fuming. Was my father spying on Tori as well, or had Dmitri double crossed me? Either way, he was going to need to be replaced. Even if he wasn't sending pictures to my father, he was clearly a shit bodyguard if he hadn't noticed other people hanging around and taking pictures of my wife.

"Do you know about this?" my father roared, stabbing the page with his finger.

Tugging it out from under his finger, I made a show of examining the photo again.

"I'm not sure what there is to know." I sat back down in my chair, crossing my arms over my chest, looking him in the eye. "She goes to school. She's in a study group. This is a picture of her studying, in that group. Is there something significant about that?"

My father looked like he wanted to punch something. Like he wanted to punch me.

"My son is an idiot," he sneered. He picked up the photo again and held it in front of my nose. "You know who this is? This is Gavin fucking Chase."

"Okay?" I kept my expression blank, not indicating that I already knew Gavin's name.

"His brother works for the DOD!" my father exploded. "As an agent against trafficking. And he's hanging around your wife!"

He was pointing at me now, and I had to shake my head. Inside, I was in shock.

"So what do you think this means?" I asked carefully.

"It *means*," he said, pacing the office now, "that this little shit is trying to infiltrate our operations through Tori. Or at minimum, he's trying to get information out of her."

"We don't know that for sure," I said.

"This isn't a coincidence, Stefan," he shot back. "Get your head out of your ass."

I leaned back in my chair, trying to look casual. It was taking everything in my power to keep the panic from my face. I'd had no idea that Gavin was an actual threat of any kind.

At the same time, I was chastising myself for being so foolish. My contact at the DOD was Frank Chase. I'd never made the connection. Chase was a common enough name, and I had never considered the two were related. How had my men missed this? Obviously the fact had been hidden. But I couldn't worry about that right now. Not with my father raging in front of me.

"They're study partners," I said calmly, even though I knew he was right—there was no way this was a coincidence. "Gavin is one of *many* people that Tori studies with. And even if he were trying to get information from her, she doesn't know enough to spill any details. And she wouldn't risk telling anyone what she does know."

I was lying through my teeth, but the whole plan—and Tori's life—depended on convincing my father that she wasn't a threat. That she was harmless.

But I could tell he wasn't buying it. His fury didn't abate. Instead, he slammed his hand back down on my desk, crumpling the photos beneath his meaty palm.

"My children are destroying everything I've worked

for," he seethed. "I can tell your head isn't in the game. If it was, this wouldn't have slipped right past you."

"Everything is under control," I told him, keeping my tone as convincing as possible. "I agree, it looks bad, but the reality is: this guy has jack shit on us. He's got nothing. Zero."

My father was shaking his head. "It's you two who are going to bring us down," he said, grinding out the words. "I've got Luka acting like an ignorant child, drowning himself in booze and blowjobs, when he should be manning up to take a spot at the helm of this business. And now here you are getting so cocky you're willing to ignore an obvious threat."

Thinking about Luka, a wave of empathy and guilt hit me. We were brothers, just a few years apart, but we'd always reacted to things in completely opposite ways. Realizing just how vile the family business was, I had hardened and buckled down, determined to take down my father at any cost. Luke, instead, had cracked.

"I'll get Luka under control. He's my responsibility now," I said evenly, hoping it would appease my father.

It didn't.

He leaned across the desk toward me.

"Fuck Luka. You have to be the strong one here. Your wife is going to be a liability. You're enamored with her pussy, but now that she's not standing in front of you to distract you, you need to remember why you married her—and it wasn't to get your dick shined."

I bit back the rage boiling up inside. "Just stop—"

"This is about the company!" he cut me off. "Remember your loyalties here. You need to get your priorities straight and keep your wife in line. Don't think for a second that she isn't disposable."

"My priorities *are* straight!" I stood up, my fists clenched. I couldn't help myself—I'd stayed in line for his man, but threatening my wife was crossing the line. "My wife comes first, the company second." Even if the company I was interested in protecting didn't look like the company my father wanted to run. "And don't you dare ever insinuate that she's disposable again. She's part of me, and if you want me at your side, you accept her as well."

We glared at each other, at an impasse.

Both of us knew that my father needed me. Even though he still maintained control of KZM, he had conceded enough responsibility to me over the years that he wouldn't have been able run it without me.

But he was stubborn and cruel and never, ever apologized. I didn't expect him to back down from his threat, but he knew that he couldn't do any of this without me, which meant that I had leverage against him. I could keep Tori safe. For now.

My father swept his hand across my desk, scattering the photos across the floor, and then turned to stalk out of my office without a word.

I gathered up the pictures and threw them in the trash. Nothing was resolved between us, but I was resolved to get the ball rolling on ousting my father from power. I had allies in place already—and as the adrenaline left my body, I realized that my father had unknowingly given me more than just threats today. He had given me a lead, a connection that I could use to my benefit. I knew exactly how I could use Tori now, and keep her safe at the same time.

Sitting back in my chair, I immediately assembled a list of things that needed to be done. The sooner, the better.

First things first, I called Dmitri and let him go. I told him he'd get a nice severance bonus for keeping his mouth shut, and that I'd hunt him down if he didn't. I knew I'd have to find Tori a new bodyguard, but I could handle that after my next task.

Although I disliked prying into her things, I reasoned that when it came to Tori's safety, it was okay to do a little digging—so I got on my computer and accessed her cell phone records. When I had the number I needed, I left the office. There were too many eyes at work and not enough of them were trustworthy. My father had spies everywhere.

I had my driver drop me off at Maggie Daley Park, and I walked to an empty bench far from other people. I didn't want to take any chances. Then I pulled out my phone.

I knew I was taking a risk, but I had a feeling this was someone I could trust with Tori's security, and that alone was enough to make me dial the number.

Gavin Chase picked up after a few rings. "Hello?"

"This is Stefan Zoric," I said.

"Go to hell," he told me.

"Wait." I didn't blame him for the less-than-warm response. The last time we'd spoken, I had threatened to kill him if he went near my wife again. "I think we both want the same thing."

"And what's that?" he asked, his voice more cautious now.

"My wife's safety," I said. "And my father's demise."

CHAPTER 29

Once upon a time, my father had been my biggest fan, the most avid supporter of my love for languages and word puzzles, and my strongest protector. I could still remember the time he and Michelle had taken me to a county fair when I was six years old, and I'd begged to go on the miniature roller coaster with its flashy blinking lights and multicolored flags that hung from the posts marking the first drop. It was hardly more than a hill, that drop, but sitting in that roller coaster car, it seemed like a mountain to me. As the nose of the car tilted upward, and we clinked along the track, getting higher and higher above the fairgrounds, I was instantly panicked. My stomach was full of butterflies. I'd grabbed for my father, who was sitting next to me.

"I want to get off the ride," I told him. "I changed my mind."

"Shh, I've got you," he had soothed me, taking my hand in his large, strong one. "You're a brave girl. After this little hill, it's all smooth sailing."

It turned out he was right. That first drop felt like flying to me, and I hadn't just gotten through the ride—I'd loved it, laughing with every swoop and curve. My dad held my hand the whole time.

But now that I knew the truth about my father, about his involvement with KZM, the world had dropped out from under my feet. I had no father. I had no hand to hold.

Except I did. I had Stefan's. I hadn't just grown apart from my dad—I'd grown up. The most important man in my life was now my husband. And now that he had confided in me—about how he felt, and about his family's business—I knew we were strong enough together to face anything.

I came home from school Monday night to find the condo empty, the cleaning staff having come and gone and Gretna's dinner waiting in the stove for me and Stefan to enjoy. It was nice knowing that everything was taken care of, that I could just sit back and unwind as I waited for my husband to arrive.

When I heard the front door close, I looked up from the homework I had spread out across the table. He looked as handsome as always, wearing one of my favorite suits and a sleek silk tie. It made me want to tangle my fingers in it and pull him close for a nice, long, welcome home kiss.

But as I got up and approached him, I noticed that he looked more tired than usual, lines visible at the corners of his eyes and mouth. In the past, he would have put on a brave, stoic face and pretended that everything was okay just to avoid questions from me. Now, he was honest.

"Long day," he said, setting down his bag.

"Good thing you're home now," I said with a smile, wrapping my arms around his neck and pulling him in for a tight hug.

He immediately hugged me back, burying his face in my neck.

It made my heart soar with pleasure and love.

"You look tired," I told him gently after I pulled back.

I smoothed his hair back from his face and he smiled at me, some of the exhaustion and tension easing from his forehead.

"Rough day at the office," he said. "But I have some good news."

I perked up immediately at that. "Tell me," I demanded.

He laughed, relaxing his face even more.

"Come sit with me," he said.

He poured himself a drink and then settled into the big leather chair in the corner of the living room that I often studied in. But it was big enough for the two of us, and I crawled into his lap, my fingers working to loosen his tie and undo the top button of his shirt.

He let out a sigh of contentment.

"Better?" I asked.

"Better," he confirmed before dropping a kiss on my cheek.

"So what's the news?" I asked.

He laughed again, shaking his head. "You're not going to believe this, but I had a chat with your friend Gavin today."

My jaw dropped. "What?"

I knew that Stefan hated Gavin, so I could only imagine that his good news had something to do with him scaring Gavin away from me for good. But if my husband thought that was going to stand with me, he was about to realize he'd been wrong.

"It's not what you think," Stefan assured me, clearly seeing the concern on my face.

"You sure I don't need to call someone to retrieve the body?" I asked, only half teasing.

He smiled. "Trust me, it wasn't like that. Do you know anything about his family?"

I shook my head. "I know he has a brother, and that they were raised by a single mom. But we never really got too deep into it," I said. "We mostly just talked about school stuff."

"Gavin's brother works for the DOD," Stefan told me. "His name is Frank Chase. He's actually my contact there, but I never made the connection between the two."

I absorbed the information. "So does that mean...?"

Stefan nodded. "Gavin wanted to get close to you for more complicated reasons than it seemed," he said. "Not that I doubt he was attracted to you—but I that's not why he befriended you to begin with."

It all made sense. The way Gavin had shown up midway through the semester, the way he'd been interested in me right from the start, how he'd worked so hard to maintain our friendship, even when I gave him the cold shoulder. And despite the fact that my ego was a little bruised, I couldn't help remembering what Gavin had said the night we went out for pizza. Something about how his interest in me hadn't been part of the plan. This had to be related.

"So he's working for the feds, too," I said.

Stefan took a drink from his glass. "I met with him this afternoon. Apparently after I made contact with the DOD, they planted Gavin in your life, trying to use that connection to figure out if I could be trusted, or if I was a bigger part of the trafficking ring than I'd led them to believe. If I was somehow trying to play both sides."

"That's pretty smart," I admitted. "Using me to get to you. I never saw it coming."

"They're good at what they do," he said. "Gavin told me that if it had turned out I was involved in the trafficking, they were going to try to convince you to testify against me. Or give up evidence, if there was any to give."

It wasn't a great feeling to realize that all these months I had been manipulated by both sides—and kept completely in the dark. But now everything was finally coming to light.

"But there isn't any evidence," I said. "This is all your father's doing. Not yours."

I should have known that Gavin was keeping something from me—especially after everything that had happened that night at the club. No wonder he'd tried to convince me that Stefan was the one responsible for drugging me. He'd been trying to turn me against my own husband. It was a lot to take in. I understood Gavin's motivations, but I still felt betrayed.

Stefan continued, "Now that I've proven myself, I can use Gavin to pass critical proof against my father to the feds. It's all coming together."

All this new information was a shock, but I was thrilled that my husband trusted me enough to bring me on board.

"So what happens next?" I said.

He looked at me, and I could see the emotions warring in his eyes. "I've been thinking about your request. And I hate the idea of putting you in danger. But you're right—you're a valuable asset. So...I've found a way you can help me bring down KZM."

"Tell me. I'll do anything," I said.

"I've already arranged everything with Gavin. He and I met on the UChicago campus today, in plain sight of plenty of witnesses. We discussed how the situation would work, but mostly we made it look like I was a jealous husband confronting him about his interest in you. We made a big scene, and I threatened him. I said I'd kill him if he ever touched you again."

"I bet Gavin didn't like that," I said. Even knowing it had been staged, I was a little turned on. I loved it when Stefan was possessive.

Stefan laughed. "He actually let me give him a black eye." He held up his hand, still curved in a fist. "Just to make sure it all looked real."

I took Stefan's hand and kissed his knuckles.

"But that was a one-time deal. I can't be seen in public with him again," Stefan told me. "And that means I can't hand over any documents to him without it looking suspicious. That will have to be your job. Anything I get that will be of use to the feds will have to go through the two of you. You'll have to pretend you're exchanging class notes."

"Of course." I nodded eagerly. "I can do that. I'm grateful to be able to help."

He reached up to take my face in his hands, and he kissed me softly.

"Thank you."

Then he kissed me again, deeper this time, until I was almost out of breath.

"There's something else," he said, looking into my eyes. "I owe you an apology, Tori. I'm sorry I kept in you in the dark for so long about your security. Everyone in your life has been keeping things from you, and I don't want to be that man anymore. I don't want there to be any secrets between us. I'm only going to be honest going forward. Because I love you."

"I love you too," I told him before kissing him again.

But before we could take it anything further, he pulled away and stood, tugging me to my feet. Then he led me across the living room and through the foyer, to the front door.

"I need you to meet someone," he said.

He opened the door. There was huge man standing out there, with the bearing and crewcut of an ex-military soldier, waiting patiently in the hall with his massive arms clasped behind his back. He nodded at me. I could see he was chewing gum.

"This is Bruce," Stefan said. "He's your new bodyguard. He'll be with you at all times, prominently visible. Even when you're at school."

"Okay," I said to Stefan, and then I held out my hand to Bruce. "Hi. I'm Tori."

The man shook my hand, firmly but gently. "Good to meet you, Tori," he said. I'd been intimidated at first, but when he flashed me a small smile, I smiled back. I liked him.

"He'll be with you even when you're with Gavin," Stefan went on. "So if my father has anyone watching, he'll believe there's no way you could be saying anything you shouldn't. My father is well aware that Bruce works for me, and he'd never think that he or I would betray him.

"It's important that we make a big show of the fact that I'm watching you. My father's more inclined to trust me if he knows I'm keeping an eye on you 24/7."

"I understand," I said. "So he'll be standing outside the door all night, too?"

"Yes, ma'am," Bruce said. "Barring short breaks, as needed."

Stefan nodded at Bruce, who gave him a brief nod in return, and then Stefan and I went back into the condo together. We sat down on the couch, and Stefan took my hand.

"There's one more thing," he said. "Even with the cover

I've set in place, we have no chance of making this work unless you can convince my father that you've accepted the situation. So you're going to have to pretend that you're on board with the business, or at the very least, that you're not concerned with what my father and I do behind the scenes."

"How am I supposed to do that?" I asked, my heart beating faster now.

"We'll figure something out," Stefan said. "But this is vital. Otherwise, he'll be watching everything we do with a magnifying glass, and we won't get away with anything. We won't be able to see this through."

I put my hand on his arm. "We may not, regardless," I said. "But we have to try."

My hand was tight on Stefan's knee as we sat in the back of the Town Car on our way to Konstantin's penthouse. My father-in-law had invited us over for Sunday dinner with the stated intent to discuss my role in the family. The timing was almost too good to be true—Stefan and I knew we wouldn't get a more perfect opportunity to put our plan into action and convince my father-in-law that I didn't care what he or KZ Modeling did behind the scenes.

But I was going to have to act my ass off convincing Konstantin that I wasn't completely disgusted by what he and his company did to women. Stefan's years of hard work depended on me pulling it off. It was the only way we'd have a chance in hell of taking KZM down.

Luckily, I'd had days to prepare.

Stefan and I had practiced endlessly for what I'd be up against when I spoke with Konstantin. I knew exactly what I would need to say to convince him that I was a team player.

As I'd dressed for dinner that night, I was so nervous I

could barely put on my dress, my hands were shaking so badly. As he zipped me up, Stefan had kissed the back of my neck, making me shiver.

"You're going to do great," he had said. "My father's ego is so big, he's going to eat up every word you say like candy."

"I know," I said. "I'm just nervous."

"I'll be by your side the whole time," he reassured me.

I nodded, trying to take a few deep breaths. Then I looked myself over in the mirror for a final once-over. I'd chosen to wear something simple and demure. A modest black dress that covered practically everything and went down past my knees. It was cotton—no silk or satin or lace tonight. I didn't want to look expensive. I wanted to look as if I knew my wealth, my privilege, was a gift that Konstantin and his family business had bestowed upon me. A gift that I was aware could just as easily be taken away.

My heels were modest as well, nothing like the sexy stilettos I usually wore when I got dressed up. No labels. No designers. My hair was pulled back in a smooth, nondescript bun, my makeup subtle. I needed to look innocent and contrite. Like the kind of girl who'd consider herself lucky to be included in such a wealthy, well-situated family. Regardless of how dangerous—or illegal—their activities were.

Now that we were actually sitting in the car, though, I was nauseated with anxiety.

"Can we go over the lines one more time?" I whispered.

Moving my hand from his knee to his lips, Stefan gave my knuckles a soft kiss.

"Of course," he said, squeezing my hand. "First of all, he's going to start with a lecture about how you've behaved. Probably saunter around the room with his chest all puffed up. And I can guarantee you he's been going over his speech all afternoon. So don't interrupt."

"Right." I nodded, my knee bouncing rapidly in time with my racing heart. "Contrition."

We had run through this over and over again. How Konstantin would chastise me for my selfish behavior and how I would pour on the apologies.

"He'll call you ungrateful and spoiled," Stefan prompted. "He might yell. It's okay if you're scared. Don't hide it. He'll like that."

I hung my head, practicing how I would react.

"I'm sorry," I recited. "I know I've been acting like a child. Everything in life has been so easy for me up until now, and...I guess this is the first time I've had to learn that this kind of money doesn't come from legitimate businesses. It's been a hard lesson."

"Good," Stefan said. "The entitlement angle is good. It'll make it more believable for him when you play the shame card."

What made this part of the speech so easy was that it was partly true. I had been given a lot of opportunities and financial help in my life, and I was well aware of that fact. And there were times I did feel ashamed about it—especially now that I knew what kind of man my father really was. Stefan had coached me to lean into my feelings, to let some honesty bleed into the lies I would tell. Otherwise my words would ring hollow and false.

I cleared my throat and continued. "But the truth is, I love our lifestyle. And more importantly, I love my husband —and I'll stand by him and whatever methods he chooses to provide for us. I have no plans to interfere or fuss about any of your dealings ever again."

"And?" Stefan gestured for me to continue.

I swallowed. "And I will be more grateful and understanding going forward. I will be nothing but supportive."

It made me sick to say the words even in practice, but I knew it was for the best. That this final lie would hopefully be exactly what was needed to lay the pathway to Konstantin's end.

It was all for the greater good.

Thank god Stefan and I were doing this together. I knew I wouldn't have been able to make it through the night —let alone the car ride over—without him supporting me.

"I believe in you," he said now. "You've got this down. What you're doing is incredibly brave and it's going to make a difference."

Nodding, I tried to smile, but it was strained. We were minutes away.

"I have something for you," he said, pulling a small square box out of his pocket.

When I opened it, I found a pair of sparkling pendant earrings nestled in the velvet. Their beauty nearly took my breath away. The drops were round clusters of pavé diamonds set in platinum, and they had an Art Deco look to them. Subtle but incredibly sparkly.

"They're gorgeous," I said, taking them in with wide eyes. "I love them."

"I wanted these to be a symbol of the two of us," Stefan said, unhooking them from the velvet. "That we're a pair now."

I felt my chest get tight with emotion, and I blinked back the sting in my eyes. "Thank you," was all I could manage.

"We belong together. Always," he said. "Deal?"

"Deal," I told him.

He swept my hair aside and helped me put them on.

Somehow, having this gift from him, feeling it close to my body, calmed me in a way I hadn't expected. I felt ready to face my father-in-law. Stefan and I were a team, and we would take down his father—and mine—together.

The Town Car arrived at Konstantin's apartment and dropped us off in the front of the luxurious building. Our fingers entwined, Stefan helped me out of the car and we headed inside.

It was quiet when we entered the penthouse.

"In the library," Konstantin's voice echoed through the marble entryway.

"The library?" I whispered to Stefan.

Something was wrong, I could sense it. Judging by the way that Stefan tensed, I could tell that he was on edge as well. What was going on?

We made our way toward through apartment, my hand gripping Stefan's the whole way.

When we entered the library, we saw that Konstantin wasn't alone.

There were two people with him. One was a boy who was playing on his iPad, his attention fully focused on some kind of game that I could see reflected in his pale green eyes. Vaguely familiar eyes. He looked to be around seven or eight years old.

But it was the sight of the woman that made Stefan go still at my side.

I looked at her, at the way she looked at Stefan.

She was beautiful—there was no denying that—and she was beautiful in that particular way that KZM models were beautiful. Tall and leggy, with long, shining black hair and striking eyes that were a stormy shade of blue-green that was rare in someone with her coloring.

I'd never seen her before, but I could tell by the tension in the room that she was someone important.

Glancing at my father-in-law, I took in the way he was standing in the middle of it all, a drink in his hand and a triumphant, cruel sneer on his face. It was that expression that had my stomach sinking to the floor. He had planned all this, and even though I still didn't know exactly what *this* was, I could tell it wasn't good. Was this one of the models that Stefan had helped to escape? Had she betrayed him, or been caught? If Konstantin was onto Stefan, our plan was dead in the water. Before he could ever bring the feds the bulk of the evidence against his father.

My heart was hammering in my chest, and I didn't know what to say or do.

Finally, someone spoke first. It was the woman.

"Stefan," she said, her voice like a whisper. She was staring at my husband with tears in her eyes.

"Anja," he said, his eyes fixated on her.

Realizing who she was made me feel like the floor was tilting beneath my feet. This was Anja Borjan. The model Stefan had fallen in love with when he was seventeen. The model who had disappeared after Konstantin discovered that his son wanted to marry her.

Stefan's gaze shifted and I followed it to the boy sitting on the couch. The boy who was still so engrossed in his video game that he didn't even bother to look up. Stefan's eyes moved back to Anja's and she nodded.

"He's yours," she said, so quietly that the boy didn't even hear her. "Your son."

I heard the gasp that came out of me as my entire world shattered.

My knees went weak. I felt Stefan's hand tighten around

mine, but he said nothing. How could he? What could he say? Just when our lives were finally beginning to come together—when we had finally found the love and trust and connection we'd been seeking—the woman who Stefan had loved, who he had been searching for all these years, was back.

And she was the mother of his child.

Stefan had a child.

He now had an impossible choice. Would this tear us apart? Would he choose a life with Anja and his son? Or me?

Everything was about to change.

Tori and Stefan's entire relationship has been threatened. Where does Stefan's heart belong? With Tori or his first love?

≈

Find out in The Choice.

On the day my husband and I committed to each other, I didn't wear a white dress.

We didn't exchange rings.

There was no audience or minister to witness our union. Only the two of us.

We swore to put each other first, to take on the evils our families had perpetuated together. Side by side.

But that was before the past returned to haunt us.

Now everything has changed.

Stefan can't have both his past and my future.

I can't ask him to choose.

And neither of us can do what has to be done without the other. It's an impossible choice, but we've run out of time.

The Choice

Dear Reader,

Thank you so much for reading The Secret. Stefan and Tori have been on such a roller coaster of a ride and just when their bond begins to strengthen, a past love threatens to tear it apart. Read the emotional conclusion to the Arranged Series, The Choice.

Thank you again for reading Stefan and Tori's story. If you enjoyed The Secret , I would greatly appreciate it if you let a friend or two know and leave a review. It's the best way to thank an author and just a few sentences is all it takes to show your support.

Sincerely,
Stella

Want to be up-to-date with all my releases? Sign up for my newsletter!

ALSO BY STELLA GRAY

~

Arranged Series

The Deal

The Secret

The Choice

Convenience Series

The Sham

The Contract

The Ruin

Charade Series

The Lie

The Act

The Truth

ABOUT STELLA GRAY

Stella Gray is an emerging author of contemporary romance. When she is not writing, Stella loves to read, hike, knit and cuddle with her greyhound.

Made in the USA
Columbia, SC
22 September 2023

23215258R00171